NEVER BE ANOTHA: *REDEMPTION*

Book 3

Troii Devereaux

Never Be Anotha: Redemption Book 3

By Troii Devereaux

This is a work of fiction. Names, characters, places, and incidents are the product of the author's imagination or are used fictitiously. Any resemblance to actual persons, living or dead, events or locales is entirely coincidental.

First paperback edition July 2020

Book design by SheerGenius

ISBN 9781953267009 (Paperback)

Published by **AKT Publishing, Inc.**

Contact us and leave feedback about the book at www.AKTPublishing.com.

ACKNOWLEDGEMENTS

For TaKesha. Rest easy, little big sister. You will never be forgotten.

This book is dedicated to the memory of my late mother, Deleatrice A. Knight.

Table of Contents

Chapter 1

Sam

Keith opened me up to a whole new world of sexual exhibition. Not that he knew that. I waited almost twenty-seven years to lose my virginity, officially, and now I just cannot get enough of it. I wanna 'fuck' all the time. Keith likes when I say 'fuck', he said it sounds sexy coming out of my pretty little mouth. So, I oblige him and be sure to say it quite a bit. I always wanted him inside of me. "You ready babe?" We were on the way to a nightclub called Silk's. Tonight, was R&B night, and I was in the mood for some good music and some great food.

Keith

"Damn baby... you are absolutely stunning. Not sure I'll be able to keep my eyes, or my hands, off of you all night." Was I imagining shit, or was my mouth watering at the sight of her?

Sam

I was wearing a black lace belted dress that hugged my modest curves. It had a nude lining under it, which made it look like I had nothing on underneath. The shoulder straps were thin, and my Giuseppe Zanotti black sandals were four inches high with black lace on the satin material across my toe area.

"And I don't want you to keep your eyes or your hands off of me. So, don't you dare try." I went over to him, grabbed him by his tie and kissed his lips. "But we've gotta go if we want to get to the club at a decent time."

Once we arrived, Keith pulled up to the front door where the valet attendants were stationed. He exited the driver's side to open my car door. He then took my hand and escorted me into the club. It was live up in there. Nice ambiance, lights weren't too dim, but weren't overly bright. Beautiful people everywhere. Sexy voluptuous ladies and fine ass men, who I'm sure had big bank as well as big dicks of all shapes and sizes. Keith seemed to know quite a few people there. How did a guy who owned a project management company know *these* people? Some looked like bankers, others looked like gangsters. But one man in particular that Keith was talking to, caught my eye.

Keith

"Samantha, I'd like you to meet an associate of mine, Jerrick Houston. He owns a few businesses and specializes in sales. Jerrick, this is my lady, Sam."

Sam

"Nice to meet you, Jerrick." As I took his hand in mine.

Keith's friend, Jerrick

"Likewise. My friends call me Benny. Jerrick is my father's name." Damn, Slim was fine. I was hoping she wasn't here with anyone, but she just had to be fucking Don's brother. Damn. I guess that's out.

Sam

"Okay, Bennie. Would you like to be my friend?" I said as I licked my red stained lips. By this time, Keith was talking with someone else, so I'm sure he didn't hear my question. Benny was a tall, slender baby-faced man. But behind that innocence, I felt it in my bones that he was hardcore. He was chocolate, had a low cut, and dark brown eyes with curly lashes. He was beautiful, and he was swagged out to the max.

Benny

"Yeah, I wouldn't mind a friend that looks like you." As I licked my lips in return. This couldn't be his *lady*, the way she just winked her pussy at me. I guess we'll see though. "I'm sure I'll see you around, Sam. Have a good night."

Sam

"Yes, yes you will." I planned on seeing Bennie again very soon.

Aubrey

"Why won't this baby come out already? Mommy, tell them to take him out NOW!" My contractions started as soon as I walked into the hospital. I wasn't prepared for this pain. At this point, fuck this birth plan. "Give me the epidural. I want it, please. Give me the epidural. Mommy, please! Make them give it to me!" I started to cry; I was in so much pain.

Dee Dee

"Baby, it's already too late for the epidural. You're at eight centimeters, you have to just let the birthing process flow." I said as I patted her face with a cold damp rag to cool her off. I felt so bad for my baby, but she originally told them that she didn't want the meds. She wanted to have the baby naturally. "Nurse, is there anything you can give her? She's been at eight centimeters for almost three hours."

Nurse

"I'm sorry ma'am, it's already too late. The doctor will be in shortly to assess the situation. My apologies." She said so nonchalantly.

Aubrey

"Mommy, can you pass me some more ice chips please?" After she gave me some ice, the nurse walked back in to ask my mother if she could speak with her privately. I didn't have the strength to panic. They walked out into the hallway after my mom ensured I was okay.

Dee Dee

"Is there something wrong with my baby? Tell me! What's wrong with my baby?" I knew I wasn't allowing her to speak, but why was she taking so long to get to the point? At that point, I heard Aubrey scream out in pain yet again.

Aubrey

I felt another contraction coming on and I gripped the sides of the little bed that I was in. "Nnnnnnnnnnggggggggggaaaaahhhhhhhh!!" I was sweating so much, and I was so thirsty. "Mommy, ice chips, please!" I screeched.

Dee Dee

"One second nurse. Here Aubrey. I'm not going anywhere baby, I'm just gonna step into the hallway really fast. I'll be right back." I stepped out into the hallway in front of Aubrey's room, but she wanted me to come into a room across the hall. I followed her, "What is this about? I have to get back to my daughter." I said as I folded my arms across my chest.

Nurse

"Ma'am, there has been an incident. A gunman came into the hospital and started shooting blindly. No one died, but your husband was among the people shot. He's being wheeled into surgery with a shattered clavicle as we speak, but he's expected to make a full recovery."

Dee Dee

I just realized he still hadn't returned from meeting Monroe in the lobby. "Why weren't there any alarms that went off? Are we safe in this unit of the hospital? What floor is my husband on? When can I see him? What happened to the gunman?" What am I going to tell Aubrey?

Nurse

"The gunman is no longer here. He was taken away, maybe apprehended. Your husband is going to be placed in recovery on the fourth floor once he is out of surgery. That's all the information that I have, but I will ensure that you're updated. I'm so sorry."

Dee Dee

When I went back into Aubrey's room, I knew she was going to ask about what the nurse and I spoke about. I never lied to Aubrey before, but in her condition, she was under enough stress. "Mike slipped and fell. He hurt his shoulder so he's being seen for that. He's fine and should be out soon."

Aubrey

"Well damn, Mike is supposed to be here to cut his grandson's cord." That was the part of my birth plan that I still was interested in, unfortunately.

Monroe

"I'm here to cut my son's cord." I said as I walked into her hospital room. I had just finished getting my arm bandaged. That nigga Rob can't shoot for shit, but he'll get dealt with. This time for good.

Aubrey

"What are you doing here, Monroe?" I turned my attention to my mother. "Mom? Did you call him? Why would you do that knowing how I feel right now?" I felt betrayed and I started to cry.

Monroe

"Mike called me. Which is what you should have done. Why would you deliberately keep this from me Aubrey? I've done nothing but respect your wishes, I would have continued to do so. This is something that I should have been able to experience as well. He's my son too... and my first child." I said I wouldn't get angry, but I couldn't help it. She was acting like I hurt her or something.

Aubrey

"I cannot discuss this right now with you, Monroe." He started to object, but at that very moment, another contraction felt like it was searing through me. "Ahhhhhhhhhhh, gggaaaaaahhhh! NURSE! Please check me again, it feels like I have to push right now."

Monroe

I went over to the side table and wet a cloth and placed it on her forehead. The nurse seemed to be moving way too slow for me. "Nurse, please call the doctor, she said she's experiencing pressure that feels different from the pain she was already having." Her mom gave her more ice chips and was rubbing ice along her neck and chest.

When the doctor entered the room, he washed his hands and sat between Aubrey's legs.

Doctor

"She's crowning, let's get this show on the road, shall we? Now, Ms. Collins, I'm going to need for you to push only when I tell you to. It is very important that you do not push any other time. Understood?"

Monroe

Aubrey shook her head yes. It was eleven thirty-nine pm, so maybe my son would share my birthday with me. Aubrey probably didn't know that, but my son did. That's my little champ already. I couldn't wait to see him.

Doctor

"Grandma, dad, I'll need your help for this next phase. She's going to need to focus on her breathing and we'll probably need to help with pushing her knees as far back as she can comfortably stand. Ok Aubrey, I see that your next contraction is about to start, you'll need to start pushing on the count of three. One, two, three… push!"

Monroe

"Come on Aubrey, you got this. Push, baby!" My son seemed like he wasn't budging at first, but after some strenuous pushing, his head was out! After the doctor was doing whatever it was that he was doing down there, it only took a few more minutes for the baby to be out completely. Just shy of my birthday by two minutes! "Aubrey you did so well baby." I kissed her on her forehead, and I felt her hand touch my face. I expected her to slap me, but in that moment, I think she was grateful I was there.

Dee Dee

"Look at my grand baby! He's so beautiful! Aubrey you did great!" I looked back and she was hugging Monroe with tears streaming down her face. It was absolutely beautiful! And guess who had their camera ready! I captured the moment of their first kiss, their first embrace since her accident. And the first few moments as parents to this beautiful little boy.

Doctor

"Dad, are you ready to cut the cord?"

Monroe

Currently, I wasn't ready to break away from my embrace with Aubrey, but it was time to meet our son. "Yes sir, I am." They placed my son onto Aubrey's chest while I cut the cord. Mrs. Roberson was just snapping away with her camera. We were just all so overcome with joy! My son weighed eight pounds, eleven ounces and he was twenty-two inches long. He is huge! And he looks just like me. It's crazy, Aubrey carried my little man and he looks just like me. After I cut the cord, they weighed him and cleaned him off.

Aubrey

"Happy birthday, Monroe. I love you."

Chapter 2

Free

I dropped Tamia off with my friend Crystyle from the club, so that I could go to the hospital. James was injured in a shooting at Southern Maryland and that was all the information they would give me over the phone as his next of kin. I raced there; I didn't care about police pulling me over. It was almost midnight and I needed to get to my husband. This year couldn't end fast enough. With the kidnapping, the baby's health scare and now this? It was time for 2017 to get the fuck on!

I parked my car, grabbed my purse and ran to the information desk. "Hello, my husband was shot here tonight. James Casey, I'm his wife, Fresia Casey. Can you tell me his status? Is he okay? Can I see him please?" I was so worried, and this bitch was the least bit accommodating.

Receptionist

"Ma'am, may I see your identification please?" She asked.

Free

I handed her my driver's license and she handed it back. She ruffled through some files until she came across the folder she was looking for. She told me the floor he was on and pointed to the elevators. I took it up to the fourth floor where I came to another desk and realized that I was probably going to have to repeat the same procedure again. So, I gave them my driver's license to start with, told them my name and who I was there to see.

Receptionist #2

"Yes ma'am, your husband is in recovery and is a little sedated. He was shot in his right-side flank, but the doctors were able to stitch him back up. You're welcome to go and sit with him, he's in room four twelve.

Free

"Thank you." I walked quickly until I got his room. He looked like he was sleeping, so I just sat beside him and held his hand. He opened his eyes once he felt my hand on his and I hugged him. "Hi baby. I was so scared. Are you alright? What happened?" Tears poured down my face as I quickly scanned his body.

James

I didn't dare bring up that fuck nigga's name to my wife. She was finally able to get rid of her nightmares and live normally again. "Hey my love, I'm ok. It was just a random fool from what I understand that just started shooting in the lobby. No one died though. They're just monitoring me for now, since a bullet grazed me on the side. They had to stitch me up, but I'll be okay. I should be going home shortly. Sorry I couldn't call you myself. I left my phone in the car, for obvious reasons." We never have our phones on us when we're handling business, and that's why thought I was here. "Money's old girl, Aubrey, was in labor with their baby. That was what we found out from her stepdad when we got here."

Free

Hmmm, I wonder why she didn't tell him before. I know she lost her memory, but did she think it was someone else's baby? I know she's not like that, or at least not while she was in college. "That's a good reason to be at a hospital, but I wonder why some crazy person would just start shooting up the place. Anyway, do you think it would be a good idea for me to apologize to her again while she's here? I really want to make amends with her, even if she doesn't want to resume a friendship."

James

"Baby I think that's a great idea. Especially since Money and I are so tight. Why don't we head down there together once I'm released? Or maybe we can come back during the day once she's had some rest. I'm hoping she had the baby by now, because we got here around eight o'clock."

Free

"Sounds like a plan, but for now, you need to get some rest too. Did you need anything? You thirsty? Hungry?" He declined, but he squeezed my hand and then drifted off to sleep again. I decided to find me something to munch on. I knew there had to be a vending machine around here somewhere. I ran into Mrs. Dee Dee and she looked at me as if she recognized me, but didn't, which is understandable since she hadn't seen me in a long time. "Hello Mrs. Dee Dee, it me… Fresia." Oncc I said that, she came to me and hugged me. I was so relieved that there was no bad blood between us. I knew that she knew about what happened between me and Aubrey over Rob.

Dee Dee

"Free, you are looking good girl! I see you with the snap back! Aubrey told me you were pregnant the last time she saw you. And please don't be embarrassed. Life is too short for all of that and I've damn sure made my share of mistakes. I just hope after tonight, they put his ass under the jail."

Free

"Put who under the jail, Mrs. Dee Dee?" I'm confused at this point because I knew she was referring to Rob. But what did he have to do with tonight? I didn't get it. James didn't come out and say it, but I believed Rob was dead.

Dee Dee

"Robert's crazy ass. Why he would come in here shooting everywhere like that is beyond me. My husband just got out of surgery behind that mess. He's alright, Monroe is too. How's your husband? He's on this floor as well, right?" Free looked as if she saw a ghost, and I looked in the direction she was staring in as well. "Free, are you alright honey? Come on, let's sit down sweetie. Can I get some help over here?" I yelled to whatever hospital staff was near me.

Free

I can't believe James would deliberately lie to my face that way. He told me they took care of his ass months ago. How was that true when he came in here and shot at them? What the fuck? "I'm alright, but did you say that Rob was here? And shot them tonight? I thought he was dead! Are you sure it was him? How did he find them here?" I feel like I've lost my security blanket. I now know that I can't trust my own damn husband. "I gotta get out of here. I'm sorry Mrs. Dee Dee." She kept asking me if I was alright and wanted me to sit down and speak with her, but I had to get out of there. I ran back to my car with all my might so that I could go get my baby and figure out my next move.

Taisha

"You like that daddy? You like the way that pussy looks, huh?" I bent over in front of my newest customer and clapped my ass as he inserted as many fingers as he could ram inside of me. He was stroking his dick as I danced for him, and hopefully I could make him nut even faster now that he's already gotten started.

Trick

"Aiight little mama, turn around and get on your knees. I want you to suck this dick."

Taisha

"Okay now, do you need a run-down of my rates? To get your dick sucked, it's one hundred and fifty dollars. For me to top you off, it's two-fifty. So, what do you want me to do for you baby?" I slurred.

Trick

"I want just like last time, top that shit off baby."

Taisha

I did just as he instructed. But how did I not remember doing this for him before? I deep throated his dick, letting it continually hit my tonsils while I kept it real wet for him. My mouth and my hand were in perfect sync with one another.

Trick

"No hands ma, ooohhhh, you about to make me cum all down your throat. Spit on it, bitch, make it real nasty for me."

Taisha

I ignored him, if I stopped to do all that, it would prolong the inevitable. I removed my hand, let my head go all the way to the base of his dick and kept repeating that motion. I'm so glad I have no gag reflex. About a minute later, I felt his warmth threatening to suffocate me as it coated my throat. I jacked his dick off to get the remainder out as I spit that shit out beside him. I grabbed my towel and wiped my hand and mouth off once I was done. Then I held out my hand.

Trick

"Come on Tai, how about I give you some of that good shit instead?" He asked, trying to play me.

Taisha

He then removed some heroin from his pocket and was trying to give it to me. "If that's what you wanna do, at least give me the equivalent of two-fifty. This ain't even a hundred dollars' worth. He shook his head while laughing and gave me the drugs and two hundred dollars cash. I was cool with that. He pulled his pants back up and left while I went and got ready for my next one.

Travis

"Mami, where's the money? You ready to please my next friend? You lookin' real good today mami. *Tu culo esta bien bueno mami.* That ass is phat baby. *Meterme dentro de ti.* I gotta get in them guts tonight."

Taisha

"I got a hundred dollars for you baby. And yeah, I can't wait for you to fuck me again." I lied. Travis' dick only felt good when I was high because I ain't know no better. But I didn't mind. As long as he kept me high. And he let me keep half of the money I made. I knew he was dogging me out but fuck this life. I still belonged to Don, so I just didn't care anymore.

Travis

"Sí, sí... check it mami, Curt from the club is here. He told me that he was looking forward to seeing you. I want you to do him right, he's gonna pay five hundred *dólares* for the *especial*. He said you know what that is?"

Taisha

"Yeah, I remember what the fat nigga likes. Lemme just wash the last nigga off my face; he was sloppy. But stay close. Curt may try something on some get back shit. And I need a hit papi. Can you do that for me, *por favor* papi?" He agreed and went and got his kit. I brushed my teeth and washed my face. Once he came back, I tied myself off and he located the big vein for me and injected it for me. I could never find the big vein by myself, so I loved him for that shit. "Ah yes papi! Mmmmmmm, this is soooo damn good. Mmmmmm."

Travis

"Mami, no nodding off. I need you to perform for this money. This fat ass negro looks like he cum *en un minuto!*"

Taisha

Travis laughed, but that nigga Curt was sitting on a schlong! It was at least nine inches and took him a long while to cum. And he wanted way too much all the time. I'm just glad they prearranged the amount. I went into the room where I would fuck him. I started putting oil all over myself like I remembered. He walked in the room and he looked different for some reason. "Hey Curt, what's popping daddy?" I slurred as the drug continued to work its magic.

Curt

"Bitch I ain't been the s-s-s-s-s-same since you pulled that shit on me the last time I saw you. But when I heard you was tricking f-f-f-f-f-for money, I knew I was gonna come out here to s-s-s-s-s-see your ass. You f-f-f-f-f-fell off a lot huh? Ha, I can tell from the track marks that Travis added you to his stable. Come on over here and get this party s-s-s-s-s-started, bitch. You-u-u-you know what I like." He stammered as he laughed at my downtrodden appearance.

Months Ago

Curt

"Hey Sapphire, you came to twerk that ass on this dick for a real nigga?" I instantly smiled at the prospect getting up in some of the best pussy I've ever had. Of course, she didn't need to know I thought that. I told her that, because she was getting older, that she needed to prove to me that she deserved to be here. And that was in the form of a lil sample after a private show every now and then. Truth be told, it was hard for me not blow my load just off of watching her dance.

Taisha

I almost threw up in my mouth at the memory of our last encounter. "Curt, I came to tell you that I will not be dancing in this piece of shit club anymore." His facial expression looked like his dumb ass was confused or something. I hope he doesn't try and jump bad or nothing, because I got my taser with me today and I will light that ass all the way up! If I can, I'll place that shit right up to them nuts!

Curt

"Fuck you mean you not dancing here no more? Your shift starts in an hour. Who I'mma get to fill that spot on such short notice?" Curt asked, genuinely confused.

Taisha

"Not my problem. I'm out." And with that, I turned around and chucked up the deuces just before the debut of my elegant middle finger. Then his ass had the nerve to grab me by the arm! It wasn't rough or anything, but the audacity of this fool!

Curt

"Sapphire, look, just let me sample that pussy one more time and I'll let you leave. You know you like it." I said while grabbing on my dick. "I'll pay you this time and everything." I

took my stash out of my pocket that totaled about fifteen hundred dollars. I was willing to give her everything in my hand, too. She was that good!

Taisha

This was just what I was waiting on. "What would you like me to do?" As I licked my lips seductively. He started pulling his pants down revealing that he was semi-hard. With that big ass, ugly ass dick. "Money first though Curt. I'm not playing with you, today."

Curt

"You know what I like baby. Come on over here and let Big Curt feel that wet pussy."

Taisha

He tried peeling off a few twenties, and I wasn't having that. "All of it if you want anything from me today, nigga." I was dead serious too.

Curt

"Alright Sapphire, damn. Here." I didn't care about that little bit of money. My shit was hard as a brick now. I sat down on my couch after pulling my shit out to show her how ready I was for her. Nobody worked that shit for me like she did. These other bitches in here were lazy. And most of the time complained that I was too big. I still made them give it up though.

Taisha

After I stashed that money in my Christian Dior purse, I sauntered over to him and he leaned his head back on the back of that nasty ass couch that was in his office. It was like a grayish colored, microfiber piece of shit that appeared like it hadn't been cleaned in twenty years. It was all sticky and I made sure never to touch it. He had his eyes closed in anticipation of the pleasure I usually put on him, but he was in for the shock of his life, literally. I pulled out that taser, aimed it at his nether region and let it flow. He couldn't even make any noise at first. His face was fashioned into the most grotesque image I'd ever seen. There was no sound at first, and then after what seemed like forever, he let out this high-pitched squeal.

"Yeah nigga, you will never get none of this good shit again! Ole nasty ass, perverted ass nigga. Kiss my muthafuckin' ass and don't you ever speak my name again!" With that, I grabbed all of my belongings I packed from my locker and ran out of the building. As soon as I got in my car, my phone rang, scaring the shit outta me!

Present Day

Taisha

I knew he was only trying to make me feel bad about what I was doing, but I was way past that point months ago. I was halfway hoping he brought a gun in here and just blew my brains out to get me back.

Instead of fucking me, because he said I was too "dirty" now, he pushed my head down on his dick while he wrapped my ponytail around his fat ass hands and fucked my throat, hard. It took him a while to nut as usual but once he did, he held my head in place. I couldn't breathe, I couldn't move, and I was trying my best to get away from him. I tried not to panic, but I realized he was doing this on purpose with each breath I tried gasping for.

Curt

"You bite me b-b-b-b-b-bitch, and I'm gonna blow your muthafuckin head off. Take that nut and s-s-s-s-swallow ALL of it. Don't let not a drop come out your f-f-f-f-filthy ass mouth, hoe."

Taisha

Yep, I brought this shit on myself. I almost passed out, until I felt him take his hand outta my hair. I then proceeded to choke as the tears fell from my eyes. I tried catching my breath as I gagged and coughed until my airway was clear enough to breathe deeply.

Curt

"I'll s-s-s-s-see you next week hoe. Make s-s-s-s-sure you ready for me." And he threw the money at me while I was still trying to catch my breath on the floor. I was humiliated once again.

Chapter 3

Aubrey

After they cleaned my son off, they taught me how to get him to latch on to my breast while encouraging our "skin to skin" bonding, just like the pregnancy book I read suggested. Monroe was right there through everything and was so helpful. Before I delivered, Monroe took charge, ensuring that I was taken care of despite his arm injury. It looked fresh, but with all of the excitement and commotion, I didn't have a chance to ask him about it. The fact that he showed me so much care, regardless of the way I treated him this last year since my coma, was endearing.

During the delivery, there were flashes of things we experienced together before my car accident. I guess the trauma from pushing out a whole human being had some type of effect on my brain. I can't say I remember everything about our relationship in the past, but I remembered enough to know that I loved him with my entire soul. At the doctor's words, "it's a boy", I knew I was in love with Monroe again and that he, my baby boy and I would be a family forever. I'm not letting him get away from me ever again. Those feelings of love, safety and fulfillment absolutely consumed me. And I was excited about the future.

The baby slept peacefully after they ensured that everything was ok with him. I stayed up until the nurse came in at about six in the morning to check me again. I was sore and super tired, but I couldn't stop looking at my son. He was so cute. I still didn't know what his name was going to be, but I knew it had to be something strong. And I also knew, he would have his daddy's last name, King. I would ask Monroe for his input, once he woke up a few hours from now.

About an hour later, the nurse came back in my room to check on me and the baby. She helped me get him to latch on again since he didn't eat much the first time. "Are you hungry baby boy?" He looked at me and I noticed he had my hazel eyes. "I'm glad you got something from me, because the rest of you is all daddy." He was the spitting image of Monroe with a head full of hair. I was very happy about that because of Rob forcing himself on me a couple of times before I was able to get away from him prior to the accident. I also remember that he pleasured me even though I hated him so much, and that's why I was so distracted when I was driving away. I was already at least six or seven weeks pregnant when all of that went down, so I'm very happy about not bringing that demon's spawn into this world like Free did.

I left Rob with no word of where I had gone, not a 'thank you, next', not a fuck you very much. Nada! I was in a three-year, violent and possessive relationship with him and I never looked back. It wasn't until one night when he called me crying about being held hostage and needing my help, that I spoke to him again. But like I should have known from the start, he wasn't just going to let me go on about my life once I helped free him. Had I listened to my friends and not gone to see about him, everything still would have been perfect in my little world with Monroe. I remember and regret that day like it was yesterday.

Earlier this year

Rob

"Oh, so you ain't got nothing to say to me? You just take all your shit and bounce without leaving a note or anything else? Like fuck me, huh?" I manhandled her ass til we got up in my apartment. If she kept fucking with me like this tonight, she was gonna make me hurt her ass.

Aubrey

"Rob, you said if I helped you, you would leave me alone. Can you please just let me go? I need to find out what happened to Joe!" Aubrey cried. I'm so very scared in this moment, I know this look in his eyes. I've seen it too many times before.

Rob

"So, you fuckin that nigga too? You just out here being a whole entire hoe, huh? Since you giving the pussy up to every muthafuckin' body else out here, come here and get my dick wet too." She got me fucked up if she think I'm gonna let her go that easy. I knew she was fuckin that dude. While she up here crying for him, she should have been crying for me while that crazy ass bitch was holding me hostage. And if it wasn't for her ass not being at work that day, I would have never even paid attention to her ass! It was her fault that I got tangled up with that crazy bitch! "Aubrey, don't make me ask you twice, take them got damn clothes off, NOW!"

Aubrey

"Nooooooooo! You can't do this to me! I helped you get away from Marie! Please let me go, Rob. PLEEAAASSSEEE!"

Rob

"So, you wanna do this shit the hard way? Ok!" I punched her right in her eye and she fell to the floor. I then kicked her in her side and got down and started punching her some more.

"I don't give a fuck about how you look in public now! Since you out here giving this pussy up to them niggas, and you have a nerve to tell me no? You serving up this pussy tonight!"

Aubrey

I was numb at this point from all of the pain. I couldn't see straight, my eye was swelling shut and my ear felt like it was split open. I prayed that I didn't have any broken ribs from him kicking me so hard. I felt him tugging at my shoes and then my joggers. Then I felt the coldness from the floor below me. He ripped my panties off and made me turn on my stomach. I winced as he shoved himself roughly into my vagina.

Is this my karma for giving him so many chances to hurt me in the past? Is this what he did to Sam? Will he kill me when he's done? I heard him grunting in my ear and he had the nerve to ask me if I liked it. When I thought he was done, he turned me over and pushed himself inside me again, but this time he lubricated his dick with his saliva. Please hurry up! And please don't let my body betray me by getting wet. I can't believe that I used to absolutely live for this man less than a year ago and he's now raping me.

Rob

I knew she wanted me for real. I can feel her pussy gripping my dick from the inside. I missed this pussy, but why is she still laying there not saying nothing? "I know you miss me too baby, stop fighting me and just enjoy it. I'm sorry for hitting you. And this pussy feels way too tight for somebody else to be hittin' it. Damn girl, ooooohhh. You know I love you Aubrey and I know you still love me. This is where you are supposed to be. I'm glad you're back home. Mmmmmm..."

I was kissing on her neck and her back as I continued to pound in and out of her sweet pussy, and even though she didn't answer me, I know that I just heard her moan. I reached underneath her sports bra because I missed those titties, too. I guess she wasn't pregnant after all, because I could tell she had lost a few pounds. Why the fuck did I have to hit her in the face though? I'll just buy her something pretty tomorrow and everything will be okay. I felt myself about to nut, so I spread her legs open as wide as they would go, so I could be deeper inside of her.

"Damn, you feel so good baby. Uhhhhhhh ooooooohhhhh mmmmmhhhhhmmm, baby. I love you so much! I'm so sorry baby, please forgive me for hurting you again." I said as I felt my dick start to throb and release inside of her. I really meant it; I know my temper is ferocious. She didn't say anything, she just laid there and continued to look into nothingness. I took my time to regain my senses and pulled out of her slowly, then pulled my pants back up. I scooped her up off the floor and took her into the bedroom and laid her down on her side. I pulled the covers up over her and laid beside her and went to sleep with my arm draped over her.

Present Day

Once I saw an exit that day, I took it. No pants on, no panties on. Just the top I had on the day before. I jumped in the car and sped off with my mind going in so many different directions I wasn't able to think straight. I wasn't paying attention as I sped through a red light and I woke up in the hospital, with no recollection of who or what Monroe was to me.

I decided I was going to look ahead and thank God for allowing me to come out of all of that craziness. I am alive, I have a beautiful son and my man is right here beside me, despite it all. It just can't get any better than this and I would live the rest of my days with that in mind. I would forever be grateful for this second chance, no matter how extraordinary.

Monroe

I woke up and watched as Aubrey fed my son and talked to him. "Aubrey, you are so beautiful to me. Thank you for my son. I know you've been through so much this year, and you were probably unsure of what to do, but you will never have to be his parent alone. I love you, regardless of whether or not you want to be with me. I will always love you."

Aubrey

I didn't even know he was awake, but another thing I remembered is the fact that he's always made me feel protected. "Come here. Sit with us." By this time, the sun was up, and it was going on eight o'clock in the morning. I was starting to get a little sleepy, but I didn't want to take my eyes off of my little man. "We need to name him, Monroe. Any ideas?"

Monroe

I didn't want to be presumptuous with suggesting that he be a Junior. I just told her I would think about it. She looked up at me and then pulled my lips to hers and kissed me. My dick automatically sprung to life. Although I didn't fuck Taisha, I had a few women that would open up for me from time to time. Nothing serious though. But I never experienced the type of satisfaction that I did with Aubrey. Everything was always on another level with her, I still knew she was the one for me. When she kissed me, it was like I could breathe again. I could hope for a future with her again. I still wanted her to be my wife, but I didn't want to rush things.

We continued to kiss, like we both were hungry for one another. She kissed me like she couldn't live without me. I felt the very same way. I'm glad there was no one in the room but us, because I started caressing her breasts underneath the gown. Got a little milk on me, but I didn't care. There was a light knock at the door and in the midst of us gathering ourselves, me removing my hand from her gown and trying to adjust my dick so it didn't salute whoever came in, there was a beautiful young lady that had flowers and a teddy bear for Aubrey.

I could tell she was from an island with her long, curly hair, smooth caramel skin and green eyes. She wasn't helping my situation either. She wore some jeans that highlighted her wide sexy hips and I believe I saw that ass from the front. Once I made it back up to her face, I could also tell she wasn't happy but I would have never guessed why on my own. And looking at Aubrey, she wouldn't make eye contact with either of us but homegirl was not dropping her stare. I guess it was my job to break up whatever awkwardness was happening here. "Baby, don't you want to introduce me to your friend?"

Jordan

"Yeah, 'baby', don't you want to introduce us?" I said with a menacing stare.

Sam

I was back at my place because Keith was out of town this week. He wanted to me to stay at his house, but I declined. He asked Benny to keep an eye on me, and I was very excited about that. Keith let me know that Benny would be stopping by sometime this evening to check in on me. Benny knocked on my door around seven, and I was *definitely* prepared for his arrival. I made sure I wore my matching lace bra and panty set, with my *Desert Rose* style garter belt and thigh high sheer stockings from La Perla with the lace band around my thighs. I remembered how my ex, Joe, said high heels made my legs appear longer and how my ass looked a bit plumper, so I wore my nude Louboutin pumps as well. My red hair was freshly shampooed and styled. I knew I was looking and smelling good.

When I answered the door, Benny was speechless, as I knew he would be. "Come in handsome, I prepared some food for us if you're hungry. I also took a note of what you were drinking in the club the other night and purchased some Hennessy for you. Would you like a glass?"

Benny

"Damn." This threw me off guard like shit, but she know she was looking so good. That ass was sitting right and she wore them "come fuck me pumps" with her lingerie. Red bottoms. Stomach was flat, titties looking scrumptious. I could tell that all the shit she had on was expensive. "What are you trying to do, little mama? Keith is not to be fucked with like that. I don't know what your plans are with him, but he considers you his lady."

Sam

"Never mind all that." I poured Benny a drink and went over to him. "May I take your coat?" He smirked and shook his head as he removed it and then sat on the couch. I joined him, by sitting on his lap and kissing his neck. He continued to sip his drink as I circled his ear with my fingertip. Once he finished, he asked for a refill. I obliged him. When I came back with his drink, I removed his expensive gym shoes and began unbuckling his jeans.

Benny

"Yo, you mind if I blaze?" This shit is wild. On the one hand, I don't want to disrespect Keith, but *she* was pushing up on *me*. I just hope I'm not signing my own death warrant by fucking with his bitch.

Sam

"Sure, I don't mind. Can I have some too?" He told me it's whatever. Once I was able to undo his pants, I saw that his dick was semi hard and was already a nice size. He wasn't as well-endowed as Keith, but he was bigger than Joe. I removed his penis from his boxers and proceeded to lick the tip. He just stared at me while I swirled my tongue around his love stick and inhaled his smoke. I put him all the way into my mouth and sucked and licked while he kept watching me. I felt a little insecure, because he wasn't moaning or anything. But he placed his hand behind my head to keep me from letting it come out of my mouth. At that point, I kept sliding up and down on his dick until he told me to get up. "You want me to stop?"

Benny

"Hit this blunt lil mama, I wanna see something. When you inhale, make sure you hold the smoke in your lungs at least 5 seconds." This was that Sativa Haze, some good shit, and I wanted her not to be in her head for what we were about to do. She started coughing immediately and I laughed a little bit. "Have you ever smoked before?"

Sam

"No," I said as I coughed some more. I drank some water and when I settled down, he told me to try it again. He thought I was nervous and wanted me to relax completely. I indulged him and held it in my lungs like he said for about 5 seconds like he told me to. I did it three more times with way less coughing and he said he was impressed.

Benny

"Now that you're a pro, try sucking my dick again. Like you like it." No more of that timid shit.

Sam

That turned me on so much and now I was starting to feel the effects of the marijuana. I felt so good, it was like an outer body experience. Kind of like I was watching myself perform the sacred art of fellatio and I'm cheering myself on from the sideline. He pushed my head all the way down where I felt his penis obstruct my airway. He let up a little, but I had to get creative with it so that I could still breathe.

Benny

"Are you gonna let me release on your face, like a good girl?" I wanted to see how far she would go for me. She didn't look like a hoe, but most of them don't. She nodded her head yes while she was still bobbing on my dick. Watching her watch me was sexy as fuck even though her makeup was running down her face from the tears that sprung up from gagging. "You gonna let me fuck that pussy? I wanna see what you're working with little mama. That ass looks so good to me." Again, she nodded her head yes without stopping.

I felt that nut building up and instead of putting it on her pretty face, I wanted to see how she would react to me letting loose in her mouth. Once I was at the point of no return, I grabbed her head and started pumping from the bottom while my seed filled her throat. I let go once I started settling down from that sensation. She swallowed every fucking drop. Oh, I was gonna have fun with this little bitch.

James

I guess Free went home to check on Tamia, but she didn't wake me. I was discharged from the hospital around eight am. That process took about thirty minutes to ensure I knew how to clean and dress my wound and when to take my medications. Before leaving the hospital, I decided to go and check in with Monroe to see if the baby was here yet. I stopped at the information desk and they gave me Aubrey's room number, but as I got closer, it sounded like World War III had broken out. I remembered just then that I had given my gun to the young boys prior to being seen after the lil nigga went crazy last night, so I had nothing on me in case things got outta hand. I was trying to figure out what I would be able to use if something really popped off.

I heard arguing and it sounded like Monroe was trying to calm everyone down. Once I got there, Monroe was holding back a little Spanish chick trying to get at Aubrey. The nurse passed by me with the baby in her arms and Aubrey's mom had just walked in the room and was trying to figure out what was going on just like I was.

Spanish Chick

"So, you trying to play me now that your man is back? Who was there caressing you and making sure you ate so your baby wouldn't come out malnourished? Who helped you regain full use of your arm and leg after the accident? And who was there for you, loving on your *culo*, making you feel good when you were lonely? I only asked you to be truthful and you up in here letting this nigga feel you up? You just had a fucking baby, for Christ's sake? Ungrateful nasty bitch."

James

At that time, a security guard came in. Monroe looked over at me like he wanted to laugh, but he didn't as he tried escorting her out of Aubrey's hospital room.

Security Guard

"Ma'am, I'm sorry, you have to go. The only reason you were allowed in here before visiting hours is because you said you were the patient's girlfriend. You cannot be in here causing all of this turmoil as there are other mothers and babies trying to get some rest. I'm sorry."

Spanish Chick

"Yeah, I'm sorry too. Aubrey, don't you ever call me or come near me again *puta*." I can't believe I let this bitch get under my skin. How could I have allowed myself to fall in love with someone that didn't remember her past? When I met her, she was all fucked up! But it was just something about her that I couldn't resist. Damn, I hate her!

Monroe

I stepped into the hallway with James to allow my lady a chance to get herself together. I let the nurse know that it was okay to hand the baby back over to her and I apologized for the trouble. "Damn lil mama was strong! I'm sure the security guard wasn't anticipating all of this commotion in the maternity ward. I only got one good arm right now and I think she was trying to break that one trying to get at Aubrey. I guess they had a little thing while Aubrey thought she was a lesbian. And walking in on us kissing set her off. I didn't know shit about Aubrey being with her, she just went the fuck off."

James

"Damn, Boss, this shit sounds like a soap opera. I just wanted to come by and say congrats man." I dapped him up and he had this big ass smile on his face. "What you have, a little boy or girl?"

Monroe

"I got a son man!! Seven pounds, eleven ounces. Big boy! Looks just like me but has Aubrey's eyes. He's beautiful man! Thanks so much!"

James

"What's his name? Monroe, Jr.? MJ?" I was so excited for my friend!

Monroe

"We don't know yet. Hadn't gotten to that point by the time ole girl showed up." We laughed. "Let me get back in this room to make sure everything is straight. You comin' in to say hello?"

James

"Yeah man, I'm right behind you."

Chapter 4

James

After congratulating Aubrey on the new arrival, I headed out of there so they could enjoy their new son and address whatever issues they needed to. It was late morning by that point and the sun was beaming by the time I exited the hospital. It was still a bit brisk outside, being mid-December and all. Once I got to my car, I tried calling Free. She didn't answer. She may have been feeding Tamia or taking a nap since she was up so late. I went home so I could take a shower. I missed my daughter. I was so glad that Free allowed me to adopt her so that she would have my last name too.

I got to the house and Free's car wasn't there. Well maybe she decided to stay at Crystyle's house. I went upstairs and got in the shower, careful not to get my bandages wet. I used the handheld shower head and let the warm water cascade down the left side of my body and wiped off what I could near my wound. When I noticed Rob with that gun last night at the hospital, I just knew we were all dead. It's probably time for me to find a less stressful line of work because this shit is for the birds, I surmised. I remained in the shower allowing my stress to drift away until the water started getting lukewarm. I'm just thankful that that bullet just grazed me. At that specific location had it actually penetrated me, it could have caused some serious damage to my organs. I've been thanking God all night long.

I got out of the shower and laid down in my bed. I redialed Free and again, she didn't answer. I left her a message. "Hey baby, I'm home. Call me, I love you." I drifted off into a much-needed sleep after taking the medication that was prescribed to me this morning. When I woke up hours later, it was dark outside. It seemed like I was still home alone. I checked my phone and there was no return call from Fresia. I dialed her again and she still didn't answer. I decided to leave her another message, "Baby, I'm getting worried about you, what is going on? I'm home, please call me." I called Money to see if he knew anything about the lil nigga's whereabouts.

<<ring, ring>>

"Money, I haven't seen Free since last night at the hospital. Do you know what happened with Rob? Did the goons take him?" I was almost frantic because I knew Free probably wouldn't recover from another hostage situation.

Monroe

"No, Goldie tackled him after he started shooting us and then they carried him outside after disarming him and beat his ass. Before they could take him away, the police came and arrested him. His arraignment is scheduled for tomorrow morning at nine. Have you called her friend, Crystyle? She took the baby over her house, right?"

James

"No, but I'll do that now. Thanks bruh." I totally forgot about her.

Monroe

"In the meantime, I'll put the word out and have Benny look for her as well. I got you."

James

I called Crystyle to see if she knew where my ladies were.

<<ring, ring>>

"Hey Crystyle, how are you? I'm looking for Free and Tamia. Are they there with you?"

Crystyle

"Umm, James, she came to pick Tamia up last night. Are you doing okay? She said you were shot. She was very upset when she left here with the baby. Should I do something?"

James

"Did you she say anything about why she was upset? She seemed relieved that I was okay last night when I saw her and at the news I would be coming home." She told me no. Now I knew they weren't with the lil nigga and wasn't with Crystyle either. I didn't know what to think nor did I know what I was going to do next.

Kristin

"Thank you for calling Mountainview Smiles, how may I direct your call?" These patients always forgot their damn appointment dates and times. And I was always expected to be so cheery and polite to them while repeating myself over and over and over again, just because I'm the damn secretary. Like damn, write that shit down when you make the appointment. Since moving from Tennessee to here in Maryland, I feel lucky that I was able to find this position so quickly. I think one of the dentists has a crush on me but there ain't nothing he can do for me that I'm not already getting from my man. Dr. Saul is super short in stature, but what he lacks in physicality I know he more than makes up for with his money. I know I could get material things from any man, but believe I've always sought out love from men because my parents didn't exactly shower me with love or anything. I'm not looking back though.

I've been with my man since his ex, Samantha, decided she wanted to be with someone else. I know, I know, maybe I could be considered a rebound to some, but we've had a connection since before pursuing anything sexually. My ex came here to "retrieve" me, as he said but I refused to return to Tennessee. Joe was there for me and it made me want to pursue him even more.

A few months ago...

Joe

Sam didn't return home by the time I left her place around four pm. I was angry, but I would get over it. I drove home, and on my way, I saw a woman that resembled Kristin very closely trying to get away from a man with some tired ass braids that I had never seen before. Once I saw him slap her face, I pulled over, exited my car and placed myself in between the two of them.

"Is there a problem here? Why are you putting your hands on this woman?" I asked as I approached him menacingly.

Dude

"Aye man, what you need to do is mind your muthafuckin' business. This ain't got shit to do with you, period. This between me and my bitch." He snarled.

Kristin

"Joe, please. Please go." I cried.

Joe

He tried to charge at her as she ran away from him trying to get behind me and he lost his footing. I'm sure he felt embarrassed and that's why he charged at me next. I punched the shit outta him and he was dazed for a minute.

Kristin

"Joe. Can you take me home, please?"

Joe

I opened the passenger door and let her get in first before walking around to get in myself. He was staring a hole into me, but I silently dared him to do something. Don't no female deserve to be treated like that. And how the hell you doing all this fuck shit on the street so everyone can see you. Niggas these days are so fuckin stupid.

"You alright Kris? Is there anything that I can do?"

Kristin

I was so embarrassed. I broke up with him months ago. Why the fuck was he here? I bet my stupid ass mama told him where to find me. Taz probably gave her some drugs or money. She don't give a damn about me. That bitch never has. I'm so scared right now. "I appreciate you for taking me home. But honestly, I'm good." I said as tears streamed down my face silently. We arrived at my apartment complex. "Would you mind walking me inside please?

Joe

"Yeah, I'll walk you in. It's no problem." I saw that she was really scared and trying not to cry but I certainly was distracted. It felt insensitive for a second, but that quickly dissipated. I parked my car and walked behind Kristin as we went to her building. Her ass is super swole and those hips look so good to me. I hadn't gotten my dick wet in some time.

Kristin

"Joe, would you mind staying, just for a little while? I'm not feeling safe at all. I thought that once I got here, I would be okay." He agreed. "Would you like something to eat? Something to drink?" It was getting late and we both had to work tomorrow, so I decided to cook because he was being so nice to me. "Do you like spaghetti? It's something quick." I asked as I handed him the glass of water.

Joe

"Whatever you fix, I appreciate it. Thank you." I couldn't take my eyes off of her. She removed her jacket and had this little tank top on with no bra. She passed me the remote. She got dinner started and took a shower before we ate. She came out in this little short set. She's killing me, her butt was coming out of the bottom of them shorts and I couldn't stop staring at her. I decided

to ask her about ole dude to distract me from her body.

"So, who was that, Kristen? Why was he all in your face like that?

Kristin

"We met in high school and we were together on and off from the time I was fifteen, up until a few months before I came here. I used to hide from my family because of how he would beat my ass. I would leave, and he would sweet talk my mom into letting him in our house even if I told her not to. Once he figured out that my mom was getting high, he would bring her a little something when he came over. She wouldn't bother us. She didn't care that he was forcing me to sex him.

"When I turned eighteen, he convinced me to live with him. After I moved in, I found out that he had not one, but two girls pregnant. And one was fifteen years old. The older one moved in shortly after. It was a totally toxic environment. He would get high and want to fuck. Needless to say, if I didn't want to, he got violent. Neither of the girls ever helped me or came to my aid and honestly, I don't even know how Taz convinced me to stay. He had my mind so twisted up and always told me that no one would want an ugly little white girl with nothing or no one, so I just stayed. He made me go to work and I would come home late at night and they would either be laid up sleep in my bed or

fucking. I would just wait until they were done to see if Candace was going to go get in her bed or I would just lay on the couch. When I got paid, the money was used for the house. I never was able to do anything for myself.

"After three years of living in that situation, and four more kids 'on the side' later, I left with no money to my name and just the clothes on my back. I came here for a new start and it had been good until today." We talked just a bit more and then Joe said he would see me tomorrow, and that if I needed anything to give him a call. "I really appreciate you, Joe. See you tomorrow."

Joe

"Good night, Kris. See you tomorrow and lock this door behind me." I left and while heading home, I saw that Sam was calling. Good, because I needed to get some pussy after being around Kristin's fine ass.

Present Day

Kristen

Joe doesn't have much money or anything, but I've been getting that good good from him for the past few months and I was addicted. It was almost time for our afternoon "mouth session", as we call it. Speaking of my honey, he strolled to my desk right on time.

Joe

I always come around that corner all smiles because it's my favorite time of the day. Our routine was that I would enter the storage room first, and then she would transfer the phones during her lunch break and enter after me. I think it was the thrill of possibly being caught at work while she gave me that good ass top. And Kristin *loved* giving me head. She even told me that my nut tasted good. I was like, who says that? I realized I still missed Sam, and I believed that Kris knew this and that was why she wanted to fuck and suck on me before I even had a chance to ask for it. She thought that was what I needed, but I missed Sam because she encouraged me to be a better me. I just didn't listen to her until now, and it's too late. Kristen was fine with how things were between us. We are just fooling around for now, it's nothing serious. I'm not interested in being with nobody else, but I'm open to whatever. We having fun!

Kristin

"Hey baby, I thought we could try something different today. My pussy is in need of a major tune up and I was wondering if you would just let me sit on it and go crazy?" He didn't seem excited about it, but I was gonna get my way. "Just pull your scrubs down and lie back. I'll do all of the work." He did as I asked, and I already was super wet, so I pulled up my skirt revealing that I wasn't wearing any panties. His eyes were wide with surprise at that and I enjoyed every bit of it! I climbed on top and straddled him slowly. It always felt like the first time when he entered me. I opened my shirt because I knew he loved my breasts.

And crazy did I go! That little twin bed made so much noise with all that creaking, but I didn't give a fuck. I knew there was no one here during the lunch hour and I locked the door behind me, or so I thought. I was moaning, Joe was moaning, and we were absolutely oblivious that Dr. Saul was watching me ride Joe's dick. It wasn't until I looked up and I tried not to alert Joe to my surprise, because that would have been a whole other situation. I don't know how long he was standing there, but he was rubbing his dick from the outside of his scrubs. Joe wasn't facing the door, but I was. I kept going and decided to make it a show. I turned around on the dick and made sure that Dr. Saul could watch me twerk this big white ass on Joe's big black dick. I also wanted to show him that this was the closest he would ever get to my pussy.

Once Joe told me he was about to nut, I hopped off of his dick and made sure that I caught all of that good spunk in my mouth. Since he liked it nasty, I even let a little dribble down my chin while I swallowed the rest. I made sure I licked my tongue out to show him and Joe that it was all gone. When I looked back up, Dr. Saul was gone, and Joe and I got ourselves together to go and eat some actual food for the rest of our lunch break. That was absolutely a great time for me... I liked being the star of the show.

Marie

I can't believe Robert would do this to us! Why would he leave the babies and I all alone to exact some half-witted revenge, when he had to know it wasn't going to succeed? I just left his arraignment and I recognized a couple of the guys from Monroe's warehouse there. I guess they just wanted to make sure Robert wasn't coming out or something. I wasn't able to visit with him, but he knew I was there because he looked back into the crowd. When they escorted him out of the court room and he made eye contact with me, he turned his head very quickly. He ignored me as I called out to him. I stopped one of Monroe's goons out in the courthouse parking lot to inquire about what happened last night.

Goldie

"Yo, don't touch me bitch if you know what's good for you. I know what you're into and I don't want none of that voodoo shit on me. How you get pregnant though? Your nigga ain't even got a dick!"

Marie

He and the guy he was with started laughing at my expense. I walked away as fast as I could because I refused to allow them to see me cry. I sat in my car, that I had to pick up from the Southern Maryland Hospital parking lot the day after the shooting and bawled my eyes out. I don't see any way out of this for him and I'm not sure at this point what I could do.

"Ow, ow, come on babies, be nice to mommy. We have a little while longer and then you can come out okay? Calm down with the kicking. I'm mad at daddy too." I had to figure something out and fast!

Rob

Why was she here? Embarrassing me, yelling my name and shit. I never wanted to see her again. Damn, she could've kept her ugly ass at home. I don't know what happened with them niggas, but I was hoping when I read about my story in the paper this morning that they were both dead. I still hadn't heard anything. This shit is annoying as fuck! "Aye yo, what the fuck you looking at homeboy? You better get the fuck on somewhere before I beat the shit outta you."

Prisoner

"I'm looking at you 'Fish', you got a problem with that? And you might wanna watch your mouth talking to me like that. You in my house now. Be careful, Fish. I'm here with you after lights out. Don't you forget that shit either."

Rob

"Whateva my nigga, try me if you want to with that 'Fish' shit. I don't give a fuck about who you are. Fuck outta here with that dumb ass shit."

Aubrey

I'm so embarrassed that Jordan would come up here and show her ass like that. And in front of my momma? It's bad enough that Monroe had to find out like that too. Shit!! I'm sore as I don't know what after pushing a baby out of my body with no damn medication. I mean my entire body is aching. What did I think I was going to do to her with my out of shape ass?! "Mommy, I'm okay. I'm going to lay back down, can you just tell the nurse to bring me my baby please?" I appreciate the nurse being concerned, but both of his parents were in the room, I wasn't gonna let nothing happen to my baby.

Dee Dee

At that moment, the nurse walked back in letting us know that my grandson was in the nursery for his safety. "Nurse, I need to get my grandson from the nursery. What do I need to do?"

Nurse

"Ma'am, we have to ensure the safety of the child and the environment is your daughter's room was *not* that earlier this morning. It is my responsibility to report this incident to my supervisors. The baby's father requested that he be brought back to his mother, but I have to consult my superiors."

Dee Dee

"Ma'am, I can understand that, but I'm not concerned with what you are talking about in this moment. Give me my grandson, or there will be another 'incident' in here and you will *not* like the outcome." She got her little ass up out of that chair and retrieved my grandbaby, I know that. I haven't put my hands on someone in a long time, but it doesn't mean they still can't rock.

"Awww, there's my baby boy. NeNe came to get you baby. You ok? That mean lady was trying to keep you in there with those crybabies. But you don't belong in there with them. No, you don't… no, you don't!" I said to him in a sing-song voice.

Aubrey

"Mommy, what you talkin' about now with my baby?" I asked as my mom walked in with my son. It was so precious to see her loving on her only grandbaby.

Dee Dee

"I was telling my baby boy that his NeNe got him. Yes I do!"

Aubrey

"Mommy, you just determined that he's not gonna call you grandma huh?" I was laughing and she threw a pillow at me. "Owww! Not nice 'Grandma'!" I was really cracking up now!

Dee Dee

"While you're talking about what he's gonna call me, I would love to know what my grandson's name is so I can know what to call him! Hmmmm... Cat got your tongue huh, smart ass? Yeah, I thought so." I said as we laughed together.

Aubrey

"Okay ma, you got me. We still haven't had a chance to talk about that with all the commotion. What am I going to say to Monroe about Jordan?" Monroe walked into the room and we got quiet. "Hey, we were just talking about you. I really want to apologize for all of that earlier." He put his hand up as if to say, 'not right now' and went over to my mom to play with the baby.

Monroe

"Hey Junior, you miss your daddy? Daddy missed you baby boy."

Chapter 5

Monroe

"Mrs. Dee Dee, what did you say the baby was going to call you?" I heard her, I just wanted her to say it again because I thought it was cute.

Dee Dee

"NeNe...", we laughed together this time. I could tell there was some tension between Aubrey and Monroe. I thought this was a good time for me to go back to my husband's room. "Alright y'all, I'm going to go see my boo. I'll come back later." I kissed my grandson and left the room.

Monroe

I played with my son for a bit longer to see if Aubrey would start the conversation, but maybe I'm being a bit hard on her. I don't know. "So, let's talk Aubrey. You know where I stand with you, but that situation with your girlfriend was way too heated to be around my newborn son. What do you want to do?"

Aubrey

"Monroe, I didn't remember anything about you until I had our son, hours ago. I can't explain it, but when those memories came flooding back, there was no choice to make, there was only you. I remembered going to Silk's with you on our first date. I remembered the first time you made love to me. I remembered how you always made me feel so safe all the time, but there are still some holes in my memory. I'm hoping that it doesn't take for me to go through labor with our next child to remember every single thing." I laughed a bit hoping to lighten the mood. He didn't, he just continued to listen. I cleared my throat and started again. "I truly hope that you can be patient with me.

"After the accident, I was confused. I didn't know you, but I had everybody including my mother, the person I trusted the most in this world, telling me that I was in love with you and that we were going to get married when I woke up from my coma. And I just felt like something was wrong with me. Everyone was rooting for you, but it seemed like no one was on my side and was trying to understand how I felt. No one could identify with what *I* was feeling!" I was crying at this point, but I could tell I was getting through to Monroe. "And when I found out that I was pregnant, that just threw everything even more out of whack. I was depressed, I even sent my mother home. And you know how much I love her being around. I would even love for her to move back here.

"But this little boy was absolutely meant to be! He brought us back together and I know this is where I'm supposed to be. I'm sorry about the way I carried things, I know I will never be able to make that up to you. But I will spend the rest of my life trying to do so. I love you so much, baby. Please tell me that we can get through this. I cannot, I don't wanna live without you."

Monroe

I was totally blown away! I wasn't sure earlier about how much she remembered, although I knew that she remembered something. "That is truly the best thing you could tell me on my birthday. Consider your slate wiped clean, because there's only one thing that I want from you and that is forever. That's your whole heart forever. Are you sure that this thing between you and ole girl is over?

Aubrey

"I am sure. I will need to give her some time to cool off, so that I can meet with her and tell her in person. I hope you don't mind."

Monroe

"I don't. I think she deserves that. But I have just one more question for you baby?"

Aubrey

"What is it my love?" He was so damn handsome and sexy to me.

Monroe

"Did she suck your pussy better than me though?" She got so embarrassed in that moment and all I could do was laugh!

Aubrey

"*BABY!* Don't talk like that in front of Junior." We laughed some more until he realized just what I said. I heard him say that earlier when my mom was in here. He wasn't slick!

Monroe

"Are you saying that you're okay with naming the baby after me?" She nodded her head yes and we resumed what we started this morning while Junior slept. I love her so fucking much! We just continued our making out session and loved on our beautiful son, Monroe, Jr.

Taisha

I woke up in my bedroom and my head was spinning. I ran to the bathroom because the contents of my stomach were threatening to emerge. I was dope sick. This is how most mornings go for me, but whatever. Cold sweats, diarrhea, and body aches weren't too far behind the nausea, but I have to get myself all the way together. Today was the first day of this week that I had to go see Don. I had to actually put some thought into what I was going to wear. "Damn, I need to wash clothes. And clean up this dump." Dishes were overflowing in the sink and clothes were everywhere in my bedroom. My clothes wasn't the only shit all over my house. There were syringes, used needles, spoons and wine bottles everywhere. I just really needed to get my shit together. This is reminding me of my college days all over again.

Five years ago, I met a tall, petite white girl named Hannah in college. Hannah was a lesbian and she tried to holla at me one night at a party where I met her. I refused her that night and numerous times after that, and eventually she wore me down enough to hang out with her crazy ass. She claimed she understood I wasn't gay and just wanted to be my friend, but she would always try her hand on the sly. Hannah always had the hookup on the weed.

One night, she had given me something else though. We drove out to Rehoboth Beach in Delaware for a house party. I didn't know anyone else there, because these were her friends that lived in this big ass gorgeous house. They all were from her hometown in Pennsylvania. Had to be at least six or seven bedrooms there and in each one, there was another drug featured and had a whole 'nother set of people in them. I was one of the few black people in the house, but I was used to that hanging with her.

We ended up in a room with two girls, one of which was a gorgeous Hispanic girl with some of the prettiest gray eyes I had ever seen and an Asian girl with a big booty! Picture that! There was a guy there too, I guess he was the connect because Hannah went and spoke to him privately as I curiously watched the girls. The Hispanic girl was smoking a joint and I saw the Asian girl rubbing something on her gums before she took the joint from the pretty girl. They were almost finished with their joint when I started watching them and their eyes were glazed over by the time they were done.

Once they finished, both of them starting undressing, and the big booty girl went down on the other one. The Hispanic girl was staring at me with her pretty ass eyes, while rubbing her titties and licking her lips. By the time the Asian girl made her cum, I swear my pussy was wet. After I realized that I was turned on, I stopped watching them and started looking for Hannah. The guy had left and Hannah was just sitting there watching me.

I walked over to her. "Hey, you get the weed?"

Hannah

"Yeah girl, I got a special type of weed. You down?"

Taisha

"Yeah girl, I'm always down. But let's leave them in here so they can handle their business."

Hannah

"Okay, cool."

Taisha

We then walked around the house people watching. I really didn't know too much about drugs back then. But later on, I realized that they were doing cocaine, shooting up heroin, taking pills and all kinds of other shit. And we all were drinking too. Hannah kept bringing me some kind of homemade punch that was sweet and didn't really taste like it had much alcohol in it. She fired up the joint and took a pull of it and handed it to me. We got so fucked up at that party, that we decided to rent a room and drive back in the morning. I told her to make sure she got two beds, but of course you know we ended up with a room that had only a queen size bed in it. She claimed it was the last one. It was cool though; I was going straight to sleep.

Anyway, that joint mixed with that alcohol had me so high that apparently, I agreed to let Hannah to do whatever the fuck she wanted to do to me that night. I remember her mouth on my neck, her playing with my titties and finally, she ate me out. After all that, we fell asleep and I woke up to Hannah fondling and kissing on my ass because she was fascinated with how big it was. I was still high from that party and let her eat my pussy again because of how turned on I was. We left hours later, and she didn't seem to be acting any different from before going to this party.

Over the course of the next few days, I noticed for the first time that Hannah was an avid drug user. Not just a weed smoker, as I thought. She wanted me to smoke the special kind of weed with her again, that I later found out was mixed with cocaine, but I declined. She didn't like that very much, but she got over it, or so I thought. She just went the fuck off and forced my shorts off of me and tried to put her face in my pussy again. I told her to get out of my dorm room. It got physical and when I threatened to press charges on her, she retreated.

Over the next few weeks, she would stalk me, break into my room and ruin things and when she stole my purse, I had no choice but to press charges on her. I couldn't believe that things turned out this way. But I vowed that I would never do drugs again. And with this present situation with Don, I'm always paranoid. Looking over my shoulder everywhere I go. And having to fuck him on demand, and whoever he decides to tell me to fuck, with no say so is why I turned right back to drugs. I know this is not me, but what can I do? I'm feenin' right now though.

<<ring, ring>>

"Hey papi, can you come over real quick please? I need to get a hit before I run this errand. You got some time for me papi?

Travis

"Mami, as long as you give me the culo, I be there. Necesito sentir te mami. Give me that pussy. I need to feel you mami."

Taisha

"Yes papi, I'll be ready when you get here." I made an attempt to clean up so that he wouldn't think I was dirty too. Not like Curt, my old boss at the strip club now thought of me.

Sam

That week with Benny went way too fast. Keith came back and was all over me, and I loved his dick, so it definitely wasn't a problem. But Benny was younger, he was wild and he tore this pussy up! We even got another female to join us, and I believe I may have enjoyed her more than he did. She was this dark skin stripper that we met at Sugar's. Yes, he took me to my first strip club! Her name was Candy, and she had full succulent breasts, a very juicy booty and an unbelievably small waist. I was in love at first sight! I made sure to get her number before she left.

She made love to my pussy and my breasts with her tongue while Benny sexed me. Then we switched roles and he sexed her. Once we were done with all of the sex games, Benny spread his seed wherever he wanted, while doing what he wanted. It was some real porn star stuff, from what he said, and he seemed very excited about it. At that point, I realized I had never watched pornography. But once they left, I explored some things courtesy of the worldwide web. I even found a secret club in the city that meets once a month where anything goes. I'm going to go by myself first, and then maybe bring it up to Keith.

Monroe

It was discharge day for Aubrey and the baby and we could finally go home. I hired a cleaning company, had fresh tulips placed throughout the house and a personal chef was employed to create a special meal of all of Aubrey's favorites. There was catfish, crab cakes, loaded mashed potatoes, chicken skewers, ribeye steaks, broccoli and cheese and various desserts. She was tired, so after feeding the baby, she took a long shower and a nap. MJ and I played until he fell asleep and then I took my shower and got dressed. I still had a bit of work to do for Aubrey.

My parents took the news better than I thought they would when I told them about the baby. My mom had actually pulled me to the side and let me know that she thought Aubrey was getting fat the last time she saw her months earlier. I told her to be nice. My sisters were there with their boyfriends and we brought Mrs. Dee Dee and Mike as well. It was a family affair for sure. But I had a surprise in store.

After we all ate dinner, everyone continued loving on Monroe, Jr. I went to the car to get what I needed for the surprise and gathered everyone in the family room. "As you all know, this has been a rough year, but it is definitely ending on a great note with my lady, my new baby and having you all here to witness it. I wanted everyone to be here when I did this officially." My sister unbuttoned my son's shirt and revealed his oncsie that said, "Marry my daddy, mommy." I got on one knee and asked Aubrey now that she was out of the coma, "Will you do me the honor of being my wife? Will you marry me?"

Chapter 6

James

"Fresia, baby, please call me back." I put two and two together after Money told me that Free ran into his mother-in-law at the hospital the morning after the shooting. She knows that Rob is the one that shot us, and I know she feels betrayed. The lie was simply to protect her, not just to cover it up. Now I can't find my ladies. I'm fucked up inside. If she doesn't feel safe with me, I'm doing something completely wrong. I called her again. "Baby, I know it was fucked up that I didn't tell you that it was Rob that shot me. Please talk to me baby and let me explain. I didn't want you to return to that dark place you were in before. I don't want to lose you and Mi Mi. Please come home. I miss you and my baby. Please Fresia. I love you."

After calling for what seemed to be the millionth time, I just sat there in the dark for hours. That was my calm place. Otherwise, I was going to figure out a way to get locked up myself and go kill that bitch with my bare hands. Just then, it sounded like the front door was being unlocked. "Fresia!"

Free

"Be quiet James, Tamia is sleeping." Damn. He keeps blowing up my phone and shit. I don't wanna talk to his ass. "Save it! I listened to your bullshit over the voicemail and I don't care what you have to say now. You should have been truthful with me the first time. I don't want to talk to you right now. MOVE!" I handed him the baby and went into one of the guest rooms and locked the door behind me. I went to a hotel for a few nights, just to clear my mind. I loved James with my whole heart, but if I couldn't trust him, there was nothing more for us. I'm glad I didn't come home before now, because I was liable to say some shit I was going to regret. I just went to sleep. Fuck James and his excuses.

James

Damn, Free ain't never been this mad at me. But I'm glad she's home. I hope she talks to me in the morning. I want to tell her everything. I'm not keeping shit from her no more. "Hi baby girl, daddy missed you so much." Tamia was still sleeping, so that was good. I looked in the diaper bag and took out the bags of milk to refrigerate. I cleaned the breast pump so that it would be ready the next time Free was ready to use it. I took the baby to the room with me and let her lay on my chest. I soon fell asleep until I felt Tamia moving a few hours later. I knew what she wanted, so I took her to the nursery and changed her diaper and then I was on my way to the kitchen to make her a bottle.

Free must've heard me moving around, because she was already in the kitchen warming the bottle. "I'm sorry, I didn't mean to wake you. I was trying to move around quietly." When she looked at me, I could tell it was a mixture of sadness and disappointment. I knew that I was the cause of it, and it made me feel even more like shit. She spoke to me before I could think of anything to say.

Free

"James, more than anything, I'm sad that you feel that you can't trust me. I know that I was in a very bad place before, but when I told you that I love you and Tamia more than myself, I meant that. I'm supposed to be your partner, the one you call on when you need help, the one you can share everything with. But this... this made me feel as if you're trying to save me. I don't need a savior Jay! I just need to feel safe with you. I need to feel that I can trust you and that you can trust me back. I want no secrets between us, even if they are hard to say. Let this be the one time that you keep something from me. I won't tolerate anything less. Good night."

James

Free went back into the guest room for the night and I sat there feeding the baby, all alone with my thoughts.

Keith

"Damn Sam, yesssss… oh, fuck! Keep that shit going babe!" I would have never guessed that Samantha was this insatiable. I thoroughly enjoyed my sex life with her, but I swear she had me tired as fuck throughout the day. I mean, I am not complaining, but I am glad that this project manager shit is just the front for my distribution business. "Sssssss, I'm about to explode baby. FUCK!!" She just kept sucking that dick like she was in a contest. I'm only thirty-four, but soon I was gonna have to pick up those little blue pills to keep up with her.

Sam was lots of fun, and I could see myself loving her, but there were times that she disappeared for stints of time and I didn't know what she was doing. She would tell me she was visiting her family, or her friend that just had a baby, but I wouldn't hear from her sometimes until later on during the next day. It's not that serious that I feel I need to follow her, but I do know that I need to be careful.

Sam

I just couldn't get enough of Keith. It was like even when he was in my mouth, I would experience an orgasm just off of his pleasure. Benny doesn't have that effect on me and neither does anyone at my sex meets. I was just enjoying myself so much. I'm glad that he hasn't brought up having an exclusive relationship, because I wasn't ready for that right now. "Mmmm baby, that was good. I love seeing your face when you orgasm. It's so sexy." It was getting late, and tonight I was meeting up with Candy and one of her men. I hadn't met him yet, but she said I would enjoy him. "I'm gonna get out of here because I have an early morning. I'll call you tomorrow sweetie." I put my tongue as far in his mouth that it would go, while he squeezed my ass. I wasn't trying to start nothing, so I broke the embrace. "Talk to you tomorrow?"

Keith

"You sure you don't wanna stay, baby girl? I miss rolling over in that pussy in the middle of the night."

Sam

"I'll stay over this weekend, and I'll be sure to make it worth your while." I grabbed his hard dick through his pajama pants and walked out to my car. He watched me from the porch until I waved goodbye as I was on my way. Once I got home, I took a nice bubble bath, and when I got out, I put on my shimmering lotion that made me smell edible. I brushed my mane into a wild, sexy ponytail after slipping on a red satin teddy. It left nothing to the imagination, and that's what I was going for. I put on my black, shiny Manolo's and my ankle length, black silk trench coat and headed back to my car. I drove the 25 minutes to Candy's condo in Laurel,

Maryland. When I got to the door, she opened it before I could ring the doorbell and she looked so fucking sexy.

She was wearing a long red, satin gown that dipped down to her navel in the front, showcasing her perky D cups. Her gown had two slits that started at both sides of her clean-shaven pussy and you could see it with every step she took. The back plunged down to the top of her gorgeous ass that I liked to rub, lick and kiss on so much. I stepped in and we kissed so deeply, as I palmed both of her ass cheeks as if I would die without it. We were so hot and heavy, that I forgot all about her friend joining us as my hands made their way around to her wet pussy and her supple breasts. I kissed her neck, sucked on her ear lobes because I knew that was her spot, then our tongues initiated a dance in each other's mouths.

"Ooh Candy girl, you look tasty."

Candy's male friend

"May I join in the fun?"

Sam

When I looked at him in the candlelight, I noticed he was a white boy. He had a chiseled face with sharp, but very sexy features. He was tanned, looked to be about 6'2" or so and his chest and abs were to die for! He had dark hair, steel gray eyes, and a beautiful smile. All he was wearing was a towel, but from what I could tell, me and Candy's performance *really* turned him on. I walked over to him and started kissing his neck and shoulders as I removed his towel.

"Yeah, I can work with that baby." I said as I eyed his package. Candy had the champagne on chill, and while she was rolling the blunt, I decided to sample the goods. "Lay on your back, sexy." As he laid down, I sat on his dick reverse cowgirl. "Now, come here gorgeous and let me put my face in it." Candy did as I said and propped her leg up on a chair and put that pussy right on my tongue. We pleasured each other over and over for hours until we all decided to tap out. I was feeling nice from the weed and the champagne, and my body was blissfully satisfied beyond measure. All I kept thinking on the ride home was, when am I going to get to do that again?

Aubrey

After the initial excitement about the wedding and gushing nonstop over our son, I decided to reach out to Jordan. I really felt bad about the way things went when she came to visit me in the hospital. She agreed to meet with me, and I headed to her at her apartment in Temple Hills, Maryland. When I got to the door, it smelled like she was cooking a meal. And she looked so beautiful. I tried not to get distracted, but she had on a white cropped blouse with no bra underneath, so her nipples were standing up from the breeze that entered the apartment with me. The blouse also showcased her beautifully bronzed four pack abs, and her long flowing wrap skirt had white, baby blue and turquoise in it. The wrap part was shorter in the front and I was secretly hoping it would open as she walked so I could see her pretty pussy one more time. She was always so effortlessly sexy, and I could tell that she had just gotten out of the shower not too long before because her curly hair was still wet. She fingered it up in a ponytail and the ringlets framed her gorgeous natural face and sea green eyes.

I handed her her favorite bottle of wine as a peace offering after I entered the apartment. She didn't say a word to me, yet she reached for my coat as I passed it to her to hang up in the hall closet. She walked back into the kitchen to continue stirring whatever it was that she had in a big pot. All I could do was watch her ass swaying from side to side along with those beautiful wide hips of hers.

Jordan

"So, you just came over here to stare at me or what? You wanted to talk, so talk."

Aubrey

Her accent, her spiciness, and her attitude made her even more sexy to me, but that was not what I was supposed to be thinking at this moment. "I wanted to apologize to you for the way things went. I didn't want to disrespect you, nor did I want to hurt you. You were right, you got me through the toughest time of my life, when I didn't even know how I was going to make it through the night. I truly appreciate you for that and I love you dearly, and I always will. But something clicked inside my mind once I began delivering Junior. All of these memories of my former life started flooding back to me, and at that time, I realized then how much I loved Monroe before any of this happened.

"Right as I looked into my baby boy's eyes for the first time, I knew he wasn't a mistake. I knew he was made out of love. I truly, truly didn't mean for you to be a casualty in this love triangle, but I cannot explain how sorry I am for hurting you. That car accident changed my life and I would be lying to myself if I said I was sorry that I ever met you. I love you, Jordan. And I'm sorry." I felt the tear escape my eye and I wiped it away as fast as it came. Jordan stood in front of me and pulled my face up to look at her and she stroked my hair. I could smell her sex mixed with her body wash through the slit in her skirt and my pussy started throbbing. I hugged her around her waist, and we stayed in that position for what seemed like hours, but I know was only a minute or two. I looked up at her and she told me she loved me and forgave me.

I was so thankful, and I couldn't help myself any longer as I parted her skirt and began to kiss her flower. She moaned softly and continued running her fingers though my long, thick hair. I tapped her inner thigh, to tell her to open her legs just a bit more, while I grabbed her plentiful ass with both hands underneath her skirt. My tongue found her center and I licked her softly. Her legs started trembling, so I guided her to the couch, where I unwrapped her beautiful skirt like she was my present. She spread her legs open wide and I placed my face back into her soft folds. I suckled her clitoris gently while I pleasured her the way I knew she liked. She arched her back like she usually did when she was close to orgasm. I continued to lick and suck, lick and suck as I plunged three of my fingers in and out of her wetness. I massaged her g-spot from the inside as I continued the assault with my mouth from the outside. As her orgasm began to spill out of her, I continued devouring her until the last drop entered my mouth. Once I was done, I began to suckle her breasts one by one, back and forth while she felt on mine. I looked up at her face after a few minutes and noticed that she was crying.

"What's the matter, Jordan? Why are you crying?" As I kissed her face and then her lips softly. She didn't kiss me back, so I looked at her and waited for an answer.

Jordan

"Get out." She said softly. "Get *OUT*!! How dare you make me fall in love with you and then you tell me you're in love with someone else. Get the fuck out, Aubrey! Don't ever call me again. I hate you!"

Aubrey

She wouldn't let me say anything else, and she handed me my coat and opened the door for me. She wouldn't even look at me, she just closed the door as I stood there waiting for her say something, anything to me. I heard her sobbing softly through the door and after about five minutes, I turned around and headed home to my fiancé and my son.

Chapter 7

Don

"Why the fuck you coming up here high again, Taisha? I already told you about that shit and you're not taking me seriously. What the fuck is wrong with you? You falling way the hell off. And are those track marks on your fucking arms?" I'd been hearing rumors about her out in these streets getting pimped by this Spanish nigga named Travis. I got a hit out on his ass as we speak. My bitch was beautiful, she was clean... Now she was wasting away, she had to have lost at least ten to fifteen pounds. But that ass still looked right and them lips was still able to suck on this dick. I just hoped she still made them other niggas wear condoms. I wasn't having that shit though, I wanted to feel everything. But I knew she was pretty no-nonsense about that shit before me.

"Tai, do you hear me? Come on, you need to tell me what's going on and how I can help you fix it. Am I not taking care of you enough? Why you out in these streets the way you are? How the fuck did you end up shooting this shit into your veins?" I said as I raised her sleeves. She was embarrassed at that point. I don't know why she can't get it through her head that I got eyes out in these streets. "If I hear about you fucking with that nigga Travis and shooting this junk into your veins again, I'm cutting you the fuck off. I mean that shit too." Her eyes started to water and at that point, I knew there was something that she wanted to say.

Taisha

"Do you think I like being like this? Do you think I like being addicted to this shit and letting niggas do whatever they want to me? I just don't give a fuck anymore! Can't you see that? And can't you see that it's because of you? Shooting up helps me not to think about the messenger you sent to remind me of what happened to Renee. I know you have people watching me. I'm paranoid all the fucking time because of it. You got me up in here tricking for your fellow inmates like I agreed to do that shit in the beginning. That's when I started to fall off. And if I'm doing it for you, why can't I do it on the outside? I mean, what's the difference? At this point, if I died tomorrow, it would be welcomed. This shit ain't me, *you* did this to me! Now am I here to fuck you and whoever, or what? We wasting time with all this small talk."

Don

Tai started to undress while looking me directly in my eyes. She was still a very beautiful woman, and my dick still responded to her immediately despite what we were just talking about. She undressed slowly and swayed to whatever music was playing in her head. It was just going to be me and her from now on. I'll make one of my other bitches fuck the other niggas in here.

They weren't as special as Taisha anyway. I was just mad at first because she was trying to get back with Money, and that's why I told him about the arrangement that she suggested. I knew he was disappointed, but I also knew that he was loyal and recognized that she was now my property.

I got up and cupped her breasts from behind as she grinded her ass on my dick. She reached up and started to caress my head and neck while I continued playing with her nipples. I moved one hand down to her pussy and she was dripping. I turned her around, picked her up and slid her down on my dick while her legs were draped over my arms. I put her back against the wall and she wrapped her arms around my neck while I drilled her pussy to my heart's content. This is why I couldn't let her ass go. That shit had me sprung.

After my twins were born from one of my young girls, my wife stopped fucking me. They were now five years old, and Stacia and I had an unspoken agreement. Once my kids with her were old enough, they didn't want to come and see me in prison anymore, so she didn't make them. But she came faithfully, every Friday at ten in the morning. She was still so beautiful. As beautiful as the day I met her. But without physical love, it was just aesthetics. I made sure I took care of her so that she could maintain the lifestyle that I created for her so long ago. The only rule I had was that she couldn't fuck no other niggas for the first ten years. It's been eight.

Tai was riding the shit outta my dick and I was about spill all of my seed inside her walls. Her pussy brought me right back to reality, and out of the funk that my beautiful wife no longer desired to fuck her husband. I was just going to continue to enjoy the young pussy that I got on almost a daily basis. I had two others that came on the days that Tai and my wife weren't here. But Tai was paid much more for her services. She was good at making me feel young again at almost fifty years old. I'm just hoping that she can recover from whatever she's experiencing, because I wouldn't hesitate to leave her ass stinkin' somewhere.

Benny

It was Tuesday morning and I was out making sure that the deliveries were on time while Monroe was out of the office. He was due back on Thursday, after being home with his girl and his new son for a few weeks. That shit was crazy, he came in here one day and had a whole son that he knew nothing about in the days before. He looked so happy though and I thought that shit was beautiful. My phone started ringing and it was this nigga Keith again. I usually only did favors for this nigga because of Monroe. I looked up to Monroe, he was there when my father walked out on us because his wife wouldn't allow my mother access to any of their money. Monroe didn't know who my father was, or that the real reason I started working for him was to get back at my dad. No one ever knew his true identity, because I was the spitting image of my mother. After he left her, she began using the product he floated around the poor neighborhood that we were forced to live in. Now, my mother was just a shell of her former self, and I was still working my way up in this business to ensure she would be forever taken care of, courtesy of the same muthafucka that left us to rot in that ghetto, years ago.

<<ring, ring>>

"Yeah"

Keith

"Damn nigga, why you let the phone ring so long? Am I disturbing something with your girl?" He chuckled.

Benny

"Nah, nothing like that. What's going on?" I was getting annoyed that he thought it was okay to keep calling me like we were friends. "Are you looking for Money?"

Keith

"Not at all. I wanted to meet with you about a business proposal. I respect the way you handle yours, and I know that my brother trusts you as well." Right now, he worked for Money, my brother's protégée, but I wanted this young man on my security team. He always looked after Samantha when I wasn't here, and she only provided glowing reviews about his professionalism. "I need only people that I trust around me at all times, and you have quickly become one of those individuals. I know that you have a very good relationship with Money, but I was hoping that you and I could sit down so that I could detail all the benefits that a new business relationship between the two of us would bring."

Benny

He didn't even realize that he was just inviting me to continue to run through his girl the way she continues to ask me to do. I don't know who rung my phone more, Keith or his bitch. "Respectfully, I must decline. I can and will continue to do favors for you and your brother when I can, but I'm very satisfied with my current employer." This nigga thought that he could call me and try to sweet talk me into a new partnership. Nah, I'm good. I ain't one of these clown ass niggas out here, but people often underestimated me because I was twenty-two years old. What I lacked in age, I possessed in experience.

Keith

I kinda expected for him to decline, but I also expected him to extend me the courtesy of meeting with me to discuss my terms. "I can respect that, and I'll be in touch." After that, I hung up the phone as I heard my lady enter into my office. She had really blossomed over the years, and I'm glad that I was able to witness this side of her. We were both products of mixed heritage, and very successful in our own right. She would be a perfect wife, on paper, but there is still the matter of the times when she was missing. There was something she wasn't telling me, and I had to be creative to get it out of her.

"Hey sexy, how was your day?"

Sam

"It was great, but I'm super tired and I just know I'm gonna crash this evening. I still have to go over these plans to finalize the interior finishes for the clinic. Other than that, I can't wait to relax. I don't want to worry you with what I have going on, so I just wanted to come by and drop this dessert off to you. I know you love it." Tonight, was my monthly meeting with my sexual friends at the club.

Keith

"I think I'll join you, I could use a change of scenery, besides I'm done with my work for the evening. I'd like to be in your space tonight. That's unless you have other plans."

Sam

Shit. I wasn't counting on him offering to come to my place. He never offers to do that. I've been looking forward to this all month to let him fuck this up for me. "Well I have to stop by my parent's house. My mom said that I hadn't been coming by as often as I should. So, I'm not sure tonight would be good. How about tomorrow evening?"

Keith

I just looked at her for a minute. "What are you up to Sam? What are you rushing off to do every night you're not with me? You were just talking about how tired you were and now you're going to visit your mom? Something isn't making any sense. I have my ways of finding out information, so telling me now would probably be for the best." She looked at me curiously after my last statement. She knows nothing about what I really do, and I plan to keep it that way. But I refused to allow her to keep insulting my intelligence.

Sam

"Keith, there are nights that I want to spend time with you, and then there are nights that I do not. We have never claimed to be exclusive, so what is the narrative here? Let's not make this into a big thing. I mean, what would be the point. We're having so much fun, please don't ruin that for me. At this point, let's just leave it at that. See you tomorrow?"

Aubrey

Ever since I left Jordan's apartment, I couldn't stop thinking about her. Her beautiful face, her pretty pink pussy and her golden bronzed body. What it was like to feel her lips on mine, her tongue on my center, the curve of her hips. Her scent, her softness, the way she spoke Spanish when we made love. The way she fucked me. After seeing her that last time, I have been calling and texting her, but she won't answer. I want to be with Monroe, but I still want her too. I'm trying my best to keep my cool around Monroe, but inside I'm going absolutely crazy. To abruptly have my memories flood back to me weeks ago, does not dismiss the feelings I developed during the last four months of my pregnancy. In a sense, Jordan saved my life. I don't want to start my marriage off by keeping secrets, so I have to talk to Monroe about how I'm feeling.

Monroe

Something is going on with Aubrey, and I can't tell whether it's postpartum related or something else. I really hope that it didn't have anything to do with that Spanish chick. I am intelligent enough to understand that there were feelings involved. I want to ask her about it, but I don't want to be invasive. Besides, she still has no idea what I really do. I do know, that I will have to tell her before we get married. It has to be her choice though, to remain here with me.

Aubrey

"Baby, there's something we need to discuss."

Monroe

"I agree."

Chapter 8

James

Free ignored me for a good while. She went about her day as usual, but with no contact with me. We shared the responsibility of baby watch at night, but she still wouldn't sleep in the bed with me. She remained in the guest bedroom, for now. She technically didn't take much maternity leave since going back to school, but she went there part time everyday so she wouldn't be away from Tamia all the time.

I tried everything from buying flowers, cards that say "I'm sorry", "I miss you" and even jewelry. I know she saw the stuff, because she just put them all in the same place each time. She wouldn't open the cards or the gifts. I was at an absolute loss for what I should be doing to get my wife to talk to me. I decided after the fifth day of this silent treatment, that I was gonna figure out how to make her talk to me.

"Baby, can we talk please?"

Free

"I'm listening, James."

James

"I now understand why not telling you about Rob hurt you. I thought you would understand after

I explained to you why I did what I did, but you're still giving me the silent treatment and I don't understand why. What can I do to prove to you that I will never do it again?"

Free

He still didn't get it. I sighed and took a minute to gather my thoughts. "James, women are emotional creatures and we're also very sensitive but not *weak*. What I thought you knew about me, is that for me to be totally responsive, one hundred percent into you, is that I need to trust you and that I need to feel safe with you. You knew how the situation with Rob affected me. I wanted to die, but you brought me out of that darkness. You had me thinking that he was dead. I officially closed that chapter of my life, but when I heard about him shooting you, that fear came flooding right back to me.

"You still don't understand that simply saying you're sorry is not enough for me to forget how I felt in that moment. I felt that if he could find you and Monroe and get passed Benny and them, how hard would it be for him to come and do exactly what he told me he was going to do to me. I was raped, humiliated and in fear for my life, and all while my daughter was in the same room with me. I wouldn't wish that even on the devil! I felt like less than a woman, and those feelings resurfaced when I found out that not only was Rob still alive, but that he shot you as well.

"You think I don't miss being in your arms every day? Loving you, kissing you, feeling you inside of me? That's all I've wanted every single day and for the rest of my life since the day you came to check on me when I was pregnant with Tamia. There are no gifts or words that can make me feel safe with you. Only your actions can make me feel that way." At this point, tears were falling down my face, which is what I have been trying not to let happen. He came over to hug me and I could tell that he was unsure. I allowed the embrace. Like I said, I have missed him so much. All I want to do is feel like the only person that I trust in this world loves and trusts in me the same way.

James

"Baby, I hear you and I promise you that my actions will not only match, but I will ensure you and Mi Mi's safety and that you both can trust in me forever. I love you baby, and I always will." I tilted her head up by her chin and she let me kiss her. I wrapped my arms around her, and my world was complete again. She kissed me like she missed me, and I matched her tongue, swirl for swirl. She reached into my pajama bottoms to stroke my dick with her soft hands, as she kissed and sucked my neck. I moaned in pleasure as my hands began to explore her body as well. The baby was safe in her bassinet in the master bedroom, so I picked Free up and laid her on the bed in the guest room. She removed her shirt and I did the same. And we were back at each other, kissing and such.

I removed her pants and dove face first into her pussy with my lips and tongue. I blew on her center because I knew that drove her crazy and then replaced that sensation with my lips between her folds, teasing her pussy. She pushed me off of her and then told me to lay on my back. She then mounted my face and I was able to watch her watching me pleasure her. Once she came in my mouth, she turned around so that we were in the sixty-nine position and she went to work on the dick. She grinded her wetness on my face and I was able to palm that phat ass I so loved until she drained and swallowed me up completely.

We made love all over the house for the rest of that day and talked throughout the night. Tamia must have known that her mommy and daddy were making up because other than wanting to be changed and eating a little bit, she was right back to sleep shortly after she woke up. For the first time in almost a week, I saw my wife smile again. I heard her laugh again. I vowed then that I would ensure she did that daily, until my time on earth was done.

Rob

My first few nights had me on edge being locked up. I knew a couple of niggas from back in my days of hanging on the block. Some of them were in here off of petty crimes like burglary, joyriding and being late on child support. Others weren't so lucky and were doing big time for rape, murder and even child molestation. The ones that fucked with children got it the worst up in here and I ain't even fuckin' with them. Even if I knew them, because you're guilty by association in here, I kept my distance.

Older Male Correctional Officer

"Williams, new bunk assignment, grab your shit and let's go."

Rob

"Man, this the third time y'all moving a nigga. Wassup?"

Older Male Correctional Officer

"This ain't a fuckin' democracy inmate! Get your monkey ass up and let's go. And if I have to come in there, it ain't gonna be pretty."

Rob

"Whateva nigga." I gathered my shit up and let him cuff me. He took me to a new cell, and like I thought, I was gonna have to be on the top bunk because it was already somebody's shit in there. "FUCK!" Whoever it was, wasn't currently in there, but I started putting the rough, scratchy ass sheet on my new bunk.

Inmate

"Wassup 'Fish'? You finding your new digs alright? Anything I can do to make you feel more comfortable?" He said, as he licked his lips and looked at me like he was sizing me up.

Rob

I turned around to see that big ass nigga that I've been trying to avoid since I've been here. He was smiling at me like he won a prize or something. "Man, I done told you about calling me that. What are you doing in here? Go back to your fuckin cell dawg." Why was it always the biggest, most menacing looking niggas that was the fruitiest though? I was truly disgusted, because as much I loved slipping my dick into a woman's phat ass, pussy was where it was at. I ain't never understood a man's attraction to another fuckin' man though. Where the fuck these niggas learn this nasty ass shit?

Inmate

"Fuck you mean, Fish? This is my cell. I live here with you. Welcome home! Oh, and my name is Freddy, but you can call me Daddy."

Rob

"Nah nigga, fuck that! Get the fuck away from me before I hurt your big ass." I squared up as he started walking towards me. Once I felt how strong his ass was, I had a sudden sense of dread. He grabbed at me and I just started swinging at him. If he thought he was going to get me without a fight, he had another thing coming. "Aye nigga, back the fuck up. It ain't like that."

At first, it seemed like he was taunting me. I'm swinging wildly, and barely connecting because he was bobbing and weaving like he was a professional or some shit. Then I saw a CO pass by.

Younger Male Correctional Officer

"What the fuck in going on in here, inmate Johnson?"

Freddy

"Oh, nothing much boss, just trying to welcome my cell mate. I think he wants me to play around with him for a bit before I open him up though."

Rob

"Aye, officer, tell this nigga to leave me alone man! He all up in my fucking space and he bout to get fucked up!"

Younger Male Correctional Officer

“Oh no, I think you have it all wrong Williams. It seems like you’re about to get fucked. Carry on Johnson, enjoy your night Williams. *LIGHTS OUT ON D BLOCK!*”

Rob

What the fuck? How he just gonna leave without offering me some type of assistance? He see that this nigga two times my size. “Aye officer, you can’t let him do this! Nigga back up! GET THE FUCK OFFA ME!”

Freddy

“Stop fighting me, Fish. I promise you’ll enjoy it. I’ll take it slow at first if you just let me in. Because you are letting me in there *tonight*.”

Rob

I fought him like I was fighting for my life! I was able to connect with his face a few times, but he just took that shit like it was nothing. I just kept swinging on him and then I started getting tired. He noticed that I was slowing down and took advantage of the opportunity to lock me in a headlock. I was losing consciousness faster than a muthafucka. I was hoping that he would just kill me until he whispered in my ear.

Freddy

"You ain't going out that easy my nigga, you gon' take all *nine* inches of this dick. Oh, and Money sends his regards."

Chapter 9

Marie

It was Christmas Eve and I wasn't feeling too festive this year. I was only eight months along, but I knew that the babies were ready to come. I had contractions throughout the day, but they weren't close enough before to go to the hospital. My contractions jumped from about twelve minutes to nine minutes apart, so I gathered my bag and headed to the hospital. "Hold on babies, I'm almost there." I had been so stressed about Robert and his situation that I couldn't concentrate. My readings were off, so my customers at the boutique were slowly dwindling. The owner, Shawna, said that she wasn't going to fire me because of my pregnancy and she also knew about the shooting because she saw it on the news. She made the right choice, because I didn't want to have to murder anyone while I was so big.

Robert wouldn't accept any visitors and I really wasn't sure why he wouldn't want to see or speak to me. Why wouldn't he want to know about how our babies were doing? How I was doing? We were so happy over the course of the last few months. I just didn't understand. "Owww, owww, owww..." Another contraction. Who was supposed to be my coach? I didn't have any friends. I should have slipped something in Shawna's drink, to convince her to be my friend. Why didn't I think of that before? Shit, because I was stressing out over Robert. I really hope Robert's okay. I love him so much. I know he would have wanted to be here to see his babies being born. I finally pulled up to the emergency room exit. I didn't park because I wasn't sure that I would make it from the parking lot on my own. "Please help, somebody. I'm in labor!"

Attendant

"Ma'am, I have a wheelchair here for you. You can give me your keys and I will park your car a little bit later for you. Just turn your car off and I can wheel you inside. Is anyone going to be joining you today?"

Marie

"No, my husband is out of town at the moment and I wasn't able to contact him. I'm not due until February, but I guess they may be Christmas babies, instead. Ooooh owww, owww...". And another contraction. I just hoped their meds worked on me, everything I've ever used has been spelled in some way. I'm not sure if I will have the strength to cast one while the contractions are draining me.

Attendant

"Tammy, this woman is in labor. Approximately thirty-four weeks along, her due date is in February. What room do you have available in the maternity ward?"

Tammy

"Ma'am, did you bring your insurance card and identification?"

Marie

"Yes, I have it right here. Ahhhh, owww, please, I need some meds. My contractions are closer together now."

Tammy

"Yes ma'am, I understand. Paco, please take her into room three. That one is clean and ready to go. Ma'am, what is your doctor's name?"

Marie

"I don't have one, I haven't been going to the doctor." I said embarrassed. Why didn't I think to come to the doctor? I already knew my babies were perfect. But they don't know what I'm capable of.

Tammy

"Ma'am, are you sure you have insurance."

Marie

"Yes bitch, I just told you that. Paco, please give her this. Hopefully, she can see because obviously her ass can't hear." I said as I handed him my ID and insurance cards.

Paco

"Ok ma'am, I'm going to wheel you to your room so we can get you all hooked up and get the on-call doctor in to see you right away. Shouldn't be long now before we can get you those meds." He said as he winked his eye at me.

Marie

I've never had a Hispanic man. "Maybe he can be your new daddy, babies, since Robert was acting like he lost his mind", I thought to myself. He was short, but very nice looking. Probably had some good Latin dick too in them scrubs. Glad my hair was braided up recently, I knew despite this big belly, that I was very sexy. Robert told me so!

Taisha

I truly made the effort not to hook up with Travis for another hit, but here he was taking advantage of my body once again. He had my ankles all the way by my ears this time, and all I cared about was that he found my big vein for me when he first got here.

Travis

"Oooh mami, you fuck me so good. Mucho mejor que mi esposa. Much better than my wife. Te lo voy a dar duró, que cuando te sientes te recuerdes de mi. I'm gonna give it to you hard mami that when you sit down, all you do is think of me. Here I cum mami! Ssssss, oooohhh, fuck!"

Taisha

Once he was finished, he decided he wanted more, so I told him I needed another hit. He gladly found the big vein for me again, and a few minutes later, I nodded. When I woke an hour later, I had his semen seeping out of both orifices. I knew I would be sore in the morning because I didn't allow anyone to enter my back door too often. It definitely wasn't my favorite. And he could have at least wiped me off just a little bit.

I got up and took a shower because I had a couple that prepaid for a threesome. I was still high, so when the water from the handheld shower head hit my pussy, it felt so good and I came all over myself. The heroin made all of my nerve endings super sensitive, and that was just another perk in addition to forgetting my problems briefly. I still had little over a half bottle of wine in the refrigerator, so I decided to down that before I headed to their house.

I never met them before, so I decided to put my beloved black liquid leggings on with a thin black chenille sweater. It was pretty see-through and hung off of one shoulder, so I didn't wear a bra. My nipples were definitely highlighted through it and still looked really good on me, despite my weight loss. It fastened in the back with one button, and my lower back was showing with my beautiful ass completely on display. I finished my look with some black ankle boots that had a four-inch heel.

When I looked in the mirror, I noticed the dark circles around my eyes and also that my weave was shot. How long had I been walking around looking like this? "FUCK!" How in the world did I expect to be sexy looking like this? I broke out my foundation, applied a little concealer and warmed up my face a little with a pretty ass bronzer from Rihanna's new line. "Now that's that fine ass Tai right there!" I took a sip of my Apothic "Dark Crush" red wine and it gave me the idea to wear my favorite lipstick because of its rich burgundy color. "Yes lawd, I still got it!" I just had to put a little something on and placed my hair in a messy bun. I sprayed on my Juicy Couture perfume, grabbed my coat and my bag, downed the rest of my glass and I was out.

It was cold as shit outside! I forgot it was even winter. Drug addicts ain't shit, I tell you. How was it a whole 'nother season and I didn't remember? Whatever, lemme go get this money.

Aww shit, my bitch was on the radio and her part was about to start! I turned the radio up, blasted the heat to get it warm and jumped out of the car!

"Fuck him then I get some money…
Fuck him then I get some money…
Fuck him then I get some money…
Fuck him then I get some money…

I need tongue, I need face. Give me brain, concentrate.
Apple phone, Prada case. Kill a weave, rock a lace.
Fuck the Moët, Buy the ACE. Fuck the Ghost, Drive a Wraith.

Get some money, flood the Rollie, Fuck the Rollie, Patek face
My career takin' off, these hoes jogging in place
Swear these hoes run they mouth, how these hoes out of shape?
Can you stop with all the subs? Bitch I ain't Jared.
If you really want some smoke you can pull up, you can get it

Grab a hand full of braids, make ya nigga eat me out, put a white boy on the Sazon, I might turn G-Eazy out, Keep it G from the club 'til the end, from the start. You know me, Cardi B, pussy poppin' on the charts. Ahh, ahh!"

I'm out here twerking in the snow! And sang everything word for word! Yaaaassss! Lemme get my ass on before I get too tired to fuck.

I pulled out of my driveway and thought I saw someone sitting in a car down the street, but shit, whatever they was doing wasn't none of my business. I had to drive all the fuck the way out close to Baltimore, these niggas was giving up some tip money or something. That was a hump! Anyway, I pulled up to a small mansion or something with a circular driveway. It was so pretty. I'm glad I made myself presentable, but I should have worn my lingerie instead of packing it. The doors were huge and there was a light skin woman with red hair who walked out to greet me. She was alright, but she ain't have shit on me though.

Sam

My first choice, Candy, was sick and couldn't make it, so she gave me one of her old co-worker's numbers and I arranged payment for her to pleasure us over the phone. I invited the chick out to Keith's house as it was his thirty-fifth birthday and I decided to surprise him. He wasn't home yet, but I was expecting him in about thirty minutes. I had the wine chilling for me and her, and the Coconut Ciroc on deck for him. I told her to wear all black, and to be sexy. But when she got out of the car, she looked like a hood rat.

"Hello, my name is Samantha, but everyone calls me Sam. Did you bring something to change into?" As I looked her up and down.

Taisha

"Um, yes I did." Damn, she serious and bougie as fuck! I wanted to ask her, "am I not up to your standards, bitch?" I started laughing because my ass was still high. Let me get serious so I don't fuck this money up. I wasn't sharing with Travis on this one. "I have the all black outfit that you requested. Did you want me to dance for y'all? Is there something in particular that you're looking for? I'm all about presentation of the fantasy, so whatever you want I can deliver."

Sam

"Good to know. Come on in. There's a bedroom to your left that you can change in. Would you like something to drink? I have red and white wine. Your choice." When she stepped in, I got a better look at her. She was very sexy. Nice titties, ass was just right and that gap between those beautiful thighs gave me a clear view of her camel toe in those leggings. Okay, she wasn't as thick as I prefer, like Candy, but she will do. And I know that Keith likes light skin women. I was as light as they come. She had a beautiful buttercream complexion. I couldn't wait to see her in her lingerie.

I was hoping Keith would enjoy this because he had no idea what I was into. I knew he was curious about what I was getting into in my personal time. Our last conversation wasn't so pleasant, but I was hoping this experience would make up for it.

Keith

I walked through my front door and smelled candles burning. "Hello?" It was my birthday and I knew exactly what I wanted to get into. "Come on in baby." Kai was a nice woman that I met a few years back at a conference that I attended to support my front. She had a big sexy ass, nice full double D cup titties and a small waist that I wanted to explore.

Sam

"Surprise!" And then I saw him walking hand and hand with this tramp that I just wanted to pounce on. "What the fuck, Keith?"

Taisha

"Who's been a bad boy this year? What bad boy deserves this spanking tonight?" But no one looked pleased, everyone seemed angry. And then the arguing started. I got the fuck out of there, with my five hundred dollars and no tip.

Chapter 10

Aubrey

"You go ahead baby; I want to hear what you have to say." It couldn't be any worse than what I needed to tell him, by any means.

Monroe

I was holding my son and feeding him a bottle of breast milk. He was a greedy little dude, and he had gained three pounds in four weeks. The doctor said we were feeding him too much, but what do you do when a newborn baby cries? You feed them or you change their diaper. That's what we did besides play with him so he could smile, showing his toothless gums in his mouth. He was absolutely adorable. And he had his mother's beautiful eyes, with my face.

"Aubrey...". I sighed. I knew I needed to tell her the whole truth and not hold anything back. "Baby, I-"

Aubrey

"I CHEATED ON YOU WITH JORDAN! And I'm sorry!" I felt even more ashamed now that I said it out loud and saw his face. He was truly shocked. I felt even more like shit.

Monroe

"What the fuck, Aubrey? When did this happen?" I was confused. The old Aubrey would have never cheated on me. And what did she mean? Wasn't no dick involved so what did this mean? We're tryna make it to six weeks postpartum and I thought I was going to be the first to dip into that sweet pussy. "Fuck you mean you cheated with Jordan?"

Aubrey

"It happened the day I went to tell her that I chose you. I ended up tasting her, kissing her and..." I really didn't know what else to say to him.

Monroe

"And what Aubrey? So, you ate her pussy and came home and kissed me in my mouth? You came home and kissed my son in his mouth too? That's some nasty ass, foul ass shit. The whole time you were in your coma, I never let anyone near my heart. Even after you woke up and dismissed me, I was determined to let it play out. That's fucked up. What the fuck am I supposed to do with that shit? How the hell do you want or expect me to fuckin' respond? You could have kept that dumb shit to yourself, for real. FUCK!" My son started crying, because I raised my voice. She came over to take him from me. "Nah, we alright. My son is just fine!" I went to our bedroom and rocked him so I could settle him down and also calm myself. And here her ass comes.

Aubrey

"Baby, I'm sorry. It was not what I went there for. I told her everything I wanted her to know. I let her know, that I do still love her, but I love you as well. I wanted to be honest with you and her. I love the both of you. I cannot just turn my feelings off for her. And I let her know that there was no way I could not love you, especially when my memories came back. You and I created the best part of me. I'm so sorry baby. I never meant for this to happen."

Monroe

She still wasn't telling me what I wanted to hear. "So, tell me this Bree, who the fuck are you *in love* with? Answer me that." She looked around the room as if she really needed to think about it. "Don't even worry about it. You've answered my answer with your lack of answer."

Aubrey

He started to leave the room with Junior, but stopped when I began to explain.

"I'm in love with you both for very different reasons. She saved my life, baby." I grabbed his hand. "She was there when I didn't know what I was feeling. When I found out I was having Junior,

I had no idea what to do. I didn't know what to feel. I couldn't remember this great love that everyone was trying to make me remember. It wasn't coming back to me, but because everyone told me how great we were together, it further made me feel like a fuck up because I drove myself into that car accident." I was nervous about what I was about to say next, but he had to know. "He raped me." I whispered.

Then I found my voice. "He RAPED ME! I was scared that Junior was his baby, but I could not bring myself to get another abortion!" Tears were falling down my face uncontrollably at this point now. "Jordan saved my life! I thought about committing suicide but couldn't figure out how to do it. I was depressed. It was a rough time for me, but she was there. She made sure I ate. She even made me feel like a woman again. She brought me back to life.

So, after I finished telling her I wanted to be with you, I did go down on her. I did make her feel like a woman, because that was what she did for me." I was breathing hard at this point. "I'm sorry, none of that takes away from what I feel for you, and vice versa. I love her too, Monroe. I honestly don't know what I'm supposed to do. I'm so sorry for hurting you baby, and I really love you so much."

Monroe

I was quiet for a good five minutes before I said something. "Call her and tell her I need to speak with her." And she did. Hopefully, Jordan would come and meet with me. I needed to know some things from her.

Keith

"Sam, what are you doing here? What is going on? You made it quite clear that we weren't exclusive. You shouldn't be here." Although, I was looking at the young lady that was packing up her things. She was bad as fuck yet was eerily familiar to me. "Hey miss, don't I know you from somewhere?"

Taisha

"I doubt it. Your face doesn't ring a bell for me." I continued collecting my things and proceeded to put my coat on and head home. Shit it was cold. And I was feenin'. I decided to see if papi would stop thru because my buzz was ruined.

Sam

"So, what, you're done with me because I said we weren't exclusive?"

Keith

"I didn't say that, but Kai is my company for the night."

Kai

"Keith, baby, why don't you invite your friend to join us. I mean, it is your birthday. The more the merrier, right baby?"

Keith

And after she said that, Kai tongued the shit outta me in front of Sam. Kai went over to Sam and tongued her as well and palmed her ass in front of me. Sam looked too surprised at first, and then she seemed intrigued. Sam squeezed Kai's plump ass and then squatted in front of her, lifted her dress, pulled her panties to the side and licked her pussy right in front of me. My dick sprang to life once again, and when Sam came up for air, she came over to me and then took me into her mouth. Her hot mouth felt so amazing.

Sam then took Kai's hand and led her down to her knees to take the other side of my dick into her mouth as well. They were essentially tongue kissing each other with my dick between them, it was so sexy. Sam caressed Kai's titties through her shirt and encouraged her return the gesture. They both got up and kissed each other again and started undressing each other. I poured me a glass of the Coconut Ciroc that Sam had on ice for me and watched them go at it. Kai seemed very comfortable with Sam. She poured some of the champagne on Sam's pussy and slurped it off of her. Sam looked me in my eyes as Kai made love to her body with her tongue.

I downed my glass of Ciroc and removed my clothes as I walked over to them with my dick saluting them. Kai had smooth mocha brown skin that reminded me of coffee with just a splash of cream. Her limbs intertwined with Sam's made the perfect sex sundae. I positioned Kai on top of Sam with her ass up and Sam's legs wide open under her while both of their slippery pussies were facing me. They were once again tasting each other's lips while I entered Kai from the back. When I did, she arched her back and moaned sexily with pleasure. Sam took her breasts into her mouth which I'm sure increased Kai's pleasure. Her pussy was so tight and wet, and I was in heaven as I gripped her hips and smacked her luscious ass. I loved how that phat brown ass looked as I pounded her pussy from the back. I pulled out of Kai and entered Sam's velvety pussy while she remained underneath Kai, which felt like it was made for the curve of my dick. I couldn't stay inside of her wetness for too long, or I was gonna nut too soon. I removed myself and re-entered Kai and kept that routine up, back and forth between them, for as long as I could.

I knew I was in danger of ending our night too soon, so I had Sam bend over as well so that both of their beautiful asses were facing me. Then I went around to the front of them and let them tongue kiss my dick together again so I could recover. Once I felt like it was safe enough to restart the fun, I went back around and plunged my hardness back into Kai's creamy wetness and grabbed her by her hair while I watched that ass again bounce up against me. It was such a perfect sight that I almost couldn't stop myself until Sam beckoned for me to fuck her again as well, while she was swirling her tongue around Kai's big sexy brown nipples. I removed myself from Kai and entered Sam from behind and repeated the same that I just performed on Kai's pussy, on hers. I knew this was gonna be it for this round, my nut was ferociously building in my balls as I fucked Sam's sweet pussy from behind.

"I'm about to cum... Uggghhhhhh.... ahhhhhhhhhhhh...". Sam sat up just in time to connect her tongue with my dick as I let my seed flow into her mouth. Once I was finished, Kai went over to Sam and licked the little bit that spilled down her chin. This was the sexiest shit I had ever seen while they both caressed and kissed on each other. This was one of the best birthdays that I could remember, and this was just the first of many times I busted that night.

Kai rode me into oblivion while Sam slept and then Sam did the same while she licked Kai's pussy so that I could see. Kai then sat on my face while I played with those phat ass titties and Sam went to town on my dick until I blessed her with my nut again. They spoiled me and I knew I wasn't done with either of them for a long time to come. Sam and I didn't have to be exclusive, but that pussy had my name tattooed all in it and I didn't care what the fuck she did in her spare time as long as she didn't hesitate to please me like this.

Chapter 11

Rob

I woke up and over the next few days, the assaults got worse and worse. I couldn't even fight Freddy off anymore. The only time he didn't bother me, was those shifts when the female officer was working D Block. Both of my eyes are still black, because of me trying to fight that him off that first time. I hate to say it, but he broke me. And to know Money's reach is this long, I just felt defeated. Freddy told me it was because I liked to rape women, but I wasn't raping nobody. Why would Money tell Freddy about Aubrey and Free? I totally forgot their names until he brought them up. But I never forgot their faces, or what it felt like to be inside of them. They don't cum like Aubrey and Free did, when you rape them. And I made both of them bust all over my dick. They liked it! I didn't deserve this!

I ended up in the infirmary after the first week of being in my new cell. Freddy wouldn't even lubricate his dick most of the time when he forced that shit in my asshole. I had to lay on my stomach after getting stitches until I healed. After I recovered and they returned me to my cell, he started spitting on his dick before he entered me. He said he didn't want me to be gone away from him that long again. I just wanted to die every day. I started to reflect on the shit that I had done in the past and for the first time in my life, I saw myself for the monster I truly was.

It started with my sister when I was younger, she was two years younger than me. We got along great until boys started noticing her. She had full titties and a big ass that she just developed out of nowhere over summer one year. I got in fights at school because I would hear them niggas talking about how they were going to fuck her. I decided to keep a close eye on her, so she wouldn't even think about fucking none of those niggas. I never even noticed how well developed her body was even though she would walk around the house with little ass, tight ass shorts on and shirts with no bra. It wasn't like she was doing it on purpose. We were poor and she only had what she was growing out of to wear. Plus, I was her brother and she was still a virgin, so she ain't even think that way. I was determined that she wasn't gonna be out here being called no hoe.

Years earlier, I came home from school with yet another black eye. It was the third fight in the same week over her. Nina didn't understand why I fought so much, because I never told her it was about her.

Nina

"Robbie, why you keep fighting these boys at school? Aren't you tired of this? Come here, let me clean around your eye."

Rob

[Passage omitted.] *"Put some fucking clothes on around here. Don't let me catch you in that little shit no more."* *I got up, pushed her again, and she fell and hit her head on the wall behind her. I called my girl and she came over [omitted]. I met Kiana last year at a cookout at my friend's house. [omitted]*

Kiana

"Robbie, you gotta stop letting these dudes get to you. Your sister is growing up, they gonna continue to talk, but Nina is not like that. Come here, let me make you feel better."

Rob

Since my mother was always working, Kiana was always there [omitted]. Turns out, she was my cousin on my father's side. We didn't know it at the time, because my coward ass father dipped out on us so long ago. She ended up getting pregnant, but she said it was somebody else's baby. I left her alone since she was cheating. I knew she was hoe anyway. I didn't realize that Nina used to watch us through a crack in the door. And I also didn't realize, that by doing what I did to her when I touched on her, that she became even more curious about sex.

The cycle of violence continued with my sister because I couldn't control my own fucking attraction to her. I used to come home and beat her ass off of the rumors that she was sexing niggas. My mother would take her away from the house, and I would threaten to beat her ass too. I was the true definition of a fuck nigga. How I do that to my moms and my sis, when I was supposed to be the one protecting them? And these were the thoughts that rolled through my mind every night as Freddy pounded in and out of my ass. I just let the tears fall, it wasn't shit I could do. The worst part about it, everybody in that prison knew that I was Freddy's bitch. I ain't never felt this alone, but I brought this shit on myself.

Jordan

Aubrey just wouldn't quit calling my phone. I could've blocked her number, but I was still in love with her. Call me a glutton for punishment, I guess. "What, Aubrey? I told you to leave me alone!"

Monroe

"This is Monroe, not Aubrey. Can we meet somewhere private? I would like to talk you about some things. If you don't mind."

Jordan

Why was her man calling me? I remember him being at the hospital when I showed up. I couldn't help noticing how gorgeous he was. Smooth brown skin, dimples, beautiful curly hair. And I could tell he had a big ass dick, from when he was trying to adjust himself. I just hate that I embarrassed myself like I did that day.

"What is it you want to talk about that you cannot get from Aubrey? Why are you calling me? I don't owe you anything."

Monroe

"I didn't say that you owed me anything, now did I, sweetheart? I just know that there are some unresolved feelings there between you and Aubrey and I wanted to simply speak with you about it in person. I know you're hurt and acting tough right now, but I know you love her still. Will you meet with me?"

Jordan

I wasn't exclusively a lesbian, actually, I didn't like labels. It just depended on the connection I had with a person. Whether it was a man or a woman, if we had that chemistry and I wanted to explore it, I did just that. "When and where?"

Monroe

"My auto mechanic shop on Pennsylvania Avenue in DC. I'll text you the address. How about an hour?" She agreed to meet me. Aubrey had Junior, so I went and got in the shower and dressed casually. I drove out to my shop and since it was the holiday season, we weren't officially open, we were just on call for emergencies. I heard the buzzer downstairs go off, and it had to be her. I went and opened the door, and she was just as gorgeous as the last time I saw her.

She was bundled up in a cream knee length, puffy coat with brown faux fur lining around the hood. She had a cream knit hat on with one of those furry balls at the top of it. I invited her in and offered to take her coat. She removed it and had on a brown v-neck, fitted sweater with some low-rise, cream colored pants that allowed me to see her belly button. As I escorted her to my office, I allowed her to walk up the stairs first and it gave me nice view of that ass, as well as the tattoo of a butterfly on her lower back.

Jordan

“So, what did you want to meet with me about?” He was even more handsome today, and I could see how Aubrey fell for him in the first place. He was a gentleman, and from what I could see here, a successful businessman.

Monroe

“Well first, I would like to thank you for taking the time to meet with me. I also wanted you to know, that Aubrey has agreed to be my wife, but I know there are some unresolved feelings between the two of you. Why won’t you take her calls? And it’s alright, I already know that when she came to see you that she got very sexual with you. She told me she initiated it.”

Jordan

Wow, I would’ve never thought she would have told him that. “Well congratulations on your engagement.” I said with a little salt laced in my words. I sighed, and we were both quiet for a minute. “I was Aubrey’s in-home therapist once she was released from the hospital. At first, everything was very professional, but once she made the decision to keep the baby, she was different. I could tell that had I not tried to console her she was not going to make it. She felt alone, her memories still weren’t there and she was scared she was going to resent the baby somehow, after he was born.

"I will say, that I just had the intention of being someone she could lean on. But as you know, Aubrey is very beautiful. And I fell for her. No, it wasn't professional, but once we crossed that boundary, there was no turning back. I fell in love with her, and even considered helping her raise the baby. So, when I saw you feeling her up in her hospital room that day, I saw red! I couldn't believe that after everything that we experienced, that she chose you." I had to stop talking at this point, because I felt like I would break down. I just started looking at the floor as my eyes welled up.

Monroe

I walked over to her and squatted down in front of her so she would know that there's no bad blood between us. I grabbed one of her hands. "I'm sorry for my part in your pain. I never imagined that things would turn out like this. I've loved and been in love with Aubrey for a long time, even when she didn't remember me, so I understand how you feel. But I feel like she's not going to be happy without you in her life. I don't know how this can work, but please consider speaking with her and at the very least being her friend again. I love her that much, and I can see you do as well."

This was unreal. Was I asking my fiancée's girlfriend to come back into her life? What would this mean for us? What if she ended up choosing her over me? I don't know, but I felt like this was the only way to ensure her happiness and I would do anything for Aubrey.

Jordan

"You really do love her, huh?" He nodded his head yes and walked back to his desk. "I'm not sure that I can just be her friend, Monroe. I want all of her."

Monroe

"I'm sorry, you cannot have all of her. I'm not willing to let her go. That's not an option." I said to her as I leaned against my desk. Jordan walked over to me and whispered into my ear.

Jordan

"What if she wants us both? What if I want you as well?" I massaged his dick through his sweatpants while looking him squarely in his eyes. I used my other hand to bring his face toward mine as I stood on my tiptoes so that I could suck on his lips. Our tongues danced in a forbidden way, as we both kept staring into each other's eyes. He reached underneath my sweater and massaged my bare breast, while palming my ass with his other hand.

Monroe

I didn't know what I was doing or how it got here, but it felt good. As I tongued her deeply, I heard the door to the office open. I knew she wouldn't be able to stay away, especially since I let her know that Jordan and I would be chatting today. She entered the room and remained quiet. I wanted her to see us, though I didn't know how she would react. She sat on the loveseat in the corner while Jordan and I continued kissing and touching one another. By this point, Jordan has closed her eyes, but mine remained open. I watched Aubrey watching me, and I wasn't sure what the look on her face meant. She crossed her legs and continued watching me as I stared at her, waiting for her to say something, anything. Jordan removed my dick from my sweatpants slowly, as if she wanted to ensure I was alright with it. I didn't stop her, I just allowed it to happen. Once she did, it was like she inhaled all of me.

Her back was still to Aubrey, so she wasn't aware that she was being watched, but I just kept staring into Aubrey's eyes while Jordan did her thing. I placed my hand behind Jordan's head as I fucked the back of her throat repeatedly. Aubrey walked over to me and kissed me deeply. Jordan heard her footsteps and once she was within her reach, she reached up and gently caressed Aubrey's ass. This was not how I envisioned this going, but I was serious about giving Aubrey whatever she wanted. I'm sure I would be alright with this right now, but things like this don't always end well. I guess that is something we’ll worry about later down the line.

Chapter 12

Joe

It had been a few weeks since I last spoke to Aubrey, and we decided to meet up for lunch. I still couldn't believe that she had just had a baby. I knew she was gaining weight from the last few times that I saw her, but I thought it was one of the side effects from being in a coma for so long. We were going to meet up at Applebee's, her favorite, out in Bowie. I arrived first and got us a booth by the window so I would see her when she pulled up.

I saw her drive up and she had her signature lip gloss on. I saw the sun reflecting off of those beautiful hazel eyes of hers. She wore a black, waist length pea coat and that ass looked scrumptious. Damn, I didn't think she would still look so fuckin good, but I don't know why. Aubrey always took pride in the way she looked. She went to the backseat on the other side to retrieve the baby, while her hair was flowing in the breeze. He was covered up, since it was so cold out, and she still was so beautiful to me.

Aubrey

When I got into the Applebee's, I saw Joe in the back as he waved at me. He got up and started towards me and asked if I needed any help. "Nah I got it boo, thanks." I took my coat off after sitting the car seat on my side of the booth and handed Joe my coat to put on his side. “Come over here and give me a hug, boy! I missed you so much, and I’m sorry for keeping so much from you. As I explained on the phone, I wasn’t sure how to talk about what I was going through. You see my son? Wanna hold him?”

Joe

“Man, he looks just like that nigga, Monroe! At least he has your beautiful eyes. He’s a cutie, but nah, you know I don’t do little babies. Maybe when he gets a little bigger. But damn baby girl, you look so good. You don’t even look like you had a baby.” I did notice when she took her coat off, that them titties were even phatter. She wrapped her arms around my neck and gave me a good squeeze, as I embraced her around her waist and kissed her on her cheek. And she had a nerve to have on a fitted low-cut shirt. I had to sit down before she noticed how much my dick grew just watching her. And she smelled delicious.

Aubrey

“I appreciate the compliment, Joe, but I got a good twenty pounds still on me that I need to get rid of. And this little one is always so hungry, so that keeps my boobies so full. I swear they didn’t look like this earlier when I put this shirt on.”

Joe

Mmmmm, I would love to suck some of that milk right outta them titties my damn self. I put my coat on my lap because at this point the waitress was going to see my dick straining to get free. "Did you lose something? What you looking for?" She was in what I presume was the baby's bag and couldn't find whatever she was looking for as the baby was starting to get fussy.

Aubrey

"I left his bottles at the house. I thought I packed them, because I was just going to feed him while we waited on our food. I am totally unprepared to feed him, I didn't even wear the right shirt to breastfeed. Joe, I can't feed my baby in the bathroom, I really hope you don't mind. I'm sorry."

Joe

Aubrey took the baby out of the baby seat and repositioned herself so that she was facing the window and had her back to the restaurant. She whipped one of her titties out and placed her son on her nipple so that he could eat. That shit was so fucking sexy to me, and I was glad that the restaurant was busy because I started stroking my dick under the table while I pretended to peruse the menu and while Aubrey was looking at hers.

Aubrey

"Have you decided on anything, Joe? I think I'm probably going to have a salad and some wings or something." I just couldn't look Joe in the face while I was feeding my baby, I didn't want it to be awkward. I knew he was hungry, he rarely cried unless he wanted to eat. He looked right at me while he ate. When Junior looked like he was getting full, and I removed my breast from his mouth for a second to see if he was really finished. He liked to play all day. It took him about thirty seconds to realize I removed him from my breast before he started whining again. "He does this to me all the time, little greedy self."

Joe

When she removed her breast from her baby's mouth, she let it sit there for a little bit to see if he was done, I guess. There were still a few drops that were leaking up out of her nipple and I just knew I was about to nut all in my hand. Luckily for me, when I ordered some waters for us before she got here, the waitress brought napkins with them. I snatched a few of those napkins while I stared at that big sexy ass titty leaking those drops of milk and let my seed flow into it.

I'm glad she wasn't looking at my face in that moment, because my face probably looked like

I was being tortured. Shit! As soon as I was done, I wiped my dick with the rest of the napkins I didn't use to catch my release in and threw them on the floor. I then waited for my heart rate to slow down.

After that, I was able to continue the lunch like nothing happened. I'm so glad I chose this corner booth. Aubrey finished feeding the baby and put her titties back in that sexy ass shirt she was wearing. I ordered me a couple of drinks to have with my food and we had a nice lunch. We talked about everything, from her memories coming back, and the proposal to that bitch ass Rob's upcoming trial. She said she wasn't sure if she would be coming back to work at the clinic, but that she would still be around. "Well, I miss you being around there. Have you spoken to Sam lately?"

Aubrey

"We talk like once a week, but she's been super busy with the new practice. She has stopped by the house a few times to visit with her new Godson. She told me what happened, are you okay?"

Joe

"Yeah, I've moved on. I miss her though. I just wished it could've ended on a better note. But anyway, I'm just glad to see you."

Aubrey

"Same here! We're going to be having the New Year's party soon at the club, and I would love it if you could come. And bring a date. I just want you there. It should be really nice, and I'll make sure you're on the VIP. But we really need to stay in touch on a regular basis. I know the peanut gallery is driving you crazy." We laughed about that for a good little while.

Joe

"No doubt baby girl, I'll be there. I've been missing you so much."

James

Free was at work today, so it was just me and my baby girl. She was almost seven months now, so I took her with me to the auto shop. Monroe hadn't seen his God daughter in a week or so, but I knew he would stop everything for his "Muffin" as he called her. I strapped her into the car seat and we headed to the office. Everything had been pretty quiet lately, deliveries were coming in on time, business was booming, and we had been talking about retirement lately, especially since we were family men now. That unnecessary risk we were taking just wasn't worth it anymore. We had Don to thank for that realization.

I ran into Lew once I got there and he told me about some of the corner boys having to be disciplined for some petty drama between a few of them over the same bitch. Three of them were currently at the warehouse cooling off and waiting for the boss, but I thanked him for the heads up. I made it up to Money's office, and I heard some noises. Sounded like Aubrey made a lunch time visit. I went back downstairs to wait until she left. But it wasn't Aubrey, it was the girl Aubrey was dealing with when she couldn't remember Money. She looked at me and waved as she left the shop as she adjusted her skirt. I was genuinely confused.

Monroe

Damn, I don't know how long James had been here, but I saw him when Jordan was leaving. I washed my hands and face, sprayed some air freshener and wiped down my desk before placing everything back on it. I heard him knock, and invited him in. He had this curious look on his face, as I reached for my Muffin. "Come here my Muffin!" She just smiled at me with her pretty self and reached back for me. "Uncle Money missed you baby girl!"

James

"I don't know where your mouth was just at Uncle Money, so don't be kissing on my daughter." I said as I laughed.

Monroe

"I got you Jay, I got you. So, you not gonna ask?" He shook his head no. "Well I'm gonna tell you anyway, so you don't think it's any shady shit going on. Aubrey was still a little confused about her feelings for the both of us, so instead of making her choose, we are all together. It's working so far, and I'm definitely enjoying myself."

James

"How is it going to work once you and Aubrey get married though? You sure ole girl is not gonna be jealous or feel left out?" I was genuinely curious about this "arrangement".

Monroe

"Well me and Aubrey were just talking about that and during our honeymoon, we're going to surprise her and I'm gonna marry Jordan too. Aubrey is nervous about how to tell her mom, but I told her the details of our lives don't concern anyone else. But she's definitely gonna be wondering why she's always around. We'll cross that road when we get to it though."

James

"Damn man, I would have never thought about that shit. But when y'all figure out the details for the wedding, please let me know. Fresia wants to talk to Aubrey and really wants to work out their friendship."

Monroe

"I got you man. You hear about that dumb shit happening with the little niggas on the corner? I don't know whether I wanna dead them little muthafuckas for bringing attention to our operation or just make them fight Goldie one on one. Shit is stupid over these young bitches that probably don't even know how to fuck yet." We laughed together at that. "But hey, you ready for the New Year's party in a few days at Silk's? Gonna have all your favorites there, the liquor, the dancers and that R&B group you like will perform live."

James

"Oh yeah? That's wassup, I'll let Free know when she gets home."

Monroe

And I have a nanny that is watching Junior, and she doesn't mind taking Muffin too. I already asked her. Oh, and I meant to let you know, the lil nigga is being "taken care of" in prison. Every single night. You remember Big Fred that used to work for Don? I paid one of the COs to switch his cell to bunk with him."

James

"All of that is good news. Nothing more than what his bitch ass deserves from what he's put everyone through. Shit, speaking of which, we deserve a night to just hang out and enjoy ourselves without all of the drama that was surrounding us this year. I've been waiting on 2018 very impatiently and I have a good feeling that this will be our year."

Monroe

"Yeah man, I hear that. But I got some news for you though. Did you hear about Marie having twins by the lil nigga? She was pregnant before we separated him from his shit."

James

"Fuck no. Please tell me that they are both girls. I was serious as fuck about him not leaving a legacy. I don't like killing little kids, but I'd consider making a serious exception in this case." And I was serious as fuck about that.

Monroe

"She had a girl and a boy." I saw his brows furrow as his eyes became darker. "I'm with whatever you wanna do."

Chapter 13

Dee Dee

Mike was finishing up his physical therapy session of the day and I came with him to help him put his arm sling back on and for general support. We had returned back to Miami about two weeks after the baby was born. I was already missing him, and I called every day on FaceTime so I could see him. I couldn't believe how much he favored Monroe. I just knew he would look like me at least a little bit. But I would just wait to see what my granddaughter would look like once they decided to have another baby.

<<ring, ring>>

"Hi baby, where is NeNe's Junior?"

Aubrey

"Hey mommy, hold on. He may still be sleeping. Let me go see." I walked into the nursery and there was Monroe and Junior knocked out in the rocking chair. "Mommy, look." I whispered so I wouldn't wake them up.

Dee Dee

"Aww, my son and grandson. They're both so handsome." I whispered as she left out of the room. "I'm here with Mike while he's getting his physical therapy. His shoulder is healing nicely, and he should be good to go soon. Robert's trial is supposed to start sometime soon, and the prosecutor said it would good for the victims of the shooting to be present during the trial."

Aubrey

Forget about Rob, I hope he gets everything that's coming to him. "Oh well I'm just glad you're coming back here so you can help me plan my wedding. I'm so happy Mike is healing nicely too. I want him to walk me down the aisle. But let me ask him myself, mom." She looked like she was about to cry, so I needed to change the subject with her sensitive ass. Why wouldn't he walk me down the aisle? He's been the only father I've ever known. "So, when you coming back? You can stay at my house, Junior and I have been staying at Monroe's, so you will still have your privacy. Do you want me to arrange for an in-home physical therapist?"

Dee Dee

"Oh baby, that would be nice. Mike is wrapping up his session, so I'll give you a call to let you know when we will be out there."

Jordan

"Bree, you got any more of that-", she was on FaceTime with her mom, who knew nothing about our new arrangement.

Dee Dee

"Aubrey, who was that? Is Jordan in Monroe's house? What's going on?"

Aubrey

"Hey ma, lemme call you right back. Love you, bye." I hung up real quick, my mom hadn't seen nor heard about Jordan since the day I had my son. I know she was too confused and could not wait for me to call her back.

Jordan

"Damn, I'm sorry hun. I just needed a little of that wax stuff you use on your legs." I don't know why we're hiding now that we've decided to all be together. "Aubrey, your mom is coming here soon, what's going to happen when she comes here. At your insistence, I gave up my apartment, so when are you going to tell her I'm your woman *and* Monroe's too? I'm grown, I'm not hiding what I do for anyone."

Aubrey

"I'm not asking you to hide anything. I'm just asking for your... for just a little discretion. I'm not ready to tell my mother yet. Baby, can we please change the subject?" I went over to her and hugged and kissed on her. But she wouldn't hug me back. It's ok, I was just going to keep doing it until she gives in. I licked her neck and worked my way down to her beautiful tits. Then she started responding to me. "I knew that would warm you up."

Monroe

"I can't wait to warm you up." I said as I entered the room both Aubrey and Jordan were in. "Has it been six weeks yet? Damn, I miss your pussy baby." I kissed on her, while she kissed on Jordan. We were all getting into it and then Junior started crying. "Well, that's the end of that."

Jordan

"Just for now. It's my turn, I got him."

Marie

My labor didn't progress the way it should have and after almost twenty-six hours, I was taken into surgery for an emergency c-section. I still couldn't believe that I had to do all of this by myself. They applied the oxygen mask over my nose, and it took the doctors about fifteen minutes to bring out my first baby. It was my daughter, and they cleaned her off and brought her to me so I could see her. She had my face and was so bright. She was probably going to be Rob's light complexion. I felt them tugging a little bit and then my second baby was out. He was loud!! They cleaned him off as well and brought him over to me.

And he looked just like Robert but was browner than his sister, like me. Fraternal twins, I was so happy they were here!

They were taken to be weighed and my daughter was four pounds, six ounces and my son was four pounds, two ounces. I already know he's gonna be so much bigger than his sister when they get older though, I saw it in my dreams. I don't know what their names are going to be yet, but I'm hoping I can talk to Robert to see what he wants to name them. So far, I liked Celeste Marie, for my daughter, after Grandmother. Her name was Celestine. And I was thinking of the name Marchaud Robert for my son.

After they stitched me back together, I was taken to my recovery room. There were no balloons or flowers, no fanfare, and nobody to extend congratulations. The nurses helped me into my white, sterile bed and they asked me if I was hungry. I told them yes, but I really didn't have an appetite. Once they left me alone in my room, I cried and cried because I still was all alone in this world. The nurse wheeled my babies in the room and I wiped my eyes, because at least I still had them. My milk wasn't trying to express, so for now, I fed them both with the little bottles they provided me.

Once I was done feeding and burping my twins, the nurse put them back into the little bassinet together beside me, and they just looked so sweet. Paco brought my meal in and he also had a bag in his hand.

Paco

"I know your husband hasn't made it here yet, but the staff and I decided to get you something to celebrate you as a new mother. So, enjoy your food and your gift. From all of us."

Marie

And there he goes winking that eye at me again. "I'm so grateful, thank you so much Paco." I told him as I started crying again. Once it was just me and my babies, I opened my food tray and there was a big, juicy steak, a baked potato, asparagus and a huge slice of chocolate cake. My mouth began to water immediately, and I was grateful for the unconditional love that I knew I would experience from my two babies in all the days to come.

After I enjoyed my delicious meal that seemed way too tasty to have been prepared in a hospital cafeteria, I started to feel really drowsy. I fell asleep, but not before I saw someone enter my room and sit in the chair next to me.

Unknown man

"Hello Marie, I take it congratulations are in order. How does it feel to be a new mom?"

Marie

I was so drowsy, that I couldn't speak. I could barely make out a face. The voice even sounded distorted. I saw this person walk over to my babies and pick up one of my twins.

Unknown man

"I know you didn't think that food you ate was prepared in this hospital. Oh no." I said to her with added drama. "I had it delivered special. I needed to be able to come and steal your son, so that I can eliminate him. I told that bitch you procreated with, that he would never be allowed to leave a legacy behind in this world. So, with that being said, your son will have to die." At the mention of her son's demise, her eyes tried to respond, but her eyelids were way too heavy, courtesy of the extra sleep medication her food was cooked with.

Marie

"Nnnnnnnn...". I couldn't even force the word no out of my mouth. All I could do is close my eyes and proceed to have the worst nightmare of my life. Now three days later, no one knew who the person was who stole my son.

All we know from the surveillance footage, is there was a man that entered my room and then exited seven minutes later... with no baby in hand. There was no clear shot of his face from any angle.

I fired off questions in rapid succession to the police officer assigned to my case, "Where's Paco? Where did he get my food from? He told me it wasn't prepared by the hospital. I had a steak, asparagus, baked potato and chocolate cake. Immediately after I was finished eating, I was super drowsy, my vision was blurred, and I couldn't speak!" I felt like I was hyperventilating. But I needed to remain calm for Celeste.

Police Officer

"Ma'am, the menu for the maternity ward that night was baked chicken, broccoli and wild rice with lemon creme cake." Then he started conversing with his partner. "My partner is in the process of speaking with this Paco and everyone else that was on that shift during that time. Ma'am, we're doing everything in our power to locate your son."

Marie

I haven't let my daughter out of my sight, or my arms, since this happened. I feel like she knows her brother is missing. She's had a connection with him for the past eight months, and now he's not here. I feel so sad for her. And whoever was involved in my son's abduction would have hell to pay! And that was a promise, *not* a threat.

Taisha

Once I left that cluster fuck that was supposed to be a threesome out in the boonies the other night, I called Travis because my high was completely blown. It took me almost forty-five minutes to get back home, and by that time, I was so alert and on edge from coming down from my high. If Travis didn't come through tonight, I was going to have to smoke the heroin that I had, which I do not like to do. It's way too much effort and it takes me way too long to feel the effects and get high. I was starting to get anxious, because this drive was taking too long.

Finally, I turned into my driveway and I saw Travis' car. My anxiety started to melt away immediately, since I didn't have to wait. He was already at my house! I knew I was probably going to have to suck his dick or something because he hates waiting for anyone. I looked in his car, and he wasn't sitting in there. He had a key to my home, so I just went inside and was giddy because I was 'bout to get so high!

I walked up to the door and it was cracked open. Once I walked in, there was shit strewn everywhere! My heart started beating really fast, my mouth got super dry and my anxiety returned. "Travis... papi, are you here?" I pulled out my phone to dial emergency services. Before I could press send, I heard a thump come from above my head. I started walking up the stairs, and once I got there it was eerily clean. My bedroom was a mess before I left earlier, and I know it wasn't Travis. There were also some flowers on my dresser with a card attached. The card read:

"He warned you to leave that nigga alone... Bathroom..."

I turned around and immediately noticed the subtle light coming from my master bathroom. I opened the door and threw up all the contents in my stomach at what I saw. I was so weak, but I managed to run out of my house. That car from earlier was still down the street. When the person saw me, they turned on their high beams so that I wouldn't be able to make out their face, car model and screeched past me while turning the corner. I'm smoking my shit tonight... *before* I call the police.

Chapter 14

Kristin

It had been about three weeks since Dr. Saul saw us having sex in the storage room. Ever since then, I've made sure to be super professional with him as if nothing ever happened. I was super cheery all the time and I made sure that I didn't complain about the customers forgetting their damn appointments, even though it still irritated me entirely.

"Good morning and thank you for calling Mountainview Smiles. This is Kristin, how may I assist you?" Yeah, I was being way extra, but I really didn't want to lose my job, I even started going on other interviews just in case I was fired. Joe was very disappointed that I cancelled our "mouth sessions" in the storage room. I still never told him that we were being watched that day, and I'm not sure that I ever will. He's been really salty since then, but he'll get over it. "Hi Joe, how's your day going?"

Joe

"I would be better if I could get that afternoon special I got so used to, but my girlfriend is acting funny for some reason. But anyway, Aubrey and Monroe are having a New Year's Eve party and I would like for you to go with me."

Kristin

"What are we wearing? I need to stop by the mall this evening. I don't wanna be looking busted in front of your friends... or your ex." I watched him after I said that to see what his reaction would be. He acted normal, I guess.

Joe

"Babe, why you even worried about her is beyond me, for real. You could put on a paper sack and as long as that ass is right, you good."

Kristin

"Is that all you think I am is a phat ass? Ughhh." He really had me in my feelings about that. I was way more than my ass or a "mouth session". I just went to the break room and warmed up my food. As I entered, Dr. Saul was leaving out. He looked so embarrassed and I hate that it was like this between us now. "Dr. Saul, we need to talk. May I come to your office a little later?"

Dr. Saul

"Actually, Kristin, I have a very busy afternoon today. I'm not sure it'll be a good time to speak today."

Kristin

He tried rushing off, but I stopped him. "Sir, your schedule is pretty light this afternoon.

I'll just stop by and see if you're available during one of your non-appointment times, okay?" I didn't wait for an answer, I walked back to the break room and warmed up my food. We were gonna get rid of this awkwardness today. And he was going to tell me if I was in danger of losing my job. Joe was still standing in front of my desk with that sorry ass look on his face. I wish he would just get the hell on. I wasn't making time for it today.

Joe

I'm not sure what is going on with Kristin. How you get me used to getting my dick sucked every single day to just cutting me off cold turkey though? That shit ain't right. And now, she's super fucking sensitive about me complimenting her phat ass? Fuck outta here with that bullshit. And she got me feeling bad about the shit. Lemme go to lunch, I'm sure she'll feel some kinda way about that too, but I'm not even gonna dwell on it. "Just let me know what you gonna do for New Year's Eve. I'm wearing all black." And I dipped out on that ass. Eat that bland ass shit you made for lunch today. I'm going up the street to eat me some chicken and waffles.

Free

I was not showing up to the New Year's Eve party without speaking with Aubrey first. I really needed her to know that I'm not the same bitch I was a year ago. So here goes nothing.

<<ring, ring>>

Aubrey

"Hello?"

Free

"Hello, Aubrey? This is Free. Do you have a minute to talk?"

Aubrey

Here we go. I knew she wanted to talk to me, and I know now that children can change your views of the world, but I just wasn't interested. "Yes, what can I do for you Free."

Free

I could already tell she wasn't beat for this conversation, but I was still gonna press forward. "Well, first, I want to extend my congratulations on the birth of your son. James showed me a picture and he is absolutely beautiful." I paused to let her congratulate me on Tamia, because I know she saw her in person, but it's okay. I'm the one in the wrong here, and I called to make amends with her.

Aubrey

"Thank you." I'm pretty sure she wanted me to say something similar to her about the baby she had with my ex-boyfriend. But I had time to be petty today.

Free

"Well anyway, I'm accompanying my husband to your party tomorrow evening and I wanted to call and basically let you know that I'm not the same person I was almost a year ago when I saw you last. I was nasty, I was disrespectful, and I didn't know my worth as a woman. I have grown since becoming a mom and experiencing the rape and kidnapping situation that Rob put me through. I have struggled with all of that, and I'm a stronger person now. I know we have gone through similar things with him, and I just wanted to call and apologize to you again about the disrespect I showed you because we were once friends. I really wish we could at the very least be cordial with each other, but I can understand if you don't care to do the same. Our men are really close, and I don't want to be the source of any drama for them or anyone to discuss from the outside looking in." I would own up to my shit, but I ain't kissing her ass. I don't give a shit who she or her man is cool with.

Aubrey

"Okay, thank you for calling." And I hung up the phone. I would address that in my own time. She still was supposed to be my friend first. But she chose to be trifling. I do know, I will not let

2018 start with any animosity towards anyone. Especially on account of bum ass Rob.

Monroe

"Hey baby, you alright? Where is Jordy?"

Aubrey

"I'm good baby. That was Free calling to make things right. *Jordan* is in her room chillin'. Why, wassup baby? You need something?"

Monroe

"Nah, I don't need anything baby. Just seeing where she was. So, were you being nice to Free? She's been trying to get right with you ever since Junior was born. Maybe even before that. She's been through a lot... And I'm not discounting anything you've been through, baby. I just wanted you to know." I saw the look on her face when I said that and when I called Jordan by the nickname I created for her, so I had to make sure I attempted to clean it up. "Look, after this New Year's Eve party, I'd like to take you somewhere for a few days, by ourselves."

Aubrey

"Monroe, now you know I can't leave my baby. And what about 'Jordy'?" Since this nigga giving her nicknames and shit now. Lemme stop acting jealous. Originally, he started this three-way for me. "I'm sorry baby, Free got me in my feelings. I didn't mean to snap at you. But whatever we do, and wherever we go, if you take me somewhere for a few days, how do you think Jordan will feel?"

Monroe

"Bae, this arrangement is based on your wants and needs. Anything that I experience from it is a bonus. Whatever you want, is what you shall have. We can all go as a family, I just wanted you to know that I miss us and you're still my priority."

Aubrey

"I can't wait to put this pussy on you. Two more weeks baby... I may not even be able to wait to be honest. I mean, who cares if I get pregnant, I'm about to be your wife anyway." And I kissed him and gave him all this tongue. I grabbed his dick, that I missed so much and of course he was hard. He wouldn't let me suck his dick though, and at first it bothered me. But he said if he couldn't please me all the way, it wasn't fair for me to please him that way. I guess it bothered me a little bit because he let Jordan do it, and she could have his dick whenever. That's alright, because when it goes down, it's going to be everything that he's been missing.

Monroe

"Well baby, I want you to heal, but I am impatiently waiting. And you know we make some pretty ass babies, so I'm down for whatever. I love you."

Jordan

I've been sitting on the stairs listening to them this whole time. I truly hope that Monroe will learn to love me, and I pray that Aubrey does not harbor any jealousy towards me. This was their decision to include me. And I know it would have been painful if I hadn't been back in Aubrey's life. But all it would've taken was a little bit of time. I would have eventually gotten over it. I don't want to be a third wheel, but I will enjoy this 'situationship' for as long as it benefits me. I've gone back to work, they don't ask me for money to contribute to the household, but I do purchase food and cook sometimes. Additionally, I do for the baby because I love him like he's my son too. Besides, if I'm pregnant like I suspect, I want my baby to be regarded the same way they treat Junior.

Chapter 15

Taisha

Once I was able to smoke my shit and hide my stash, I called the police. They ain't have to do Travis like that. Once I got high, I did go back into the house and relieve him of any drugs or cash he had left in his pockets. I know it seemed foul or whatever, but I had to. His wife and kids didn't deserve for him to be labeled as such a lowlife in the news. He was my friend first, a long time ago and I felt I owed him that. I mean, I know he turned me out and used my body for profit now, but it wasn't shit that I hadn't agreed to do.

Now, there was the small issue of explaining this shit to Don tomorrow during our visit. But I'll worry about that once these people remove Travis' dead and mutilated body from my home. And here they come, banging on my door like they ain't got no fucking home training. I never understood why they knocked like that. Let me replace this look of annoyance with some tears or some shit and put on a show.

I opened the door, and thee most handsome man I had ever seen was standing in front of me with his service weapon in his hands. He was brown skin, with gray eyes, a low haircut and a body to fuckin die for! That steely-eyed stare was so sexy to me. How was I supposed to be riddled with emotion over my *friend* with this fine ass man in front of me? I just hoped he couldn't tell that I was an addict and faking these tears. What I really wanted to do was tear that uniform off of him and snatch his entire soul!

"Come on in officer. My friend was meeting me here at my home, but by the time I arrived, I found him in there... dead." I was trembling for effect and I had since removed the card from the flowers and deleted the texts between Travis and I. He's upstairs in my master bathroom." I was too excited that it was clean in my bedroom. I didn't want him to know I was a fuckin slob. Downstairs looked as if I was robbed while I wasn't home."

Officer

"Ma'am, please escort me to the area where the victim is currently located. Is there anyone else here with you? Any pets? And please don't be alarmed, my partner is walking around, outside your home so we don't encounter any surprises."

Taisha

"No, officer. I live alone. And I do not own any pets." I continued my damsel in distress act, so that maybe he would feel sorry for me and want to check on me later. After leading him to the master bedroom, I acted as if I couldn't enter because I was too shaken up. Once he entered my bedroom, I checked myself out in the hallway mirror and my makeup was still on point! I look presentable even though I still had my freak gear underneath my long trench coat. He would never know I was supposed to be a hooker tonight for some well to do, bougie ass couple.

Officer

"Ma'am, I have alerted the Coroner and the Medical Examiner. I'm going to look throughout your house to ensure that the perpetrator is indeed not still here. Please do not move, stay right here. Okay?"

Taisha

"Yes sir. I will be right here." Once he cleared my home, I asked if he would be willing to check my attic for me. I hadn't gone up there yet. Once he was done, I did let him know about the suspicious vehicle that I saw twice today. It wasn't like I was really telling on Don or anything. I didn't actually know who it was, nor could I describe the vehicle in any way.

Officer

"Ma'am, do you have somewhere you can stay this evening? Your home is considered a crime scene for now, but we should be done by morning."

Taisha

"Well officer, I'll just have to get a hotel room for the night. Do you have a card with your contact information attached? Just in case I have any questions?" I cooed.

Officer

"Yes ma'am. My name is Officer Gerald Mason. My office number as well as my cell phone are attached. Please do not hesitate to let me know if you need anything."

Taisha

"Thank you, Officer. I really feel safer with you taking care of this case. My friend and his family really deserve all of your efforts." I'm sure Travis' wife knew he wasn't shit. Especially once she saw me and what my fine ass was working with. "Would you mind coming into the house with me as I pack a bag really quickly? I would feel much safer with you in there with me sir."

He agreed. I ensured that I packed some cute clothes that I would be proud to wear in his presence and packed enough for the week. I would have to get all this blood and shit cleaned up before I could stay here again. I've seen worse, so I wasn't traumatized or anything. But if "Officer Fineass" took the bait, I would have to move around in some way to keep up this ruse of being helpless.

Marie

Celeste and I were now at my home. There were no developments concerning my son, but I knew I would have to take matters into my own hands. So in between feeding my daughter and pumping enough milk to have reserved for my son in the event that I found him before the police did, he would have the nutrients he needed to be strong. Once she was sleep, I retrieved my mother's spell book. She practiced dark magic, and it was exactly what I needed to locate my baby boy as soon as possible. I took a piece of Celeste's hair and a drop of my blood to cast the spell.

"*Sumna toudis alumin... Sumna toudis alumin... SUMNA TOUDIS ALUMIN...*" Either the spell was incorrect, or the connection was not strong enough. I was trying not to use my baby's blood, so I would use her saliva, for now. I mixed her saliva, her hair and my blood together and repeated the spell.

"*Sumna toudis alumin... Sumna toudis alumin... SUMNA TOUDIS ALUMIN...*" I believe something was definitely happening now. I poured the mixture on the map and it didn't move but an inch. "Damnit!" I said to myself quietly. I was going to have to use my baby girl's blood, because they shared the same blood type. It was important with these spells that you got as close to what they called for each time, or it wouldn't work. I picked her up and kissed her little cheek. I got a sterile needle and pricked her big toe. She yelled at the top of her little lungs.

I collected the droplet of her blood, mixed the last little bit of her hair that I'd collected and added her saliva in for good measure. "*Sumna toudis alumin... Sumna toudis alumin... SUMNA TOUDIS ALUMIN...*" I felt so bad for my baby. But this temporary pain would be worth it in the long run.

"Okay baby girl, okay. Mommy's sorry honey." I soothed her and rocked her in my arms until she settled down again. I spread the new mixture onto the map, and it moved to a neighborhood north of Rockville, Virginia. Since I had to take my baby with me, I had to time it just right. I decided to head out a little after midnight. The blistering cold didn't bother me since I was so motivated by retrieving my son, safe and sound. The stars were beautiful and seemed closer to the earth for some reason tonight. I took that as a positive sign that Marchaud was within my reach. I made sure my car was warmed up prior to departing, courtesy of the starter on my key ring. Celeste was bundled up and sleeping peacefully.

I drove out to the neighborhood the map directed me to and there was minimal movement in the area at this time of night. I wasn't sure how long my baby girl, who I affectionately called CeCe was going to sleep, but I just couldn't leave my baby in the car with the possibility of her screaming her little lungs off. I waited until the third time that I fed her, and ensured she had a new pamper on. I left my car running with the heat on and played her some lullaby music. I walked to the building Marchaud's essence was lingering in. Once I got there, it led me to the small home that the map was zeroing in on earlier.

I approached the door cautiously and ensured that I tied my scarf around my head and acted like an old lady that was looking for my "grandson Andre". I had a cane, I bent all the way over, and when the young man answered the door, I realized that he couldn't be much more than about nineteen years of age. "I can't hear you young man, would you mind opening the door for an old soul?" I pretended.

Young man

"Uh, excuse me ma'am, may I help you." He asked me after opening the door.

Marie

"Yes baby, do you know my eleven-year old grandson, Andre? He didn't come home this evening and I'm just knocking on doors to see if I could find him." He couldn't hear me, because I was speaking really low on purpose, so he had to bend down to hear me. And once he did, I took my sharp blade and placed it against his throat, stood up straight and asked him exactly what I wanted to know.

"Where is my baby? And don't lie, I can smell the other two people in this apartment, so I don't need to spare your life." His eyes bucked wide open, so he knew I meant business.

Young man

"He's not here anymore. Reggie came and got him about thirty minutes ago to take him to another location because he didn't want to kill him."

Marie

"Who is Reggie, young man? And where can I find him?" I knew that he didn't know much, but I also knew he wasn't being totally forthcoming with me. "What does he look like?"

Young man

"I'm sorry, lady. They don't tell us anything, they don't trust us with that type of information. And Reggie is super dark, really tall and is scary. That's all I know."

Marie

"I have something to show you, young man. I don't think you're being totally forthcoming with the little bit that you do know." I made him walk into the room where the other young man and the young lady were sitting. I placed my blade right next to his carotid artery and demanded their attention. "Hey, put your weapons down, NOW!" They did as they were told. "Now young man, which person would you like to save, because one of them has to die?"

He hesitated, so I repeated my question. "Which of the two of them would you like to save, because one of them has to die? Hurry up and choose!"

Young man

"I can't choose. He's my brother and she's my girlfriend. Please, I'll call Reggie for you and ask him where the baby is."

Marie

"Oh no, young man, you really think I'm an amateur. Once you place that call, it will alert him to the fact that I'm here. Because why else would you call about a baby you don't care anything about? You have five seconds to tell me who you want me to save. Five, four..."

Young man

"PLEASE, just kill *me*!! I love my brother and my girl. PLEASE lady, don't kill them in front of me!"

Marie

"Three, two..."

Young man

"Alright, alright, kill my girlfriend. I can't live without my brother!"

Marie

And he started crying... "You made your choice, you have to live with the consequences, one." I shot his brother in the heart, because I knew he loved him more. And now that he chose the girlfriend, he was going to live without both because she was going to leave him.

Young man

"NOOOOOOOOOO!!"

Marie

He fell to his knees and cried his eyes out as he cradled his brother in his arms. I knew that he would be hurt, but all I could think about was how hurt my daughter would be without her twin brother. I turned and left to go back to my car and figure out who this Reggie was. Back to square one. I'm killing any and everybody that gets in my way. Damn you Robert for placing us in this position! Had I not been alone at the hospital, I would have both my twins safe in my arms.

Chapter 16

Benny

I woke up this morning to three missed phone calls from Sam. She had been calling and texting me nonstop about us hooking up again, but after the first few times of dogging her ass out, I just got bored. She ain't even know how to suck dick for real. Plus, I'm on some different shit. I'm trying to establish myself and change the game. Level up... and her hoe ass ain't the one to do it with. I'm already thinking generational wealth, for the kids I haven't even had yet. And I know she out here throwing that pussy to anyone who's willing to catch it. Had I known that shit before, I wouldn't have even blessed her in the first place.

I know Money is considering retirement, so I'm trying to ensure my position to take over his business, even though I don't plan to continue this drug shit forever. This is just my platform to get the fuck out of the hood and stay out.

<<ring, ring>>

"Hello?" It was Money.

Monroe

"Yo B, what's good? I need you at the warehouse today to help me handle some business before the party tonight."

Benny

"Aight. Imma throw some clothes on and I'll see you in half an hour."

Monroe

"Bet."

Benny

Today was big purchase and distro day, as well as preparation efforts for Money's New Year's Eve party tonight. This was easily our biggest order of the year because the Feds were usually not around like that for this holiday. The second biggest time that we worried a bit less about Federal level interference was around tax time. My job, specifically, was to ensure the product was distributed to the trap houses and the corner boys. I made sure operations was running seamlessly at all locations. I also kept them in line when they needed that shit. Recently, we had three niggas involved in some type of dispute over the same hoe. Picture that. Fuckin' up your money over a bitch that was obviously for everybody. Money gave them a choice. Either get it together, or deal with the consequences. They knew Money wasn't to be fucked with, they heard how he did that fuck ass nigga Rob.

I headed to the warehouse and when I got there, there was this fine ass Spanish chick sitting in the lobby. I was trying not to stare at her, but she had these beautiful green eyes that I got lost in, but just for a second. She said hello, as did I, but I kept it moving. When I got to the back, I spotted Money with his clipboard as he checked off the delivery as they brought it in. He was very thorough and although he had plenty of us on his payroll to do that kind of thing for him, he wanted to personally ensure that he received what he paid for.

"Wassup Money." We dapped it up. "You know there's a woman in the lobby? Is she waiting on something?"

Monroe

This was the tricky part. I never wanted anyone to have anything to say about my private life, because I don't get down like that. Truthfully, I love my lady and I have only one. Aubrey and Junior are my life! I thought this three-way shit was cool at first, but all Jordan can do for me is help me bust this nut. She looks good, and the pussy good too, but if I just wanted someone for looks and pussy I would have stayed with Tai. "Ain't shit. Oh, that's my lady's friend, she needed a ride and Aubrey was busy with the baby so I told her I would take her where she needed to go but that I had to stop off for a minute. Wassup witchu? You comin' out tonight?"

Benny

"Oh, I'm in there. Is ole girl gonna be there?"

Monroe

"Lemme check. I don't even know if Aubrey mentioned it. Be right back." I had an idea and needed to finesse this shit real quick so that she felt it would benefit our situation. I went out to the lobby and there she was playing with her phone like she usually does. "Hey Jordy, I really need a favor from you and I already know you're not gonna like it, but just hear me out." She looked a little skeptical but told me to go ahead. "Alright, you know I could give a fuck about people knowing about our situation, but Aubrey is stressed about what her mom will think. She's already in town, and it's just not a good time to spring this on Mrs. Dee Dee without allowing Aubrey to speak to her mom about it first."

Jordan

"Ok, so what are you saying Monroe? Get to the point please?" This shit was starting to get old.

Monroe

"My partner that just came in would like to take you to the party tonight. And before you start to get rowdy, just consider this for a moment. If you were at the party with Benny, Aubrey's mom wouldn't know anything about our arrangement. You wouldn't have to go out with him or anyone else you didn't want to go out with ever again. I just don't want to stress Aubrey." If she could kill me with a look, I swear at this moment right here and right now, I would be dead than a muthafucka.

Jordan

"So lemme get this straight, Monroe, you want me to pretend I'm on a date with your little friend so that Aubrey's mom won't find out about our situation? Is that right?"

Monroe

"Just for now." She looked uncertain.

Jordan

"And how much longer am I going to have to be y'all's little secret? You want me to stay at his house too? You want me to fuck him too?"

Monroe

"Baby, calm down. Of course, I don't want you to do all that. Just trust me, Benny is not disrespectful, he's not going to try anything, but he thinks you are gorgeous. Which you are." I went over to her and hugged her while I grabbed all over that phat ass which I knew would make her agree to do whatever I needed. "Come on baby, do this for me, ok? For us."

Jordan

"Ok papí, I will just this once." He tongued me down quickly and so sexy-like as he squeezed my ass, making my pussy come to life. This man had an amazing effect on my body. And when he pleasured me, muy excelente…. Definitely the best dick I've ever had.

Monroe

"Alright baby, thank you. You gonna give me that pussy before we go back home, right? You know Aubrey's mom is over there right now." She nodded her head and smiled for me. "Ok, Benny will most likely come holla at you. Be nice to him for papí, ok?" I smacked her on the booty and went back into the room where Benny was validating the numbers for me. That little nigga was the future, but I ain't wanna leave him in the game. When I retire from this shit, I got something better in mind for his life too. He's like my little brother. "Thanks B, I'll take it from here. Appreciate you."

Benny

"No problem, boss. I'm done. Everything is good here. Did you want me to get the packages out to each spot before the party? I verified all the liquor, the party favors were received this morning and some of the product will be floating around for whoever wants some. I got our best on the job tonight. You won't have to worry about anything."

Monroe

He was always on top of everything. "Yeah James told me you had everything on lock. I just want security to be top notch, my family is in the house tonight and I don't want no problems." He had all of that covered. "Aubrey's friend's name is Jordan if you wanna holla at her real quick."

Marie

After I went back home, I was able to conjure up a stronger locator spell that would track my son everywhere he was taken. The only thing was, I couldn't move the map, which meant that it was likely that I would miss whoever this Reggie person was again just like I did last time. It had to remain in place, or its magic wouldn't be as effective. I'm also sure by now that the young boy called him to let him know what happened last night, but I wasn't gonna stop until I had my son back. The good thing is, I know he's alive. I still feel a strong connection to him, and I also knew he was okay.

The point on the map was moving again, and this was the second time at this location. That will be my first stop tonight and I marked the other location as well. Because I have my daughter, I have to move around at night. I don't even know where to begin to look for a babysitter. I don't even trust anyone to ask to keep her. But I will find this Reggie and I'm gonna kill him painfully. He better not *do* anything crazy to my son.

Kristin

Knock knock... "Dr. Saul, are you busy?" Once he saw it was me, there was a peculiar look on his face. It wasn't one of embarrassment like when I asked before if we could chat, but more like bewilderment. He told me to come in and close the door. So I did.

Dr. Saul

"What would you like to discuss, Ms. Jones? That little performance in the storage room with Mr. Williams?"

Kristin

He had come from behind his desk and sat directly in front of me and it made me just a tad uneasy. Something was different about his body language. He didn't seem embarrassed or nervous. His energy felt like confidence. "Um, no sir, um, actually... I wanted to ask if I was going to be fired." I couldn't get my words out right, for some reason. I fully intended to be in control of this conversation, but it seems he has flipped the script. There was a smirk on his face that I couldn't read.

"I also wanted to apologize for that... it won't happen again."

Dr. Saul

"No need to apologize, Ms. Jones. May I call you Kristin?"

Kristin

"Uh, yes Dr. Saul, you may." I wish he would get to the fucking point and answer my question. I needed this job, I really wasn't trying to go back to Tennessee.

Dr. Saul

"After witnessing your little rendezvous with Mr. Williams in the storage room, I decided to go back and review the footage from previous days. It appears that the both of you have been having relations in there daily for few weeks now. I also saw that Mr. Williams had a sexual encounter with another young lady in that very room a few months ago, who doesn't work here. These acts are in direct violation of the clinic's policy on security of our medical inventory as well as unprofessionalism and employee conduct."

Kristin

"Am I being fired?" What was I going to do now? This was my only source of income, and I hadn't received any offers from any of the jobs I'd applied for recently.

Dr. Saul

"Well... it depends on how much you and Mr. Williams would like to keep your jobs."

Kristen

"I don't understand."

Dr. Saul

"Well, let me clarify. You have the ability to save both of your jobs here from termination. Let me remind you, you both face possible jail time as well. Unless…"

Kristin

"Unless what, Dr. Saul?" Once I asked him this, he licked his lips salaciously while adjusting himself.

Dr. Saul

"You could do some of those things for me on demand and no one will ever have to know about your indiscretions. It will be our little secret."

Kristin

He said this as he started to unbuckle his pants. I paused in thought about it for a second and considered my options. I got up, walked over to the door, locked it, then approached Dr. Saul slowly. He placed his hands on my shoulders and gently guided me down in front of him, until I was on my knees.

Chapter 17

Dee Dee

There was something off about Aubrey and Monroe, but I wasn't gonna be Inspector Gadget on New Year's Eve. I'll let them make it for now, but I just don't understand how Jordan is now a "family friend" all of a sudden. She's a beautiful, young girl, but how are she and Monroe so friendly after all that commotion at the hospital?

"Where's NeNe's baby?" Junior was whining just a bit because none of us were holding him at the moment. You know I had to fix that! "Here I come, my grandbaby. You know I wasn't gonna let you lay by yourself for too long." I held him on my chest and rocked him slightly. I was so in love! I think Aubrey's a little jealous though. "So, what's new with you, my love? You still miss working at the clinic? How is Joe doing?"

Aubrey

"Sometimes I do miss it, but I love being here with my munchkin, I couldn't imagine leaving him. But he's growing so much, huh mommy? Him so fat." As I tickled under his double-chin. "Joe is good, he's dating a white girl now though."

Dee Dee

"So, you said he went from dating Samantha to a white girl? Sheesh, and I always thought he had a crush on you. But I guess you weren't the right color though, huh!" I teased her while laughing! But I guess Aubrey didn't think that was so funny.

Aubrey

"Ha, ha, ha... that's very funny mommy. I do hope he comes to the club tonight. I have really missed Joe. I haven't met his girlfriend, but she works at the clinic as the new receptionist. I'm ready to let my hair down at the party. It's been awhile since I've been able to hang out. Are you coming to the spa with me? I need to my hair touched up. I gotta be sexy for my man tonight."

Dee Dee

"Why? You still can't give him none. Junior is only four weeks old! But you know I'm already ready for my granddaughter anyway, so y'all gone on ahead and get started!"

Aubrey

Shiiiittt, while she playing, I just might! I'm tired of being horny and watching Jordan get all my good dick. It was sexy as hell, because Monroe always made eye contact with me while he was fucking her. But I did notice how Jordan turned his face to hers and started kissing him when she knew he was looking at me. His eyes still came back to mine though. I miss my man. I wonder what he's doing right now. "I just might mommy.

Owwwww!" I said while doing a slight twerk move as she gave me the side eye. "Lemme call him real quick. He still hadn't told me if he wanted me to wear the black or the blue."

Dee Dee

"You nasty!" I said while laughing. I really missed this about our relationship. Her assault, accident, then the coma, to her recovery, the memory loss and ultimately the pregnancy she wasn't excited about initially made her a different person for a while. And I understood all of it. My baby had been through so much this past year. I'm so proud of her! "I'm down for the spa. I'll just utilize the services while you get your hair done. My faux locs are already gorgeous!"

Aubrey

"Okay ma, sounds like a plan." I dialed Monroe's phone.

<<ring, ring >>

"I guess Monroe is busy, so let's just go mom." I was trying not to show my disappointment for him not answering. I knew he had errands, but Jordan was with him. I trust my man and one of our rules is that he's not allowed to be with her sexually without me being present. "Mike, you sure you're gonna be okay with Junior while we go get all dolled up?"

Mike

"You do know I raised kids back in the day, right? I got this! Me and my grandson are gonna be fine!"

Monroe

"Damn baby, your pussy is gripping the shit outta my dick. You so... fuckin... wet!" Damn, her shit was extra gushy today. We were in the backseat of my SUV while Jordan was riding the shit outta me. "Damn girl, you gonna make me nut all up in you. Ahhhhh, sssssss, fuck!"

Jordan

I had my back to him as I was popping my ass on his dick. He would stop me every so often because he wasn't trying to finish too soon. I liked when I had him to myself, because then I had his undivided attention. "You like that daddy? Te gusta papi cómo te lo dio? Is that pussy good to you papí?" His eyes rolled back into his head as he continued thrusting into my pussy while holding my hips steady. He was hitting my spot and there was no way we were going to be able to explain my juices all over the floor in the backseat. He had my pussy squirting so much!

When he said he was about to cum, I tried to keep going, but he never wanted to cum inside of me. He would always manage to push me off, and nut on me somewhere. The only reason I got him that one time is because he was tipsy while we were all together one night. He was so into Aubrey, I guess he forgot it was me and not her that he was drilling into because he didn't pull out and fell asleep as soon as we were done. I don't even think Aubrey realized what happened. But I laid there and once they were both sleep, I raised my hips and my legs so that gravity would encourage his seed further into my womb. I wanted to have Monroe's baby, and now I was. I was about two weeks along. Hadn't been to the doctor yet, but the four home tests that I took since missing my cycle, confirmed it.

Monroe

"Oooh Jordan, raise up, I'm about to nut. Oooooooh, sssssssss, aaaaaaaaahhhh, shit baby! Suck the head for me, mmmmmmmmmm."

Jordan

I did exactly as I was told, I had already gotten my prize. I'll tell them when I'm ready. For now, I'll just keep him happy since Aubrey can't.

Sam

Keith and I were spending less and less time together now, but when we did, he always pleasured my body. His touch, his kiss, that tongue of his absolutely blew my mind every time he used it on me. But nothing he did compared to that dick! NOTHING! None of the other men, or women for that matter, could make feel like Keith did. It was just that he wanted to be a couple. I just wasn't ready for that. I had just gotten out of a relationship and besides, I was having way too much fun with all my new "friends" from the club.

Keith

"Hey baby, you almost ready to go?" When Samantha came over earlier, it was a surprise. There were always mixed signals with her. I used to see her daily, but now I was lucky to spend any time with her more than twice a week. I guess I really scared her off when the subject of exclusivity came up. But the way she put it on me when she did come over, had me thinking that I may indeed be the only one. Maybe she was just busy with her new practice.

She agreed to go to the New Year's Eve party with me after not answering my texts for a few days. It made me feel like she wanted to go with someone else. It also had me feeling like a straight bitch for even dwelling on it. Much less caring about whether or not she was doing all this for someone else. I should be glad that this beautiful, sexy woman wanted to use me for my dick. And the things she did to me, damn!

When I walked into my master bedroom, she was putting on her thigh high stockings and connecting a silk garter belt to it. I noticed she wasn't wearing any panties, so I walked up behind her, grabbed the front of her throat with my left hand as I fingered her pussy with my right. When I kissed her shoulder, I heard her moan, so I knew she wanted me to fuck her again. I just wanted to hear her say it. "Tell me what you want me to do." I whispered as I bit her on the ear. I bent her over so that beautiful ass was in the air and her pussy was saluting me. I spanked her right cheek and it started to turn red. "Tell me what you want me to do to you." I repeated.

Sam

"Mmmmmmm, I want you to fuck this pussy."

Keith

I was pulling my boxer briefs down and slapped her on the other cheek. "Say it again."

Sam

"Keith, I want you to fuck this pussy!" I cooed.

Keith

I lifted her right leg and placed her knee on top of the bed as she continued to bend over. "Arch your back for me, Samantha." She did as she was told. I teased her as I rubbed the head of my dick up and down her slit. I would push just a little bit in and then take it back as I continued that up and down motion. I waited until it started to frustrate her and then I plunged my entire length into her, while holding onto her hips. That initial moan always excited me, and I proceeded to caress her warmth from the inside out. She was always so wet and the sound of me entering her was amazing.

After she came for the second time, I turned her onto her back and placed both ankles on my shoulders. I entered her again slowly, until all of me was inside of her. I held it there while she looked me in my eyes. I made short pumps in and out of her at a steady pace because I knew I was hitting that G-spot. When the tears started to roll down the sides of her face, I long stroked her until that pussy gushed all against my stomach and legs. I continued to drill inside of her until my nut built up and trembled until all of my release was swimming around inside her walls. I laid on my back and almost said fuck that club until I heard the shower start. I knew she couldn't let her friend Aubrey down, so I wouldn't either.

Sam

After we got dressed for the second time, and while Keith was in the shower, I called Benny again. I have no idea why he was avoiding my calls but let him be at the club tonight. I was sure to find out. I went shopping for the sexiest dress I could find earlier this week. I wanted Benny to see what he was missing out on. I was wearing a beige Roberto Cavalli dress, with embellished black lace appliqués that were absolutely stunning in their placement. It was long, with a satin finish with a split that came up to right above the middle of my thigh. Luckily, I had another matching set of thigh-highs to wear, since Keith just made me ruin the ones I put on the first time. I wore some black four-inch Tom Ford pumps with the ankle strap. I admired how my perky breasts were perfectly displayed in this plunging neckline. My hair was pinned up flawlessly in a sleek and very modern French chignon. I wore diamond chandelier earrings and a neckpiece that Keith gifted me with for Christmas.

Keith got out of the shower and had on a stunning, black Cesare Attolini Italian tailored three-piece suit. He wore a tie that had just a touch of beige that tied into my dress. He looked sexy enough that I wanted to rip it off of him for a fourth session. He pulled out the black Alexander McQueen dress shoes that I gifted him for Christmas. After he applied his cologne, we both donned our coats and headed out to the car.

Keith

"This evening is special, and since you are bringing in the new year with me, I decided to have a driver take us to our destination. You have my undivided attention this evening, gorgeous." And with that, I opened the car door and allowed her to get in before entering myself. We headed to the club and on the way, I popped a bottle of Champagne. "Here's to new beginnings, in the new year, with a new outlook on our friendship." We clinked our glasses and Samantha downed her entire glass in one gulp.

Sam

"Speaking of new, I have this new lipstick on that was marketed as smudge-proof. Mind if I try it out on you?" He shook his head no, and I pressed the button to close the partition. "Excuse us, Mr. Driver." I unzipped his suit pants and pulled out the impressive penis I'd grown so fond of. "I promise not to ruin your suit, handsome."

Keith

When she lowered her hot mouth onto my dick, it was like I hadn't been inside of her three times already today. This was part of the reason that thinking about her with another man made me crazy. I didn't want her sharing this with anyone but me. "Sam, the car is stopping, you wanna finish this later babe?" She just kept going as I felt my loins tighten. "I'm gonna nut if you keep going at this pace. Mmmmmm...". I guess that was the point, because my eruption was inevitable at this point. I guess she was right about not ruining my suit and I guess that lipstick was indeed smudge-proof.

Chapter 18

James

I've been away from home for the past couple of days. The only person who knows where I am, is Monroe. I told Free that I had to prepare for the big shipment, she knew the deal. All of the guys that we worked with were trained not to talk shop in front of people that didn't have a need to know. That included wives and significant others and anyone else that didn't have clearance. I wasn't done with what I had to do, but I would come back to that in the new year.

I arrived home in time enough to change into what I was wearing this evening. I knew Free had it on lock with whatever she chose for me to wear, she loved dressing me. When I came into the house, I heard her singing. Free always sang when she knew no one else was around. She had a beautiful voice but would never sing. I went inside the bathroom and she was in the shower and still didn't know I was there. I leaned up against the door frame, while she sang one of the classics so beautifully. She put her very own twist on a song that my grandmother absolutely loved. It took me back to my youth for the duration of that tune.

"Dreams are dreams, some dreams come true
I found a real dream, baby, when I found you
You're so strong, but tender too

You're my angel, oh, angel
You're my angel, oh, angel

Love like ours is Heaven-sent
Each day a day to remember
I feel so safe, feel secure with you
You give me love, you keep right on giving
Fill me up, baby, with the joy of living
When things get tough, I can always turn to you

You're my angel, oh, angel
You're my angel"

Any song by Anita Baker would never get old, but that one was sentimental. And the way my baby was tearing it up, I couldn't help but record her with my smart phone. Once I heard her turn the water off, so I wanted to let her know I was there before I frightened her. "Hey my love, I'm home."

Free

"How long have you been standing here, James?" And I threw my towel at him, playfully. My heart still beat at a quicker pace, but at this point, I couldn't tell if it was because he excited me that much or because he startled me. My God, I loved this man.

James

Once she removed that towel, I couldn't help but admire her body. Her waist was tight, like she never even carried Tamia. Her breasts were gorgeous, with silver dollar sized nipples that looked like they were dipped in milk chocolate. Her sexy hips were perfect on her flawless frame. She stepped out of the tub and walked toward me slowly. She undressed me and took my clothes to the hamper.

Free

"Get in the shower while I check on Tamia. Don't take too long baby, I'm ready to end the year on a high note!"

James

She started to walk away and that ass was inviting me to follow. But she ain't have to tell me twice though, I jumped in that shower and was outta there in about two minutes. When I got out, I dried myself off as I walked to my bedroom and saw that she wasn't there. I couldn't yell out to her, didn't want to wake the baby. I went into the other bedrooms, but she was nowhere to be found. Here I am, walking through the house, dick swinging, when I thought I heard some movement downstairs. I should have known she was in her favorite place: the kitchen.

Free had oiled up her body and had a sexy chef's apron that barely covered her nipples. She also had some of those clear heels that she used to dance in and them legs looked like they would never end. She pulled out a chair that had a towel over it and had me sit in it. She handed me an ice-cold glass of Crown with a lime in it, just like I preferred.

Free

"First, we'll start with the appetizer. I have some sushi that I know you love. Would you like some baby?"

James

I nodded my head, she had me super curious. I love when she makes homemade sushi. She placed some of it on my tongue. Then she moved the apron over just a bit and placed one on her nipple. I thought that was so fucking sexy. We sat there for a few minutes and fed each other as she straddled me with her hot naked sex right up against mine.

Free

"Next, we'll have the main course. Would you like some of that too, my love?"

James

I nodded once again. She brought out the Surf and Turf- garlic shrimp and sliced, juicy ribeye steak. She also had some salad that was very colorful with romaine lettuce, grape tomatoes, cucumbers, shredded carrots, and other good stuff. Along with the sexiness of the situation, we were able to talk and just be us.

Free

"Lately, we have just been parents, and it's the greatest title that I've ever had! But, it's not my only title. I want you to know, that the romance and the spontaneity is not dead." I kissed my man and fed him more steak as he fed me some shrimp. Once we were through with the main course, the best was yet to come. "Alright baby, now it's time for dessert." He threw the rest of his Crown back as I brought out strawberries, orange slices, pineapple, chocolate syrup and whipped cream. "For this portion of the meal, I'll need for you to follow me." I laid him down on the covered mat on the den floor.

I squeezed some of the chocolate into a bowl and dipped a strawberry into it. He bit into it and I ate the leftover piece as I licked my fingers. I used the orange slices and squeezed some of the juice onto his chest as I licked him wherever the fruit touched. He then dipped his fingers into the tub of whip cream and did the same to me. We took our time and enjoyed each other prior to starting to get ready for tonight's party. By the time we were done, I was so tired from all this lovemaking that I even considered sitting this one out. Especially since I knew I would have to endure Aubrey acting stank.

James

The sound of a baby crying woke me from my brief nap. The feeling of dread was all over me again because I not only thought about what I was gonna have to do, I was now dreaming about it. I realized once my eyes focused, that I was in the comfort of my own home. And it was my own daughter that was crying. I went to her and picked her up to soothe her. I couldn't imagine something happening to my sweet baby. And if anyone even tried to hurt her, I would kill them twice. So how could I hurt someone else's innocent baby? I tried to reconcile in my mind, that he just had to be a casualty of war. I just had to turn James off, and get back into the character of Reggie when the time came.

Monroe

Jordan and I pulled up to the house and it seemed as if everyone was gone. I noticed that Aubrey called, but I was sure she was getting her hair done right now. "Are you heading out to get your hair done for the party tonight?" I asked Jordan as we walked into the house.

Jordan

"No, I can just straighten it myself. It's only one night. Besides, I was hoping to have you all to myself for a little more time." I said, as I massaged him through his pants. "Especially since I have to go on a "date" tonight with a man I hardly know." I said as I pouted.

Monroe

I knew she didn't want to do it, but we really needed that. "Lemme show you just how much I appreciate what you're doing for our family." I picked her up and sat her down on the bar in the den. I removed my pants and lifted her right leg over my left arm as I thrusted my hard dick into her pulsating wetness. Her shit was good before but there was a difference that I felt, and I couldn't get enough lately. She was throwing that gushy back on me as it seemed like I was going deeper and deeper.

She leaned back and lifted her shirt for me to suck on her beautiful mounds. I rotated my tongue on her right nipple with my hand on the small of her back to keep her in place. I made sure to pound that pussy, because with each stroke it just felt wetter and warmer. I got lost inside of her like nothing else in the world mattered but me busting this nut. As I felt myself getting closer, I stroked more intensely and ended up releasing my seed on her belly. As soon as I was done, I saw Mike pushing my son in his stroller toward me. He stopped in his tracks once we made eye contact and exited the room as quickly as he had come in. Not only did I just fuck Jordan in our house without Aubrey, my new father-in-law to be caught me doing it. How in the fuck was I going to explain this shit?

The current agreement was that if I fucked Jordan without Aubrey, I had to get permission. Today was the only day that I hadn't since we decided on that. And I know she's gonna figure out we were fucking when I didn't answer my phone earlier. Jordan didn't see Mike, but I let her know he was here with the baby.

Jordan

I saw Mike when he walked in, even before Monroe did, but I also didn't care. I wanted people to know about us. I deserved to be treated as good as Aubrey. But now I had even more ammunition to use against her when it came to me getting Monroe all to myself. I loved him and I couldn't wait to start my family with him. I love Aubrey too, but I needed to get her back for making me feel like shit once he returned. She broke my heart, and now I was gonna use Monroe to do the same to her.

Mike

What did I just walk in on? They had to hear me walking in the door, I wasn't exactly quiet. What was I going to say to my wife? To Aubrey?

Monroe

"Uh Mike, can I holla at you for a second? It's not what you think."

Mike

"Ay boy, I don't give two shits what y'all into around here, but what if my daughter had walked in on that shit? My wife and I ain't trying to get caught up no fucking love triangle that I'm sure you wouldn't survive." I whispered so that I wouldn't wake Junior. "This shit is so fucking disrespectful and in the middle of the day no less. It's like your punk ass ain't even care about getting caught."

Monroe

"Mike, we're together. Aubrey, Jordan and I live here together and we're in a relationship... with each other." I watched him as he thought about what I said.

Mike

"Boy, if you don't get out of my face with this dumb shit. Ain't no way that Aubrey letting you fuck that girl too. What type of fool you think I am, huh?"

Monroe

I explained to him calmly what was going on. I also let him know that Aubrey is going to tell her mom in her own time. After the new year. "Would you please promise that you will allow Aubrey to tell her mom in her own way?"

Mike

"This some sick shit here. Somebody is gonna get hurt, these things never end well. I will give Aubrey until January tenth to tell her mother, or I'm saying something. My wife and I don't keep secrets. I'll pray for you all, but I also pray none of you turn up missing."

Chapter 19

Rob

Even though I was hating life, I started to appreciate the protection Freddy gave me in here. Monroe had lots of friends in here, but because I belonged to Freddy, they let me make it when he was around. Freddy was also not as rough with my ass as he used to be, and I started to feel a little different. Not because I liked it, because I felt like he genuinely might love me. I haven't felt anything remotely close to that since I was with Aubrey. But even she didn't want shit to do with me anymore.

My charges looked like they were going to stick. I tried pleading insanity and mental illness, but the jury took one look at them sucka ass niggas Money and James trying to look all innocent in the courtroom. There was also some random nigga that I supposedly shot as well. They acted like they were dying from their injuries, and that was almost a month ago. My trial is set for early February, and I just know they are going to milk this for all they can. But we'll see. Monroe better not be fucking Aubrey again, that's all I know.

Later on, while I was in the cafeteria, some kinda fight broke out between some niggas that was always beefing with each other. I just stayed where I was and out of sight. I wasn't trying to be in no other niggas drama because I had enough of my own. I was somebody's fucking boyfriend in jail. My life is over. I'll never recover from this shit. A nigga ran over to me looking all happy and shit as he whispered something to me.

Random nigga

"Aye, they fucked that nigga Freddy up. You better watch your back because daddy look dead as a muthafucka right about now, you bitch ass nigga."

Rob

Before he walked away, he mushed the shit outta me. "What the fuck?" And he disappeared by the time the guards showed up. I walked over there to see what that nigga was referring to and the guards let me through. They had shanked the shit out of Freddy and he wasn't moving. "Aye Fred, nigga get up. You alright, get up." I started panicking, not because I was sad that he could die, I was worried about my damn self. If he was gone, these niggas was gonna do the same to me. "GET UP nigga! Come on man. Y'all do something! Why the fuck y'all just standing around, take him to the infirmary!"

After that the COs escorted me back to my cell. All types of niggas came out of the woodwork that night. Niggas wanting to fuck me because they hadn't had "their chance" to yet. Niggas was saying they were gonna fuck me up for what I did to

Money. And some of them wanted to kill me because I had done some female in their family dirty at some point or another. I hadn't prayed in a long time, but I asked God to let Freddy get better. I really needed him in here.

Aubrey

After getting my hair done at the salon, I saw that Monroe texted me to let me know that he and Jordan were home. Good, I really missed my man today. I was excited to get all dolled up for my man. I got my hair pressed and in body wave curls that are swooped to the opposite side of my dress' one shoulder strap. I decided on a royal blue sequined gown that showcased my buxom cleavage and how this body snatched back to even better than before. It was long and fitted with a slight train and a side slit that started at the top of my thigh. I decided to wear my Yves Saint Laurent silver strappy high heels that looked absolutely amazing with my dress. The back of my dress dipped all the way down to my ass. When I tried that dress on in Saks a few weeks ago, I knew all heads would turn.

Monroe has only seen me in my sweats around the house and the occasional pair of jeans and t-shirt when I ran errands. But tonight, I was going to remind him of what I had going on! I'm seriously thinking about giving him some tonight, even though I still have two weeks of healing left, per my gynecologist. I feel great though, and I've been so horny lately. Plus, I'm tired of Jordan reaping all the benefits of my good dick.

Mom and I walked in the house and Mike were already dressed. He hadn't yet put on his suit coat, so that he could continue playing with Junior. Jordan came downstairs with a short red cocktail dress that accentuated her fierce and sexy curves. Damn she was looking fly. But my stylist could have hooked that hair up had she joined us today. She just straightened it and it looked boring. But she was still gorgeous. I noticed that she borrowed my black Louboutins, but it's alright. As long as she didn't scuff my shit. "You look nice boo, I heard about Benny asking you to go with him tonight. Is he coming by the house to pick you up?"

Jordan

Here she go bringing that nigga up because her mom is standing there, but I'll play along for now. "Yeah girl, he's on his way now. He wanted to grab some food and talk a little bit. He's handsome, but I'm not sure about him yet. How you doing Mrs. Roberson? Those locs are beautiful." She gave me a dry ass thanks, but I just smiled and kept it moving. "Aubrey, I hope you don't mind that I borrowed your shoes hun. I thought they just looked good with this dress. And your hair is gorgeous. I love the swoop."

I gathered my clutch and went into the living room to wait on Benny so that there would be no more awkward conversation between her mom and I. Mike was sitting in there playing with Junior, so I decided to sit in there with them. "Mr. Roberson, you're looking dapper in your suit. I hope you have a great time tonight."

Mike

I looked around to see where my wife went because I wasn't about to play with this young lady tonight. Once I was sure my wife was upstairs, I carefully addressed Jordan. "Jordan, I'm not completely sure what's going on around here, but I'm not going to act like I didn't see what I saw earlier. I'm not trying to be rude to you, but I don't like games. You sexing Monroe and now you're going out tonight with another man sounds like games. I'll tell you like I told him, someone is going to get hurt. But it better not be my daughter. Have a nice night." I took Junior to his dad and went to the room to love on my wife while she got dressed.

Monroe

I was absolutely nervous about how Aubrey was going to take what happened earlier. I wasn't sure if I should tell her now or tomorrow, but I didn't want to ruin her night. I knew she had been looking forward to this ever since I told her about it. Her friends and her family were going to be there, so I just decided to tell her tomorrow, when there was no one else around. I heard her and her mom come in, but I was upstairs getting dressed so I could be out of her way and go feed my son before we all headed out.

When she walked in, I complimented her on her hair. This was the Aubrey I was used to. I knew she was working on getting back in shape and besides a few extra pounds that absolutely made her even sexier to me, she was trying to get back to the size she was prior to her pregnancy. “Hey baby, you look good already, so I know you’re gonna be the most beautiful woman in the place tonight.”

Aubrey

“Thank you, baby.” He kissed me like he missed me. I’m sexing him tonight just off of that kiss! “I decided to go with the blue, but I’m feeling that black on black. You look like a straight boss. Very sexy baby. How was your day? Mom and I had a great time at the salon. She’s a trip.”

Monroe

“Thank you, Beautiful. I missed you today. I just verified some shipments and of course you know Jordan went with me. That’s how she met Benny. Other than that, everything was cool.” I didn’t make eye contact with her though. Tonight, I was wearing my black tailored Georgia Armani suit, black silk shirt and tie with my silver cuff links. I was also wearing the black Armani lace up dress shoes that I purchased to complete the look. My hair was freshly tapered and I let it grow just a bit longer because that's how my lady likes my hair.

She undressed and was getting in the shower when I grabbed her and kissed her again. I just wanted to feel on those beautiful chocolate breasts and that plump ass. I sucked and licked gently on her neck and guided her to the bed so that she could lie on her back. I removed my shirt as I kissed her full breasts gently and worked my way down to her center. I suckled her love button as she arched her back at the pleasure. I held her hips as I let her wetness enter my mouth. I tried to pleasure her regularly, but truth be told, I craved her just as much if not more than she said she craved me.

Once I felt her start to tremble, I swirled my tongue around her clit feverishly until her climax was complete. She tried to get me to enter her, but I had to remind her that we had people in the house and that I needed to feed Junior. "Go ahead and get in the shower, baby." I'll see your fine ass downstairs and I delicately pecked her lips. Originally, I thought that being able to fuck Jordan would tide me over, but Aubrey was the one. And there was absolutely no substitute for her. I just hoped that she was able to understand that I made a mistake today and that it would never happen again.

Aubrey

Damn, I desired this man immensely. It had been so long since I felt him inside of me, but I remembered that he felt amazing. After my shower, I applied my shimmery moisturizer as well as the Chance by Chanel perfume that drove Monroe absolutely crazy. He always said I smelled like edible flowers when I wore that one.

I donned my gown and it fit even better now that I'd tightened up my midsection since I bought it. I swear, those women's journals that detailed breastfeeding as a way to get your figure back were not lying. But this ass seemed like it was not trying to go anywhere. My mom said I looked good and I knew Monroe preferred me this size. But if he wanted to pump some more kids inside of me, I needed to get back down to my pre-pregnancy weight first.

I put my heels on, fluffed and smoothed my hair and applied the last of the finishing touches on my face. That Fenty highlighter had my cheekbones glowing for the gods! I wore a dark berry lipstick that complimented my smoky eyes. For some reason, my eye color looked even brighter this evening and I felt beautiful. I grabbed my silver clutch and walked down the steps to join my family. Jordan had already left, and the limousine was due here within ten minutes.

Dee Dee

My baby knew she was bad. Those curves were dangerous, courtesy of my grandson. She was gorgeous before, but even more so now that she became a mother and found herself again. “Baby, you bad to the bone! And who taught you to smoke out your eyes like that? That dress... oh my God, you are wearing that dress!” She blushed and I leaned in so no one else would hear me. “Jordan and none of these other women around here don’t have nothing on you! Look at the way that man looks at you. That’s a man that is totally in love. I know that look, I see it every day in Mike’s eyes. But baby, I’m telling you again, I do not have a good feeling about that girl always being around. She needs to go. And soon! Love you sweetness.”

Aubrey

I knew my mom meant well and I also knew that eventually I had to tell her about our arrangement, but this was my life. “I hear you mom, let’s just have a great time tonight. You look gorgeous as well. Definitely who I get what I’m working with from!” At almost fifty-eight, my mom could easily pass for her early forties. She was wearing a fitted long black ruched dress that had Swarovski crystals. She kept herself in great shape due to her prior military lifestyle. She worked out regularly and she reminded me of a lighter Angela Bassett, body wise. I could only hope that I looked as good at her age.

After Monroe and I got the baby together, we all piled in the limousine and headed for the club. We entered through the private entrance so that we would be able to hand the baby over to the nanny in the secure area in the back of the club. Mike and mom went ahead into the club area while I placed our coats inside of the manager's office. As I exited, I ran into Free coming from the ladies' room. "Hello Free, you look gorgeous. Enjoy yourself tonight and I'll see you out there."

Free

Aubrey started to walk away and I grabbed her by the arm, gently. She looked annoyed at first, but I could tell she was trying not to be mean as she softened her facial expression. "Bree, I really miss the friendship that we used to have, and being that we're both moms now, I really would like to be part of your life. When we were in college, you were the only person who genuinely had my back. I know I messed that up when I betrayed you. But I was a different person then and I'm so sorry. Please forgive me... please give me another chance to be the great friend to you that you were to me."

Aubrey

"I forgive you Free. I would really like to get to know you again. I feel in my heart of hearts that you have matured. I would like the chance for us to experience motherhood together. But we do this on my terms. I can't just go all in, because you broke my trust. But I still love you, I always have." We embraced and walked into the club together to where our men were standing. There were beautiful people everywhere and knew this was going to be a great event. But why do I feel this nagging feeling in the pit of my stomach like something isn't quite right? Whatever it is, I just hope it's nothing I can't handle.

Chapter 20

Marie

I traveled to the location on the map where my son's essence appeared. It was a modest home in the suburbs and there were no cars parked there. It was New Year's Eve, so people could have been there or could have been out celebrating. All I know is, my son had been in this area a couple of times. I parked down the street and made sure Celeste was comfortable and sleeping. I felt weary, as I haven't been getting enough sleep these past few days and the stress of trying to find my Marchaud was the only thing keeping me going. I jogged lightly back to the house and went around the back to look inside to see if anything was moving. There was a cat, but otherwise the house seemed empty. I tried a few windows and they didn't budge. I decided that I couldn't bust in there, I saw the security sticker on the window. I went around to the front and tried to open a few of those windows to no avail. There was a car coming down the street and I wasn't sure where it would stop, so I hid behind a well-manicured bush. Luckily for me, it turned into the house I was currently stalking.

Once the garage door went up, I ran to the back of the car before they had a chance to let it back down. I then hid behind a couple of boxes as the couple got out of the car. This couldn't be right; these people were white. The husband reached into the back seat and removed a car seat as the wife entered the home. What would these white people be doing with my baby? I walked behind the man and blew a little of the dust from my pouch into his face. He dropped instantly and I caught the baby carrier before it hit the ground. I lifted the blanket from the baby and looked inside. It wasn't my son. I heard the wife walking back toward the door as I hurried back out onto the street and walked briskly to my car. It was the wrong house.

Benny

"Did you get enough to eat, Jordan? By the way, you're pretty good company." So far, I thought I had gotten her to warm up to me. At first, it seemed like she didn't want to come with me, but after I got her laughing at my corny jokes, it was all good.

Jordan

"I did... actually I think I ate more than I should have. I have never been to this restaurant before. Thank you so much." I was really enjoying myself. Benny seemed like a gentleman, he was very handsome, and he seemed very focused and goal oriented. He talked to me about all sorts of things, this felt like a real date. It's been a long time since someone had asked me about me. About the things I liked, versus talking about what they were trying to do for another woman. And to think, I actually loved Aubrey at one point. She was just using me because she wanted me around to please her. She wasn't interested in making me feel wanted or needed. But forget all of that. I want to know more about this man in front of me.

Benny

"Would you like some dessert? I know they have a really good cheesecake if you get down with that." Jordan was wearing the hell out of that dress and I didn't know she was stacked like that until she removed her jacket tonight at the restaurant. She seemed like a good girl. She didn't need a whole lot of makeup, wasn't rocking no weave because she had her own hair and she actually had some conversation for me. I didn't bring her out nowhere fancy, just to the Carolina Kitchen. The other women I've spent time with would have turned up their nose at this spot. But Jordan seemed really appreciative. She was fuckin' sexy.

She declined dessert so we headed to the club to enjoy the night's festivities. I'm glad she agreed to join me, otherwise I knew I would be working the floor most of the night just to pass the time. "You look really beautiful. I can't wait to get you on the dance floor so you can show me some moves. Can you dance?"

Jordan

"Oh, I'll have to do just that then! I bet I can dance circles around you." Conversation with him was just effortless. He wasn't being flirty; he didn't expect anything, and he opened my doors for me like my father told me a man was supposed to do. The only thing Monroe opened for me was my legs. We arrived at the club and there were cars everywhere and a line to get in the building. Benny pulled up to the front door, hopped out and gave the valet his keys. He came around to my side of the car and opened the door as he took my hand leading me out of his SUV.

We walked past the people waiting in line right into the club and I felt like royalty. Once we walked in, he asked for my coat and handed our things to a young lady in a server's uniform. I spotted Aubrey and Monroe right away chatting with another beautiful couple. Benny said hello to everyone and as I got closer to Aubrey and Monroe, the more insecure I became. I felt plain, although I knew my dress was cute. But she looked regal in her blue gown. And Monroe looked like the perfect King to her Queen. I saw her mom cutting her eyes at me, but I ignored her. And Mike walked past me like he didn't even know me. How fucking rude was that. I can't wait 'til I tell all of them that I'm having Monroe's baby!

Benny

"Would you like a glass of champagne?" Jordan shook her head no, but at Aubrey's insistence, she decided to have a glass.

Aubrey

"Go ahead boo, have some champagne. It's your favorite." She looked uncomfortable and I wanted her to truly enjoy herself. "Free, this is my friend Jordan. Jordan, this is my longtime friend, Fresia." They said their hellos and extended compliments to each other as I noticed a familiar face moving toward me in the crowd. "Joe!"

Monroe

"Aww here go this hatin' ass nigga," I said to James quietly. He turned to look in Joe's direction and we both stared at his date. Some plain looking white chick with curves for days. Aubrey was so excited this nigga came tonight. She doesn't know how close I came to killin' this nigga not even six months ago. I nodded my head to him, and he returned the gesture as he introduced the white girl to everyone. I extended my hand and shook hers, but she seemed a bit out of place for some reason. But considering the company she was keeping I would feel that way too.

I decided to go check on Junior and James tagged along with me to put eyes on my God daughter. They were both laying there as the nanny tickled and played with them. We decided not to disturb them, didn't wanna get the babies all riled up. We went into the office to discuss the matter from days before. James looked a bit troubled and I wanted to ensure he was alright with executing the plan. "What's going on J? Were you able to do it?" His brows furrowed and I knew he didn't. "I can get someone else to do it. I don't need you being distracted because of this. I know it's hard. We don't have to go through with this."

James

"Boss, I can do this. It's a little hard looking at my daughter and seeing that he looks so much like her. It's like looking at a brown skin, boy version of her. It trips me out. But I was serious about this nigga never being able to leave behind a legacy in this world. I don't want his name to carry on, ever! I should have just killed him and then we wouldn't even be talking about this."

Monroe

"If you killed him, we would have had to kill her too. We made an agreement to give him back."

James

"No, YOU made an agreement to give him back. I always wanted to get rid of that muthafucka." I said as I glared at him. We had never been at odds before, and I didn't want to disrespect him in any way, but this shit was on him. I would've killed the bitch too with no problem.

Monroe

"James, I understand how you're feeling, but watch how you're speaking to me." We glared at each other for about a minute before I spoke again. "Now, let's reconvene in the new year. I'll take that problem off of your hands, and if you want me to, I'll dead the bitch too. I understand you're under a bit of stress, so let's rejoin our beautiful women and enjoy the rest of the night." He didn't say anything, nor did he shake my outstretched hand. My nerves were wearing thin at this point, so I went back into the party with my fiancée and smiled through my aggravation.

Free

I was actually enjoying myself but when I didn't see James rejoin the group with Monroe, I decided to go and check on him. He was watching the baby through the glass door where the nanny had them in the secure area in the back. I couldn't read the expression on his face, but if I had to name it, it would be 'pained'. "Baby, is everything okay? You look worried about something, can I help?" I stepped closer to him and tried to rub his arm and he pulled away from me. "Talk to me baby, you're scaring me right now."

James

I'm trippin' right now, this is my wife. This is Free. "Baby, I still have some unfinished business and it's bugging me a bit. I'm okay though. And I'm sorry for worrying you." I kissed her and held her as we looked at the nanny feeding Junior as Tamia fell asleep. "She's absolutely beautiful huh, babe?"

Free

"Yes she is, and she is lucky to have a daddy like you."

James

Yeah she's lucky alright. I'm planning to kill her little brother. This is driving me nuts.

Sam

What did Benny think he was doing here with *Little Miss Salsa*? That's alright, I sashayed right on over there in all of my glory with my beautiful ass. And Joe was here with that receptionist. This shit is laughable. "Hello Jerrick. How are you? And who is your little... friend?" as I looked her up and down in her cheap Fashion Nova dress and knock off Louboutins. Who did she think she is? Cardi B? Little Miss Hip Hop? But I'd do her though. She had a nice ass. "I've been trying to reach you. Have you been receiving my calls?"

Benny

"Yes, I received all of your calls and all of your texts. And this is my beautiful date, Jordan. Jordan, this is my associate's friend, Sam. Excuse us." I said as I escorted Jordan away from the fuckery. She is a joke, I knew once Sam saw her that she would be on some other shit. I'm not playing into her shit though. "You ready to show me what you working with? I'm ready to see you dance them circles around me." She don't know that I can get down with the best of them. I'm about to make her ass dizzy.

Stevie

I wasn't at the club tonight, I was on babysitting duty. I don't know why James wouldn't just let me kill this little muthafucka and be done with it already. I looked down the street as we came out of the front door and thought I saw someone familiar. "Aye Goldie, ain't that the bitch Marie? Is she sleep in that car over there yo?"

Goldie

"Yo that is her! How the fuck she keep finding us though?"

Stevie

I kept it in the back of my mind that she had that voodoo shit going on. And I couldn't forget how she did the little homie's brother. "Aye, we need to hit up Money and James. We gotta roll out though. This bitch is on a mission. And I know she won't hesitate to try something."

Goldie

"Alright, let's roll. I don't want none of that voodoo shit nowhere near me. Let's call them first thing in the morning. I'll just send a text to Benny for now. Where we gonna take him though?"

Marie

I heard a car pull off and Celeste was getting a little fussy at the same time. "Aww what's wrong honey? You hungry? Come here baby." I picked her up and as the car rolled past us, I felt a little lightheaded. It was weird. "Mommy needs to get you home baby girl. I know I need to get some rest so that I can bring your brother home."

Chapter 21

Joe

This nigga really thinks he a big shot. Yeah, this is a nice club and everything, but don't get it twisted. You been at one, you been at them all. Kristin has been acting real funny since we had the little disagreement about what I said about her ass. She should know by now that I care about her, but you just can't change up on me after spoiling me. I'm super sexual and she knows that. I thought she was too. And I ain't had no ass in about four days. My shit dryer than a muthafucka. I don't know what is wrong with her, but I refuse to start my year off like this. She has been quiet ever since I came back from lunch the other day.

But Aubrey, got damn! She looked better than anyone in the room. I walked over to her while that nigga was chopping it up with Reggie- or James' girl... whatever the fuck his name was today. "Aye guh, you sure you had a baby a few weeks ago? You the finest thang in this bitch!" We laughed together about that and she hugged me with those big ass titties pressed into my chest. I started thinking about earlier this week when she had that milk leaking out with her titty just staring at me. "Down boy", I said to myself as I felt my shit start to brick.

Aubrey

Was he getting hard right now? I know my mom was on to something when she said he had a crush on me. I'm not going to let it get weird though, he can keep his hands in front of his dick all night for all I care. He's still my friend. "Aye, you better not let your girlfriend hear you say that! You said she works at the clinic? How long she been working there?" She was very shapely. She wasn't too much of a looker in the face, but she was very nice. A bit quiet, but nice. "Is she uncomfortable around all these black and brown people, Joe?" I really hoped not.

Sam was looking gorgeous and I told her so. I hadn't seen her and Joe speak to each other though so I just had to stir the pot and ask. "So, did you say hello to Sam tonight? I must say she's gotten a little plumper in the back since the last time I saw her. She is wearing that dress, huh?" I saw him looking, then he looked at Kristin to see where her eyes were. She wasn't paying us no mind though. "You need to speak. Don't let it be awkward between y'all. Everyone can still be friends, right?"

Joe

"Get outta my business for once, witcha nosy ass!" We laughed so hard. It was like old times at the clinic. "Lemme leave you alone, your man keeps cutting his eyes at me and I don't wanna knock his pretty boy ass out in front of all his flunkies." She punched me playfully and I acted like it hurt while holding my arm while walking away. I went to check on Kristin and she seemed to be alright. Still quiet, but I was going to try and be patient with her. I saw Sam walk to the back toward the restrooms and I excused myself as well.

I waited by the bathrooms for her to come out, while I kept an eye out for her man *and* my girl. She came out and I acted like I was walking toward the men's room that was just past the ladies' room and bumped into her. "Oh, hey Sam. Sorry about that. You look beautiful tonight. How have you been baby girl?"

Sam

"Hey Joe, I'm good." As I reached in for a hug. I felt his hand graze my ass, but I didn't say anything. "You look well, what have you been up to lately?" He really was looking good tonight, made me have some old thoughts about the fun we used to have. Not like I wanted to be with him again, but his sex was decent. I'll never forget my first. "Your date looks quite uncomfortable though. Is she alright?"

Joe

Oh, I see what kinda shit she on tonight. But Aubrey was right, she was looking plumper in the hips and ass. "She'll be alright, but I'm talking to you right now. You still with ole boy out there? He making you happy?" I started rubbing her thigh where that split stopped around the side of her pussy. She tried not to, but I heard her moan a little bit.

Sam

"Do you really wanna talk about him? Or do you want get inside of this pussy?" He looked shocked, but I was getting aroused again and I could tell he wanted me so I pulled him into the women's bathroom and started kissing him. We went into the handicapped stall, nobody here tonight needed it. I closed the toilet lid and told him to take his dick out and sit down. He looked back at it and frowned. I guess he wasn't feeling it. He grabbed me, turned me around and started kissing on my neck while simultaneously pulling up my dress. I put my hands against the wall and tooted my ass up like he liked it as I felt him thrust his dick inside me from the back.

He wasn't Keith, but he knew how to hit the right spots. And he kept hitting one spot in particular. He knew how to make me squirt and I was not about to ruin my dress. "Oooohhh baby, back up for a minute." I told him as I turned around. I lifted my leg on the assistance bar and he entered me from the front. We looked one another in the eyes as he continued to pump my pussy and as I threw it back at him. "Don't nut in me baby,

I'm going home with Keith tonight." He laughed a little bit after I said that. And I knew what was coming next.

Joe

"I won't, if you promise to swallow all this good nut for me baby. Don't make me waste it." I grabbed her throat as I fucked the shit outta her until I felt the nut building up in my balls. She nodded her head yes and I said "now", right as I thrusted one more time into her wetness so that she could squat down in time to accept all my hardness into her mouth. "Uuhhhhh, ahhhhh, sssssss. Fuck yeah!" She went to work on my dick just like I taught her. She gulped my shit down, licked my balls and sucked on my head all while looking at me. Shit was sexy as fuck. "Thanks baby girl, I needed that shit."

Sam

"Me too." As we got ourselves together, my college acquaintance Free came into the bathroom as I exited the stall. I didn't care what she or nobody else at that party had to say or think. And she damn sure couldn't say shit, having a baby by Rob's ass. I went to the sink and washed my hands. "Hey girl, you having fun tonight?" I put some water in my mouth and swished it around a few times, spit it out, and left out as Joe came out of the stall. He walked past her and went into the men's room as I rejoined the party.

Free

I couldn't believe the virgin was in here fucking another nigga in the bathroom of all places while her man is in the same party. And I already knew the nigga that came with the white girl was shady. He's been staring at Aubrey all night and adjusting his dick. I guess so no one would see him get hard. "Damn, this shit here is hilarious!"

Keith

"Hey baby, everything ok? I thought I was gonna have to send a search party." I laughed a little and she hugged me and let me know she was having an amazing time here with me. "I'm glad baby, we still got about an hour before the ball drops. Let's dance a little bit while I watch that ass twerk for me."

Sam

I had learned a few moves from Candy and I wasn't afraid to show them off for anyone. I was finally coming into my own. We went out there and I led Keith over beside Benny and his "friend". She was tryna do that salsa shit, but this was R&B and Hip Hop playing tonight. I twerked my ass all on Keith as he did his two-step. Now Benny could dance. I was surprised, because he could be so reserved at times.

I turned it up a notch and I displayed my sexy, hypnotic moves as everyone started to crowd around us. The DJ then played Stir Fry by Migos. I kept getting closer to Benny until he and I were the ones dancing together. I hiked my dress up a bit and my garter was showing as I popped my ass all over his dick. Once I noticed Keith's displeasure, I made sure to high five Benny's little date, like "tag you're it" and I walked back over to Keith.

"Hey baby, that was fun. I had to show Benny that he couldn't hang with me. I hope you enjoyed the show, Daddy." I purred. And hugged my arms around his neck as I kissed his lips. He softened up and hugged me back while grabbing all over my ass before going to the bar. I looked back at Benny and smirked at him. Then I noticed Joe's eyes on me and he laughed while shaking his head. I knew what he was thinking as I kiss on this man after I just swallowed his seed. But oh well.

Rob

I was paranoid as fuck right now. I still had not heard anything about Freddy's fate. It was New Year's Eve. This shit happened over twenty-four hours ago. I did not leave my cell even to eat. The female CO asked me if she could get me anything, but I declined. "Officer Fields, have you heard anything about Freddy?"

Officer Fields

“I’m sorry Williams, I haven’t heard anything yet. He was still in surgery when I came on shift. Here, take this water. You sure you’re not hungry?”

Rob

I never looked at her until that moment. She was a light brown skin complexion, super thick and slightly bow legged like Trina. She had thick thighs, wore her hair naturally with very light makeup. She was gorgeous. She looked so concerned for me and I wasn’t sure why. “Why are you so nice to me? I’m not a good person, I belong in here and I deserve to get whatever is coming to me. I just don’t understand why you’re so nice to me.”

Officer Fields

“I’ve read your file, Williams. I know what happened to you and my faith in Jesus is enough to know that whatever you did in the past, He can forgive you if you let him.”

Rob

For some reason, tears started rolling down my face. How is it that this stranger believes in the good that she thinks I have inside of me? “I don’t know how. Will you teach me?”

Officer Fields

“I thought you would never ask. Here is the pocket bible that I walk around with. I want you start with the book of Proverbs. Read a couple of verses each day, talk with God, meditate and pray. I’ll see what I can do about getting you some time in the prison library, just in case you need access to more reading materials. And I’ll be right back with some food. Hang tight.”

Rob

I watched her as she walked away. She was definitely stacked, but there was nothing I could do besides look. She was helping me, so I decided to be respectful. I turned to Proverbs and started with the first chapter.

Monroe

Aubrey and I went up on the stage and the music ceased. “Well everyone, I wanted to thank you all for coming out tonight and bringing in the year with us. On behalf of my lady, Aubrey, and my family and closest friends, I want everyone to grab a glass of champagne so that we can begin the countdown together in precisely one minute.” The servers were ready and started distributing glasses of champagne to everyone.

Alright everyone, put your glasses up, it's time for the countdown. "Ten, nine, eight, seven, six, five, four, three, two, one... HAPPY NEW YEAR!!" I kissed Aubrey and I knew this year was going to be a great one because she was here with me. "I can't wait until I make you my wife, beautiful. With each passing day, I get more and more excited about you becoming Mrs. King. I love you baby."

Aubrey

I was so in love with this man. "I love you and I'm excited as well." As we exited the stage, I felt some eyes on me. Jordan was staring at Monroe with her champagne glass untouched. She looked as if she was wishing that it was her being embraced and adored by Monroe instead of me. We were going to have to have a little chat. This situation seemed like it could possibly be going in a dangerous direction. And that nagging feeling once again returned to my stomach.

Chapter 22

Free

"Baby, I think it's time for us to head home." Something was going on with James, but I knew he wasn't comfortable talking about it. I wouldn't pressure him, but he wasn't gonna sit here for the rest of the night drinking everything at the bar. He didn't even do the toast, he just sat with his back turned to the rest of the club and downed shot after shot of whatever the bartender kept putting in front of him. "Sir, that's enough. Please don't serve my husband anything else. Thank you." As I slid him a fifty-dollar bill.

"Baby, I'm going to get Tamia so that we can go." He didn't say anything to me, just looked down into his almost empty glass. I walked to the back and toward the secure area where the babies were with the nanny. I spotted Kristin sitting on a couch in the lounge area with look on her face that I couldn't decipher. "Hey, sweetie, are you ok? Is there something I can help you with?" She looked up at me and tears immediately welled up in her eyes. I looked back toward the club area to ensure we were alone so that she would feel comfortable talking to me. "Tell me what's going on honey. Is someone hurting you? I know you don't know me, but I've been in some messed up situations. And I can see in your face that you are lost."

Kristin

This woman was beautiful. She didn't know me from a can of paint, but I could tell she was being sincere, not just nosy. Dr. Saul had my mind fucked up. I've been abused before, my ex really did a number on me. But this guy was sadistic. I thought that I would just suck a little dick here and there and throw it back at him whenever I had to. But he liked to hurt me, it was like if I looked like I enjoyed what we were doing, he couldn't get off. I had to be in pain or he didn't enjoy himself. "I'm alright, I'm just coming down with something and starting to feel sick. I appreciate your concern. Thank you so much."

My first time with Dr. Saul, when I agreed to have sex with him, I got on my knees and I was trying to remove his penis from his pants. He slapped my hands away. He got up and got his suit tie from his coat rack. He tied my hands behind my back with one end of the tie and connected it to my neck by tying the other end to it. I thought I was going to suffocate. Tears ran down my face as I struggled to breathe. And as I cried, he smacked my bare ass over and over until I started to bruise. Once he was done spanking me, he inserted his dick into my ass roughly while he continued to spank one cheek at a time. Once he orgasmed, he untied me and said, "until next time." He just dismissed me and I left his office. He was so degrading, but not to the point where I was going to quit or risk my freedom. And I definitely wasn't going back to Taz and that ridiculous train wreck of a life that I had in Tennessee.

Free

"Well, whatever you're going through, just know that it's not too late to do something different. That look on your face and those tears are not because you're coming down with a cold." Her shady boyfriend showed up at that exact moment and I just told her that I would see her later as I went to get my daughter.

Joe

"Kris, are you ready to go?" Why was she back here with Rob's old side bitch though? She better not have told her about me and Sam earlier. She better mind her fucking business. "What's going on? You've been acting funny for a few days now. I apologized to you for what I said, and I really meant it. What will it take to get you to believe me?" I was trying not to get frustrated with her, but this shit was really getting on my fucking nerves.

Kristin

"Joe, I'm fine, I just have a lot of things on my mind. Do you mind dropping me off at home please?" I just really wanted to be by myself and get some rest. I had to figure out how to get out of this shit with Dr. Saul. I really do believe that he would press charges on me. And with my past record, I'm sure they would believe the "good doctor" over the "white trash" receptionist with a record.

Joe

"So I can't sleep over? It's the new year baby and I wanted to spend it with you." By getting up in those guts. And I truly miss her bobbing her head on my dick. It may sound like I don't like her, but that's not true. I just don't love her. I got close to her and held her hands. "Baby, I miss you. I just wanna be with you tonight. Let me make you feel safe and protected. I know it's something you're not telling me. I just wanna be here for you."

Kristin

At that moment, Free was walking by us as Joe was pouring his heart out or whatever. Free made it a point to shake her head no as she looked into my eyes. When Joe turned around, she just kept walking with her baby until she was out of sight. "Joe, I appreciate you but I'm not feeling well, and I think being alone will allow me to get the rest I need. I'm sorry." I got up, grabbed my coat and called a Lyft. I didn't want him to feel obligated to take me home. I knew what he really wanted from me. I will have to catch up with Free another time, I feel like she has some information for me.

Aubrey

After the countdown, I decided to look for Jordan. I needed to know and understand what was going on with her. She was talking to Keith, Sam's new beau. They looked like old friends as Benny walked back over and brought her another flute of champagne. "Hey Keith, did you enjoy yourself tonight?"

Keith

Monroe's lady was very beautiful. And she was wearing that dress. "Yes, I did. You and Money definitely know how to throw a party. Thank you for the invitation." I was trying my best not to stare, but she was sexy.

Aubrey

"It was definitely our pleasure. Hey Benny, you mind if I steal your date for just a second?" He nodded, and she rolled her eyes but came with me anyway. "Hey, what's going on with you Jordan? Are you still salty about going on the date with Benny? I swear I'm gonna tell my mother about us after they leave this week. But I really just need you to be on board right now baby."

Jordan

"Look, I don't care about none of that shit. Do whatever you all are going to do. I'm going to continue to enjoy myself." I started to walk away, and Aubrey grabbed my arm. I looked up at her and she let my arm go. "Don't you ever grab me that way again. I don't belong to you, nor do I belong to Monroe. You all need to remember that. You do not want me on your bad side."

Aubrey

What did she mean by that? And why was she acting like this? She seemed to be having a great time with Benny, but I don't know what has changed. I'm not going to let her embarrass us in front of everyone, but we needed to settle this once and for all. This shit isn't working anymore. I spot Monroe chatting it up with a few people he introduced me to as his investors earlier this evening and I walked over to them. The conversation ceased and Monroe excused himself to speak with me.

Monroe

"What's going on baby? You ready to go?"

Aubrey

"Something is going on with Jordan. I'm thinking our "arrangement" is getting to her. I'm not sure it's such a great idea anymore." Then my mother and Mike walked over and asked if we were ready to go. "Mom, I'll call the car and then we can get out of here. Let me go and get Junior and then we can be on our way." I turned back to Monroe.

"Baby, I know you're still taking care of your business, so we can talk later when you get home, okay? Love you."

Monroe

"Love you too, I'll be right behind y'all." I saw Jordan eyeing me, and Aubrey noticed it too. "I'll take care of it baby, I'll talk to her." I whispered to Aubrey as I embraced her. I went back over to finish my conversation and then I noticed Goldie and Stevie walking in. I signaled to Benny to come with me. James was drunk as hell, so he wouldn't be any help at this moment. "What are y'all doing here? And where is the baby?"

Stevie

"Boss, the baby is in your office in the car seat. He sleep right now, but his mom keeps finding us. That bitch Marie was parked outside of the house, sleep in her car tonight. I'm not sure where else to take him."

Benny

"So, your dumbasses brought him here?" I said to them both. I then turned to Money, "Boss, I'll take care of this, you go ahead and tend to your family. I'll give you a call later on in the day." He agreed and left the room. "I should kill both of y'all right now. If she keeps finding y'all, what makes you think she won't come here?"

Goldie

"Benny, we didn't know what else to do or where to take him. Why don't we just kill the little nigga now?"

Benny

"That's not your muthafuckin' call. Go gas up the car, and take turns driving to different spots until we get the okay from the boss. Don't bring y'all asses back around here unless I tell you to. Now get the fuck on." I said as I stared menacingly at these dumb ass niggas.

Free

James was still sitting in the same spot at the bar, this time with an empty glass. "Baby, here put on your coat. I called the car and it's outside waiting for us."

James

"You go ahead home, baby. I need to square some shit away with Money tonight." I just wasn't ready to go home at that moment. I had to figure out what to do with this baby. I just couldn't bring myself to kill him. Free was hesitant, but after seeing that I wasn't moving, she went ahead and took the baby home. Here comes Money's side chick sitting by me at the bar. What does she want?

Jordan

"Hey, James right?" He nodded his head yes as I ordered another glass of champagne. Might as well continue the ruse since no one knows I'm pregnant yet anyway. "Did you enjoy yourself this evening?" I know I didn't. Benny is a great guy but being here with Aubrey and Monroe while they were allowed to be all over each other in front of me was torture. I was already feeling like a third wheel but having to pretend to be on a date with someone else took the cake. I saw Aubrey, her parents and the baby leave so that meant the Monroe was still here.

I started walking to the back and overheard Benny's conversation with two other guys about a baby. I've heard the name Marie before from Aubrey, but why would they want to kill her baby? I hid in the corner as Monroe left the office and continued to listen to their conversation. This wasn't right. I needed to find this Marie and let her know what was going on. This shit was crazy and I couldn't believe that they would be considering killing an innocent baby.

Monroe

I was headed back into the office and I spotted Jordan listening to what the guys were discussing. "Um, Jordan what are you doing?"

Jordan

"Oh, um, I was looking for you or Benny. I'm getting a little tired, but I can grab a Lyft or something. You go ahead and take care of your business. I'll see you later." Monroe stepped in front of me so that I could not go anywhere.

Monroe

I stared at her for a minute because she seemed nervous. "What did you overhear, Jordan?"

Chapter 23

Marie

When I got home this morning, I put the baby in her crib and checked the map. I couldn't believe what I was seeing when I reviewed it for movement. Marchaud was brought back to the location again last night during the time I must've fallen asleep. Right street, wrong house. I've got to figure this out, and someone is going to have hell to pay.

<<ring, ring>>

Shawna

"Uh, hello. Is this Marie?"

Marie

"Yes it is? Who may I ask is calling?" I knew who this was. I was just wondering what she wanted and why she was calling me. She was very rude and unsupportive to me while I was nearing the end of my pregnancy. I figured it was because of what Rob did. But after thinking about it, I don't think I would have ever treated another woman that way, going through what I was going through.

Shawna

"I um, just wanted to call you before I headed to the boutique this morning, to congratulate you. How are you doing? How are the babies? Is there anything I can do? I bought some baby items for them and I was wondering if I could bring them by? I'm really sorry I wasn't able to make some time to stop by the hospital while you were there."

Marie

"Yeah sure. All is well, my son is still at the hospital until he can get his weight up, but you can come and see my daughter Celeste." I lied. Hmmm, this might be a good idea. I may be able to strongly influence Shawna to be my sitter, since she's willing to come to me.

Shawna

"Ok, how about ten o'clock this morning? I just need to stop by the boutique and drop some things off first. See you then."

Marie

This would be my chance to move about freely during the day. And no one would miss her for a few hours. It's New Year's Day, the boutique is closed.

Keith

<<ring, ring>>

"You have a collect call from an inmate in a Federal Correctional Facility...". It was Don and it was eight o'clock in the morning, so this couldn't be good. I accepted the call and I heard the pain in his voice as soon as he started talking.

Don

"Hey bruh. The parole board denied me again. I have one more chance to meet with them in five years, but I'm just so tired of this shit. Stacia told me she wasn't going to wait for me. I don't blame her. I've put her through so much. And my new bitch, Taisha, hasn't been here to see me all week. Not since that order I put in last week."

Keith

The "order" he was referring to was that Spanish nigga Travis. I personally handled that for him because I didn't trust anyone but Benny. And he wasn't cooperating with me on this one. It was like that little nigga didn't move unless Money gave him the okay. Loyal muthafucka. "Alright, I'm on it. Why you so hung up on this bitch anyway? I can find you another bitch that will be glad to take your money. She has way too much shit with her." He couldn't answer. Don asked me to go and check her out and I told him that I would later on in the day. "Hang in there big bruh, I got you. I'll let you know what I find out. Call me tomorrow."

See this was the shit that got on my nerves. He supposed to be worried about the fact that he was denied parole again, or even worse, that Stacia was done with him. But nah, he's worried about the freak bitch that is strung out on heroin. I just didn't understand none of that shit. I'd handle all of that a little later, but for now I would go and love up on Sam. It had been a while since she spent the entire evening with me. She was still sleeping when I entered the room with breakfast. Her beautiful red hair was a wild mass on the pillow. "Sam, wake up baby, I have some breakfast for you."

Sam

"Mmmmmm, good morning baby." I'm glad I didn't say a name, I forgot where I was and who I was with. I should have known though, only Keith did this romantic stuff that I had no interest in. I couldn't get Joe or Benny off my mind after last night. It was exhilarating to rendezvous with Joe like that. And he made my pussy feel so good. And then the look on Benny's face when I twerked my ass all over his dick. Shit, now I'm horny again. "I know what I'm hungry for Keith, but it's not food." And I proceeded to devour his dick with a thirst that was absolutely unquenchable.

Marie

Shawna arrived at my apartment a few minutes after ten o'clock. She just gushed over Celeste and was amazed at how much she looked like me. I showed her a picture of Marchaud from the hospital and she thought he was a cutie as well.

I allowed her to hold the baby as I brewed a special tea for only her consumption. This tea would allow me to manipulate her mind for a few hours while I went to handle some business. "Would you like some tea?" She agreed and I brought it out to her.

Shawna

"Ooh girl, what kind of tea is this? It's delicious!"

Marie

"It's an old recipe Grandmother taught me. Drink up! I guarantee you'll want more." I went and took a shower and got dressed for my excursion today. I went over to Shawna and refilled her mug. "Shawna, stay here with Celeste and make sure she's comfortable until I get back. Do not answer the door or the phone for anyone but me. I'll be back shortly." She nodded with this blank look in her eyes. As soon as Celeste started to whine, Shawna was all over it. So now that I knew my concoction was in full effect, I headed back to the neighborhood that I was in last night.

In the daylight, I could tell which house stood out. This residence had weeds growing all over the place. The porch was littered with beer cans and cigarette butts and instead of curtains, there were sheets in the window. I went around back and looked into the windows to see what I could. There was a loud television on inside the house, so I decided to break a window near the door so I could unlock it. I entered the house and it smelled of stale cigarettes and old food. I was able to confirm that there was no one here; however, that lightheaded feeling hit me again. Much like that feeling I got this morning when that car passed me. I couldn't believe that I was that close to my baby, and I fell asleep when I should have been trying to find him.

There were no pictures in this home, I was also trying to find some mail with someone's name on it. There was nothing here. But from the feeling I got, this was a person or people that I've encountered before. I was getting closer, I just felt it in my spirit. I would just have to keep going, until I got my son back. I headed to the next spot on the map. It led me to a club called Silk's. I tried entering the front door and the door handles were chained. I went around to the back and it was the same. I went back to my car and googled the club. As soon as I got to the website, I clicked on the management tab and what do you know? Monroe's face popped up as the owner. Now I knew exactly who I needed to start with.

Monroe

"Jordan, I asked you a question sweetie. I need to know what you overheard. And please don't lie to me." We left the club ten minutes ago, and I just wanted to know how much she heard. I held her hand while we rode our destination.

Jordan

"I couldn't actually hear what was being said, I was just trying to figure out who was in the room. I heard Benny's voice, but I couldn't tell who he was speaking to. I didn't want to interrupt, so I was just trying to stay there until he came out so that I could tell him I was ready to go." It was the only thing I could come up with. Then I noticed we passed the exit to Monroe's house. "Monroe, where are you taking me?" My heart started beating fast and I tried removing my hand from his, but his grip tightened. "Let my hand go, *AHORA*! (now!)". My heart was thumping so hard inside of my chest.

Monroe

"Relax Jordan. I have a stop to make really quick." A short time later, we pulled up to the warehouse. Jordan acted like she didn't want to get out of the car, so I had Benny remove her for me. He placed her in one of the holding rooms until I decided to go and speak with her. I entered the room and she charged at me with her fists hitting my chest. I grabbed her wrists and turned her around to calm her down. Her ass was up against my dick and the way she was moving was arousing me. I kissed her neck and held on to her as she stopped struggling against me. "Shhhh, baby. Just calm down, you already know I won't hurt you." I had disabled the cameras to this room before I entered it, just in case Jordan started discussing the details of our arrangement. She started to moan as I kept one arm across her chest restraining her arms while I used my other hand to finger her clit.

"Baby, I just want you to tell me what you heard at the club. And I also want to know what the issue is between you and Aubrey." The mention of Aubrey seemed to get her riled up all over again. She started struggling against me and then I inserted my fingers into her pussy as I massaged her G-spot.

Jordan

"Get off... of... me... Mmmmmmm...". Monroe knew just how to strum my body as if I was his own personal guitar. My emotions were all over the place, I was scared, I was horny, I didn't know why I was here, I was angry with him, but I loved this man. "Oooohh baby, don't stop."

He was about to make mc cum but all of a sudden, he removed his fingers and sat down in the chair on the other side of a table where he just had me pinned against him. "What's going on? Why did you stop?" I was breathing so hard and frustrated that he would just stop while I was on the brink of cumming.

Monroe

"Jordan, something is different with you and I need to know what's up. You know I care about you and I enjoy having you around, but your attitude is changing and causing some issues for Aubrey. What is the problem?" She was still breathing hard and I know she wanted me to finish pleasing her at that moment. So, I unbuckled my slacks and pulled my dick out as I started stroking it. I knew what she wanted; she was insatiable. "You want this Jordy?" She nodded her head up and down, like a little girl being deprived of her favorite toy. "You need to tell daddy what he wants to know, and I'll give you exactly what you want."

Jordan

"I... I want you baby. I want you for myself. Please... please fuck me... please let me have all of you baby. We don't need Aubrey anymore." I started walking toward him and I got on my knees as he gripped me by my hair. I couldn't read the look on his face, but I knew that he wanted me. I started to deep throat his dick and for some reason, it felt like it was the last time. He gripped my hair with both hands as he fucked my throat. He stood up and continued this brutal assault on my throat until he was about to nut. He sat back down in the chair and I straddled him as I rode his magnificent dick until he was ready to explode. He gripped my ass roughly and pumped me from the bottom. He didn't bother to remove himself as he coated my walls with his semen which frightened me even more.

Benny

The boss was in with Jordan, but I was curious to know what they were talking about. Once I got to the office where our security camera footage was shown, I noticed that room's camera was disabled. I turned it back on and noticed that Money was sitting in a chair and Jordan was standing with her back to the camera. She was telling him that she wanted him to herself without Aubrey and it looked as if she was crying. Money was doing something with his hands, but I couldn't make out what he was doing until she went over to him and dropped down on her knees. He then grabbed her hair and she put his dick into her mouth and started sucking him off. "What the fuck?" Why would my mentor and the girl he knew I was interested in be on some fuck shit?

Chapter 24

Taisha

I had been chillin' in this hotel room for a few days now. I can't believe that I just slept through New Year's Eve. I'm usually at Money's party he throws each year. My phone had been blowing up, but I didn't recognize the numbers, so I didn't answer. I smoked up all of my stash, and I promised myself that I would leave this alone from now on. I decided to check my messages, I know that Don was looking for me.

Friday, December 29th
6:17 pm

"This message is for Taisha, he expects to see you tomorrow. Don't make me come looking for you."

Saturday, December 30th
2:03 pm

"Ma'am, this is Officer Mason, if you could give me a call back at 301-555-7879, I have a few questions to ask you. Thank you."

Saturday, December 30th
4:57 pm

"This message is for Taisha, I'm calling for him again. I'll be at your house today, bitch. And you better be there."

Taisha

Whatever nigga. I was never going back to that house. I put it on the market the day after I found Travis because I was tired of being paranoid that something would happen to me. And Officer Mason was going to be my knight in shining armor. I would tell him some sob story so that he would feel obligated to help me. I dialed his number.

<<ring, ring>>

Officer Mason

"This is Officer Gerald Mason, how may I help you?"

Taisha

"Officer Mason, this Taisha. I'm getting threatening messages on my voicemail from someone I don't know. I'm scared to go back to my home because I think that this is same person that killed my friend Travis. I don't know what to do. I don't trust anyone else and I don't have anyone else to call. Please help me!" I told him as I continued my fake crying.

Officer Mason

"Okay ma'am, please calm down for me. Do they know where you are?"

Taisha

"I don't know, but I don't feel safe here by myself. Would you be able to come here please?" I cried a little bit more to be convincing. He told me to lock my doors and windows to the hotel room and that he would be here to take my statement and make copies of the voicemails on my phone within the hour.

I was so excited, that I didn't register that I was feeling dope sick. I was jittery, my heart was racing and I started sweating profusely. I jumped into the shower and tried to get myself to calm down. Once I got out, I got dressed in jogging pants, a wife beater with no bra and brushed my hair back into a ponytail. My phone rang again, and I answered it without looking at the number. It was Don calling on three-way from someone else's phone.

Don

"Tai, baby, where have you been?"

Taisha

"What do you want Don? I don't want anything more to do with you after what happened to Travis. Please stop calling me."

Don

"Now Taisha, you know the rules. Don't talk about our business on these phones and the other is you know I will never stop calling you. You are mine, baby. When will you get that? You know what's up once I find you, right? Just come see me and I will call this whole thing off. You won't be as lucky as Renee. Hers was quick. I'll make sure that yours is slow."

Taisha

And he hung up. I was going to have to think of something fast. It would be just a matter of time before one of his goons found me in this area. Maybe Officer Mason could relocate me? I would tell him everything I knew. Yes, that's what I was going to do. Oh, here he is now. I glanced at myself one last time and checked my lip gloss to ensure it was still poppin'. I opened the door and it was that nigga from the suburbs that night. What is he doing here?

Keith

"Hello Taisha, I knew you looked familiar." I said as I injected her with a solution to knock her out. I grabbed her, carried her down to the car and put her in my trunk. I was able to track her location from the three-way call I made for Don. I just needed to make sure Don wanted me to actually go through with this.

Marie

I was headed to the only other place that I knew Monroe might be. I hadn't figured out his address yet, but it was time to show all of them I was not to be played with. I knew that warehouse most likely was going to be unmanned due to the holiday. I went around to a side door and used my key that I stole from Dre, one of the young boys that I killed months back to get my point across. Obviously, they forgot what I was capable of.

Once I entered the warehouse, I felt someone was inside. I went to the area where they held Robert and I felt no one was there. I checked the area where they tortured him, and no one was there either. I walked toward the front and as I passed a door, I sensed there was someone in this particular room. I tried the door and it was locked.

I picked the lock and opened the door to see a beautiful Hispanic young lady cuffed to a chair. She was sleeping. I caressed her face and she awoke to me standing over her. I could tell she was startled because I could feel her heart rate speed up.

"Hello, my name is Marie. Do you know who I am?" She started weeping silently and I could tell that she knew something that she didn't want to share with me. "What do you know about my son? Where is he?"

Jordan

This is the Marie that those guys were talking about. This is the one that caused so much trouble and set in motion the events that led up to Aubrey's accident.

"I have heard of you and I know what you are capable of." I remember Aubrey talking about her holding her ex-boyfriend, Rob, hostage in a closet while having him under some type of voodoo spell.

Marie

"So, you're very aware that I'm not afraid to do whatever it takes to get my son back. I suspect that you know something that you're not willing to share with me. Do you want me to make you tell me what you know?" Once again, her heart rate sped up. "No wait, all this time, I thought it was *your* heartbeat that I was hearing. Are you with child?" This is even better.

Jordan

"What? I don't know what you're talking about." I was more than terrified at this point. There was no way she could know that I was pregnant, was there? Then she placed her hand over my stomach and started telling me things I didn't yet know.

Marie

"You're approximately four weeks pregnant with a male child. Who is the father? Is it Reggie?" There was genuine confusion on her face, so it wasn't Reggie. "Do you know who Reggie is?"

Jordan

"No, I don't know a man named Reggie. How did you know that I'm pregnant?"

Marie

"I have an exceptional awareness that I'm sure no one else you'll ever encounter will have. Now whose baby is this?" She was hesitant to tell me, so I sniffed her essence.

"Oh, you're pregnant by Monroe. Here, take my phone right now and call him." She shook her head no, until I threatened her baby.

Jordan

"Alright, give me the damn phone."

<<ring, ring>>

The phone just rang and rang. I called his number three more times until a groggy Aubrey answered his phone.

"Aubrey, it's me. Can you please put Monroe on the phone please?"

Aubrey

"No, Jordan, whatever you want to say to him, you can say it to me. I'm tired of your fucking games."

Jordan

"Aubrey, I'm not playing games! Monroe left me at the warehouse cuffed to a damn chair inside of a holding room. Marie is here and-". She snatched the phone from me.

Marie

"Ahhh, Aubrey, how nice to speak with you again. Kindly ask Monroe where my son is and I will let this woman and their love child live. I promise, no harm will come to either of them."

Aubrey

What is she talking about, love child? "Marie, I don't have time for your games. Why would Monroe have your son? When did you have kids anyway?"

Marie

"Are you going to ask him or not? I won't hesitate to kill this young lady and her unborn child. You already know that I am dangerous. Especially when I don't get what I want."

Aubrey

I heard Jordan pleading in the background for me to please ask Monroe where Marie's son was. So, I nudged Monroe to wake up while I put Marie on hold. "Monroe, wake up! Monroe..."

Monroe

"What's wrong baby?" She looked so angry at me while holding my phone in her hand. "What's going on baby?"

Aubrey

"Marie is calling your phone from your warehouse where Jordan is being kept for some reason. Where is her son, Monroe?" He took the phone from me and got out of the bed. "I know you lyin'! Sit right here and put it on speakerphone so I can hear too. Seems like all of y'all just keeping up secrets around here."

Monroe

I did exactly what she said and put the phone on speaker. "Hello, Marie?"

Marie

"Nice of you to join the party. I'm here with Jordan and your unborn baby trying to figure out what you have done with my son. I'm not yet sure who this Reggie person is but I do know he was the one that came into my hospital room and took my son. Where is my son, Monroe?"

Monroe

"I'm not quite sure what you're talking about Marie, but please, can we meet and talk about this in person?"

Marie

"No, we're not meeting in person, because I'm still looking for my son. I know you have something to do with this, so you have five seconds to tell me what you know, or I am going to kill your unborn son."

Jordan

"Nooooooooo, Monroe please tell her what she wants to know. Pleaaassssseeee!"

Chapter 25

Hours Ago

Monroe

Jordan's pussy felt more and more amazing every time I was with her. Once I was done fucking her, I cuffed her to the chair and left her in the holding area. I don't know what she was thinking was going to happen once she told me she wanted Aubrey out of the picture. Had I known she was that far gone I wouldn't have touched her ass. But I don't think she would have said anything if I didn't give her this dick. And when I started walking out of the room, she had a nerve to tell me she was pregnant. I only nutted inside of her one time, and that was today, and only because it wouldn't matter once I murked her. She was trying to say anything to get out of this situation. I just left her in the soundproof room and looked around for Benny. He wasn't there though.

I headed home to get some rest for a few hours. Once I got there, I hit James up but he didn't answer. He was probably sleeping since he got so drunk at the party. I needed to take care of this baby once and for all, I didn't like this space that James and I were in. He is my best friend. For now, I'll worry about all of that later. What I did know was that Jordan has to go, I just had to concoct some story for Aubrey on why she was no longer around us.

Present time

Aubrey

"What in the entire the hell, Monroe? Is this why this bitch has been acting shady towards me? And what are you doing with Marie's son? How could you take someone's newborn when you have your own newborn son? How would you feel if she got a hold to my baby, Monroe? God!"

I didn't know what to think about this man that I absolutely adored yesterday. "Look, what you're not gonna do is sit up here like the cat got your damn tongue. You're gonna tell me what is going on right now or me and my son are out of here."

Monroe

What could I say to explain this shit? How was I going to say that my best friend wanted this baby dead and I support his decision no matter how fucked up it is?

"Babe, there is a lot that you don't know about me. But I promise you it's only to protect you. I really need for you to pack up some stuff for you and Junior so you all can go and stay with your mom until I get this shit settled. Can you please do that for me babe? Please?"

Aubrey

"And what am I supposed to tell my mother and Mike, huh? They think that I'm safe with you. And what about Jordan? Am I just supposed to leave this bitch here with you so y'all can continue whatever y'all been doing behind my back? Have you been fucking her without telling me about it? Huh?"

Monroe

At this point, Aubrey was in my face. I had never seen her this mad and I just wanted to figure out how to deescalate the situation before either of us went too far. "Babe, it has been two times that I slipped up and for that I'm sorry."

Aubrey

I had to walk away on that note. He swore that this whole arrangement was for me to be happy, and he's up here fucking this bitch behind my back. I was so damn mad and I almost gave this nigga my pussy early! Fuck this shit. I was packing my son's and my shit right now. I had to get away from this nigga before I hurt his ass.

"Stop following me. I don't want to see your fucking face right now."

Monroe

I don't know what to do. I can't lose her again, she is my world. "Baby, please just talk to me for a second. I have to tell you everything." She looked at me like she wanted to kill my ass, but she was going to know how serious this shit was. She could be mad at me later, but her and Junior's safety was all I cared about at this moment. She finally sat down at the dining room table opposite of where I was.

"I grew up with Rob. After he allowed some fuck shit to happen to my sister, I didn't fuck with him again. The only reason I allowed him to live this long was because of my mentor's relationship with this clown. I didn't realize he was your ex until quite some time after you and I started dating.

"After your accident, and finding out he raped you and Free, James and I captured him and made him pay for what he did to you both. He wouldn't have been able to make any kids after that point, but Marie had already gotten pregnant by him. James was very adamant about him not being able to leave a legacy in this world because of the fuck boy shit he had done to others. Once he found out that one of her twins was a boy, he decided to kidnap him… and I supported his decision."

Aubrey

“What… what are you into, Monroe? What do you mean, “let him live this long? I don’t know you at all! So you mean to tell me, that two new fathers of two brand new babies were going to kidnap Rob and Marie’s innocent son and do what to him? Kill him? What is that going to solve? You didn’t kill him so you decide to kill his son?

“And with Marie’s crazy ass, and the voodoo shit I heard about from Rob, what did you think was going to happen to all of us? She’s not going to stop until she gets her son back. I have to call Fresia, this shit don’t make no damn sense.”

Monroe

“Baby, please, let’s just get you and the baby’s stuff together. You can call Free on the way to your house to pick up Mike and your mom. Then we can head straight to the airport. I need to figure out what Marie’s next move is.”

Aubrey

While he was popping his gums, I texted Free to let her know that we needed to get out of town as soon as possible and that I would explain it as soon as I could.

“I can’t believe you would allow any of this to happen. I trusted you, to take care of me and your son. And Jordan! You allowed her to enter our world to get caught up with this bitch Marie? And all you've managed to do is fuck us all over. Not just me." As I was talking to his stupid ass, my phone starts ringing. I'm guessing Free would rather talk than text.

Monroe

Aubrey answered her phone and started explaining everything that was going on. I dialed James to let him know what we were up against and he answered on the first ring.

James

"Yo boss, what the hell is going on? Free is over here freaking out and packing shit talking about leaving the state after speaking to Aubrey."

Monroe

"Marie came to the warehouse today". I filled him in about the little niggas bringing the baby to the club last night and Jordan overhearing shit and her issue with me being with Aubrey. I also told him I decided to murk her ass and that's why I cuffed her and left her in the warehouse.

James

"So, what's the next move then? Where's Marie? What about Jordan?"

Monroe

"I don't know... the phone disconnected after Marie didn't get the information she was looking for."

Aubrey

After I got off the phone with Free, something clicked in my mind. "Monroe, I have one last question: what was Jordan doing at your warehouse handcuffed to a chair while you're here sleeping peacefully?"

"He started walking towards me and apologizing, saying he would explain everything. "Don't you touch me Monroe. Don't you ever touch me again." I took Junior and headed to my house.

Taisha

Where am I? I know I'm in a car trunk, and it's freezing in here. "HELP! HELP!" I started kicking and punching the top of whatever space I was in and I got tired super quickly. I threw up to the side of me, I was still dope sick. This could take days, even weeks or months to kick my habit. At this point, I just wanna die. I'm hungry but I also know that if I were to try and eat something it would make me even sicker. I felt the car slow to a stop. "HELP! HELP!" The trunk opened up and I recognized this man from the surprise birthday party in the suburbs. "Who the fuck are you? Why are you doing this?"

Keith

"My brother warned you to leave that Spanish nigga alone, but you wouldn't listen and you know how that ended. And then you decided to go missing instead of going to see him which is what you were told to do. So, you know what this is. Get your ass out."

Taisha

I sat up and looked around and noticed we were in some secluded area where no one could find us. "Please sir, I'll do whatever I need to do. I just don't wanna die like this." I was searching for a weapon of any kind that I could use. But there was nothing but rocks and weeds and shit like that around us. He pulled out a gun and told me to get on my knees. I was hysterical by this point. "Please, *PLEASE* don't kill me. I'll do whatever you want me to do." Then his phone rang.

Keith

<<ring, ring>>

I accepted Don's call and he wanted me to call it off. I already drove her way the fuck out in the middle of nowhere and pulled my gun out on the bitch. "Nigga, make your fuckin mind up! I got shit to do today as you already know."

Don

"Just disregard the whole thing. Tell her she has to come see me today." I love Taisha. I just want her to love me too. Stacia is gone, other than communicating with her about my children, she's completely given up on us. "Let me speak to her man. Please."

Taisha

While he was on the phone and distracted, I quietly snuck into the driver's seat of his car and pulled off. He started shooting at the car, but I was able to get away unscathed. I wasn't going to be nobody's 'Renee', fuck that.

Keith

"Your bitch just drove off in my muthafuckin' car! Now I gotta figure how to get back to the city. Don't call me no more this week nigga, I'm tired of your simpin' ass." FUCK!

Marie

Monroe didn't tell me what I needed to know by the time my countdown was finished. But once I disconnected the call, Jordan was pleading for the lives of her and her unborn child. But regardless of what she had to tell me, I was still taking that baby from her.

Jordan

"Please Marie, the two young guys that were talking to Benny last night have your son. Benny told them to keep driving around until he called them with further instructions because you kept finding them."

Marie

"What are these two young guys' names? And where can I find Benny?"

Jordan

"I don't know their names, and I just met Benny yesterday. I can tell you what he drives, but they all work for Monroe and James. Please don't take my baby from me. Please." I was crying so hard. This baby was all that I had left, and it was the only way that I would remain tied to Monroe in some way.

Marie

"Sorry love, that didn't help me at all." I placed my hand over her belly and recited the spell. "*Urispe fornatuce, urispe fornatuce. Chie dezie omnius*." Her body started to violently shake, and her eyes rolled into the back of her head. Once her body was still again, I released her from the handcuffs she was bound in and I told her to leave the warehouse and not to look back. I set the warehouse ablaze before I exited and ensured that the entire building was on fire. I looked directly into the camera as I left so there would be no doubt who did what. As I pulled away from the spot where there "used" to be a warehouse, I passed by Miss Jordan as she was walking away in the same direction. Too bad she will never know the joys of motherhood. She should have told me the little bit she did know when I first walked into the room.

Chapter 26

Joe

I couldn't get Sam outta my mind ever since we fucked in the club. She has matured so much since we were in a relationship with each other. That shit was funny as fuck to me when I saw her kissing ole dude after she had just swallowed my kids. Damn she was freaky, and I loved that shit. Sam enjoyed that shit, but Kristin did it because she knew I enjoyed it. Well she used to anyway. I haven't spoken to her since she abruptly left the club last night. But I wasn't gonna sweat her though. I decided to hit up Sam and see what she was up to tonight.

<<ring, ring>>

"Hey lady, what you got going on today?"

Sam

"Oh wow, I was just thinking about you. I'm about to leave Keith's right now, I'm going to have supper with my parents and brothers. What are you up to? What made you call me?" As if I wasn't expecting his call. I knew as soon as I let him get a whiff of my sweet stuff, he would be sniffing right behind me until I let him get some more.

Joe

"Not much, I was just seeing if you were getting into anything tonight. You know, I wanted to see if you wanted to stop by or if I could stop by your place. It's been a while since we've been able to kick it."

Sam

"I'm sure what you have in mind has very little to do with kicking it. Am I right? I'll tell you what, once I leave my parent's, I'll text you and then maybe you can stop over for a little more than kicking it."

Joe

"Alright, bet. I look forward to seeing you tonight. Enjoy your fam and please tell everyone I said hello." Well that was a great conversation. It ended just the way I wanted it to. Kristin ain't the only one with a pussy. That shit comes a dime a dozen. I guess I'll go and hit up my brother and them today so that I can kill some time. I haven't seen my niece and nephew since Christmas anyway.

James

Now that this bitch knew we were responsible for taking her son, she wasn't going to let this go without some shit going down. Money wanted to meet with me and Benny to figure out how to best handle this situation. She burned down the warehouse and she better be glad it wasn't yesterday before our biggest shipment was distributed. This bitch was definitely on a mission. I knew I should have killed her instead of letting her go that first time. Marie has killed people on our payroll, and she does it unapologetically. Monroe arrived with Stevie and Goldie right behind him. "Hey boss, the team will be here within the hour. Also, just a precaution, you think we should reach out to Keith for more numbers? I know she's only one person, but we cannot underestimate her by no means."

Monroe

"We still haven't figured out whether we're going to kill her or give her the baby back." I looked at the little baby and realized he looks so much like my God daughter. I realized that I couldn't do anything to that innocent baby. And I still had Aubrey's words ringing through my mind. How could I look her or Junior in the face knowing that I had something to do with killing him? "Have you heard from her? Has she called your phone?"

James

"Nah Money, she's been way too quiet. I guarantee she is formulating some type of plan to pluck us off one by one. We have to figure out how to stay one step ahead of her. Does anyone know where she lives? Maybe I can have Paco look up her information from her file at the hospital. But then what?"

Monroe

This is a tough one. I have no clue how we thought this would end, but we're in too deep to turn back now. "Yeah, hit up Paco and see what he can find out for us."

Marie

I checked in with Shawna to make sure my little mama was doing well. "Hello Shawna, how's everything going with Celeste?"

Shawna

"Hi Marie, she's good. Just sleeping. When will you be back? I have to get out of here soon."

Marie

"Oh, I'll be on my way very shortly. But in the meantime, help yourself. I have some food I cooked last night that I just know you'll love. And pair it with some more tea, I know how much you liked that." I really needed her to stay just for a bit more. I was just getting started with putting my plan into play. Currently, I was looking for Aubrey and Free. Whatever they did to my son, I was going to impart that same misery on their children.

Marchaud has now been away from me and Celeste for almost five full days.

I needed to make a quick stop and pay a visit to a handsome young man. I waited in the parking lot by his car as he exited the hospital after his shift was over. Once he spotted me, I could see the nervousness on his face that he shifted into the smile that I was used to seeing.

Paco

"Hello Miss Marie, how is everything going? I spoke with one of the officers today to let them know that whatever they needed I was willing to cooperate completely. I just want you to know that you are not alone in this and we will help you find your son."

Marie

And along with the lies he spews from his gorgeous mouth, there he goes again winking that sexy eye at me. It made my pussy jump. I finally saw his flirtation for what it was- a way to get me to feel comfortable with him. He knew I was alone; he also knew there was no husband away on a work trip. After realizing that he could have been the only one to drug my food since he was the one to bring it to me, I knew that he was in on the kidnapping.

"Oh, thank you Paco, I appreciate you helping us out." I got closer to him while he was standing inside of his car door. “But I don’t think you’ve been all the way forthcoming about what happened that night that Reggie came and stole my baby. Where can I find him?” I started to trace his jaw and around his lips in a flirty way. I know I was making him even more nervous because his heart started to race.

Paco

“Reggie? I’m not sure I know who you’re referring to. I’ve already told the officers everything that I know. What are you doing?”

Marie

“I don’t believe you’re being one hundred percent honest with me at this moment Paco. Please don’t move, this instrument is very sharp and can slice anything completely off with the slip of my hand.” I removed his penis from his scrubs and proceeded to stroke the shaft of his average sized penis. “I really need your full disclosure on the following questions. Can you do that for me baby?” He nodded yes as he closed his eyes and moaned while I performed the back and forth motion along his unimpressive dick. His breathing became choppy and his heart rate sped up.

Paco

She was stroking me and getting me so hard, it was making me lose focus. I was hoping that I could distract her enough to disarm her. Her body definitely looked good. If I didn't know already, I wouldn't have guessed she'd just had twin babies. "Miss Marie, may I please touch you? You are so sexy to me."

Marie

"You may do whatever you want to me Paco as long as you answer my questions truthfully." He then unbuttoned my shirt and removed my left breast as he covered it with his mouth and squeezed my plump behind through my leggings. "Where can I find Reggie, Paco?" He looked up at me with some of my breast milk dripping from the corner of his mouth. "That breast milk that you have the pleasure of tasting should be nourishing my son, so please help me find him Paco." I continued stroking his penis as we spoke.

Paco

"Reggie is not his real name mami. Oooohhh, ssssss, don't stop mami, por favor. He said hc was going to take the baby to his papa because you wouldn't let him see the bebé. Ahhhh mami, lemme fuck you please. Ooohhhh."

Marie

Well obviously I wasn't going to allow him to enter my healing vagina, but I decided to allow him to penetrate me elsewhere. It's been quite some time since I've had any pleasure, so I figured why not? He managed to pull my leggings down while he still suckled at my breasts. I bent over the driver's seat for him to enter me anally. "Oooohhh slow down Paco, I don't want the car to rock too much to bring attention to us."

Paco

"Mami, I knew your ass was amazing when I saw you changing out of your clothes when you were in labor. You feel so fucking amazing too."

Marie

I was trying not to get lost in the pleasure I was getting from his thrusting in and out of me, as it was a bit hard to stay on task. "Paco… ooohhh… where is my baby? Where can I, um, ooohhh find him right now?"

Paco

"Your son may be at the auto shop on Delaware Ave. Ooohhh Marie, your ass is fantastic. I'm about to shoot my load mami, ooohhhhhh shit!"

Marie

His body jerked and moaned as he held me in place by my waist while I allowed him to finish. I put my clothing back together and positioned myself next to him while he recovered himself. "Did you like that Paco?" He nodded as he leaned his back against the car next to his. "What else can you tell me about who has my son, baby?"

Paco

He opened his eyes and I guess he realized he had already said too much. “I don’t know where your son is mami. I told the officers-”

Marie

“Tsk, tsk, tsk... I know that you know more than what you’re telling me right now papi. Please don’t forget that I have this instrument in my hand and I won’t hesitate to use it.” It was the exact same sharp nail attachment that I killed Monroe’s employee, Dre, with after I was able to sample his remarkable member again. That kill was such a waste. I placed it against Paco’s throat and nicked him quickly to let him know that I was serious. “I can make you bleed so much more, so it would behoove you to tell me what I want to know and tell me quickly.”

He started sweating and told me exactly what I needed to know. Apparently, Paco just moonlights as an aide at the hospital during the night shift and the only reason I caught him at this time is because there was an emergency that required his assistance. His real job is supplying Monroe and James with information that he’s able to gather from the hospital database. He also serves the nurses with their drugs to keep them awake during their shifts or whatever they use it for. I never would have imagined that some of these "professionals" are on drugs while servicing patients.

"Well I appreciate the information and the pleasurable experience. And one more question before I let you go, have you already passed my address on to them?" He shook his head no and showed me the address he had written on a piece of paper in his pocket. I relieved him of it while simultaneously slicing through the femoral artery in his thigh. I backed up just in time for him to drop to his knees. He tried to reach for the steering wheel to pull himself up, but the sudden blood loss had him disoriented. I waited just a few more minutes to ensure that he had expired. I returned to my car, fixed my lipstick and headed to Delaware Avenue.

Chapter 27

Benny

What the fuck is this nigga calling me for though? Just because we were chopping it up at the club last night, that shit does not mean we are friends. "Yeah."

Keith

"Hey B, I don't mean to bother you so early, but I'm stranded and I can't call Sam because she's gonna have too many questions about why I'm here. And my niggas are probably still drunk from last night because they are not answering. Would you be able to scoop me? I can drop a pin to my location."

Benny

"Yeah man, drop the pin." I hung up and got up to throw something on. I might need this nigga in the future, since it seemed like I couldn't trust nobody. Money was supposed to be my nigga, so how was he fucking the bitch I was tryna get into? And James has been a bit off these last couple of days. We don't ever get drunk like he did last night. It's a rule that we're always supposed to stay sharp in case something pops off. And them dumb ass niggas Stevie and Goldie, they are lost without no real direction. I was definitely in the market for a new gig. Didn't look like I was gonna be able to wait for this nigga Money to retire. Especially since now I knew I couldn't trust his ass.

I pulled up in the middle of nowhere with my head on a swivel. I didn't trust this nigga Keith as far as I could throw his ass. I had my burner on my thigh, ready for whatever. I saw him walking toward my passenger side door and quickly scanned the area to make sure no one else would try and ambush me. He hopped in and seemed madder than a muthafucka. "Yo, you alright? What the fuck you doing all the way out here anyway?" I asked as we dapped it up.

Keith

"Let's just say I was supposed to handle something for my brother and it went south. I was stranded out here. I'm whooping ass as soon as I come across that bitch again." And I meant that shit. I don't give two fucks about Don hearing about me whooping Tai's ass. Believe that.

Benny

I didn't ask him nothing else, because it wasn't my business. Besides, if he wanted me to know he would tell me. "Yo, where you want me to drop you off at?" I was headed back toward the city but didn't want to go in the wrong direction so I wouldn't have to deal with this nigga any longer than I needed to. He asked me if I could drop him off at his house, so we headed that way.

Keith

"Have you thought anymore about my offer to join my team? I would compensate you handsomely. Money is of no object." I didn't want to seem desperate or anything, but I didn't trust anyone outside of my brother, and even that shit was shaky at this point. His mind was definitely on the wrong shit.

Benny

"Lemme get back to you on that. I'm not sure what moves I'll be making in the near future, but I'll hit you up." I knew Keith was making long money, and now that that fat ass nigga Don was locked up, I may be able to deal with him on a daily. Don was a coward and he was ruled by pussy. That's why it was so easy for me to get his dumb ass out of the picture in the first place.

When I first found out that nigga Don, and not Jerrick Sr., was my father eleven years ago, I was excited because of all of the things my mom told me about him. She made him sound like a superhero, like he was going to save us from that fuck ass neighborhood we were in and I would be living like his other kids were. Ma told me about the brothers and sisters I had and also let me know that he had a wife, but that he would be back for us. I always wondered if I went to school with any of them or if I had run into them on the street. After years of seeing my mother broken hearted and eventually using the shit he was pumping into our neighborhood, I started to hate that nigga. I realized that Jerrick Sr. really didn't stick around because he knew I wasn't his son. And when he was there, he disregarded me. Yeah, that's the best way I can describe Jerrick Sr.

In the eighties and nineties, I heard Big Don was one of the enforcers for a big-time distributor in uptown DC. He accompanied Dunbar Edwards, also known as Slick D, at all times, as his enforcer. Slick was a pretty boy and the ladies loved him. The way my mama described him in her more lucid days, he was a guy that could walk in a room and command it. At a mere five feet, ten inches, Slick was a slender light skinned dude that resembled a Black version of the Debarge's little brother Chico. He was the opposite of Don in every way; smooth with the ladies but not thirsty, he took care of his body, and even though he was into pushing that product, he invested in our community as well.

Slick D ensured his family was set and showed love to his friends as well. Money definitely reminded me of him in that way. Those dudes moved smart, and women weren't the center of their universe. Once Slick decided to "retire", Don thought that because he knew the business that he should be the next in line to take over. Slick didn't choose him, and this didn't sit well with his fat ass.

Nine Years Ago

Don

"I can't believe this nigga would overlook me. ME! I've been doing his wet work for the longest. That's alright, I'm gonna get mine. In whatever way I need to get it."

Benny

Word was that fat ass, aka Don, took Slick's successor out but no one could ever prove it. Don took over the empire, after Slick's official blessing.

I had to grow up faster than any child should have to. I made sure that the little bit of money we got from the state paid for our bills and I shopped for groceries and made sure my mother ate. I learned everything I could about Don, I even made sure to hang with a few niggas that worked for him. I studied his movements, I paid attention to the females he spent time with. I even held the door open for his wife one day when she was entering the mall. I'm surprised he never recognized my face from either looking like my mom or always being around in some way.

This nigga Money was blowing up my phone. I still didn't know how I wanted to handle that shit yet. "Yeah."

Monroe

"Yo B, I've been blowing you up. Where you been? I need you to come to the spot-on G Street. Marie blew up the warehouse. How far are you away?"

Benny

"I'll be there in a few." And I hung up the phone on that nigga. I wasn't gonna sweat it. All niggas are not made the same and I can't let a bitch get between us. I am going to talk to him about it though.

Sam

I had just left my family. It was our tradition to have dinner together on New Year's Day. Seeing my mom and dad still so in love was obviously something that I wanted some day, but right now I was just having fun. I texted Joe just like I said I would and told him to meet me at my house around ten o'clock. I wanted to surprise him and have Candy over for a threesome, but I couldn't catch up with her for some reason.

I called another girl that I met from my monthly sex club. The club advised against fraternizing with people you meet there because they were very strict about privacy. But of course, every time I saw her, I just couldn't take my eyes or my mouth off of her. She was absolutely sexy and what I imagined the perfect woman to be. She was from Jamaica with gorgeous curly hair that she wore short and natural. Her effortless curls and her smooth chocolate skin balanced her delicate features. Her perfectly arched eyebrows, her cute nose and those pouty full lips that always had red painted on them. She was about my height with average, but perky C cup breasts, a small waist and a heart shaped ass that was so perfect.

"Hello, Ionie. Are you busy this evening? Would you be able to join me and my friend tonight for some fun?"

Ionie

"Hey Sam, I've been waiting for you to invite me into your lair since we hooked up the last time. Who is your friend though? Anyone I know? And does he please your yoni as much as you do mine?"

Sam

Damn, she had me regretting even inviting Joe into our private time. "Yes honey, I believe he will please your beautiful yoni. I can't wait to taste you again sweetie. Can you come by tonight?"

Ionie

"Oh yesss... I would love to. What time and what should I wear?"

Sam

"Let's go full on dom… it'll blow his mind. See you at nine thirty?" She agreed. I decided to wear a short leather high waisted skirt with no top. I wore my fish net thigh highs with my six-inch shiny leather pumps. I brought out a table, placed a red tablecloth onto it and then organized my leather whips, paddles, nipple pinchers and feather ticklers. I also had some wrist and ankle restraints that hooked onto a collar and blindfolds. We were going to have some fun tonight with Mr. Joe.

<<ding, dong>>

I opened the door for Ionie and she had her red wool trench coat opened enough for me to see her hard nipples and she smelled delicious. She looked so sexy in her one-piece, sheer, short black dress with long sleeves. Ionie walked in and removed her coat and kissed me gently on my lips. I hung up her coat as I watched her magnificent ass and shapely legs as she went over to the table to examine the items I had on display.

Ionie

"Your candles smell divine Samantha. It puts me in the mood even more now that I'm here to explore you and this man that I have yet to meet."

Sam

I handed her a glass of Prosecco and ensured that I poured a glass of the lemon vodka for Joe. He rang the doorbell and I applied the nipple clamps to me while the chain connected them loosely. Upon opening the door, his mouth dropped as he looked from me to Ionie sitting seductively on the couch in the living room. "Well come on in handsome, are you ready for a sexy night?"

Joe

"Got damn, Sam. You look so good baby. But what's the special occasion?" She handed me a glass that I presume was vodka with an ice cube and a thin lemon slice. There was a beautiful and very voluptuous beauty sitting on the couch and I was truly hoping that I would be able to open her up tonight as well. Her lips looked like they belonged around my dick. "This is a dream babe, what did I do to deserve all of this?"

Sam

"Just follow our orders and we will ensure that you get the best experience. This is Ionie and you, Joe, are our sex slave tonight." Ionie and I started to undress Joe and chose different parts of his body to kiss. It seemed like he was too nervous to try and touch either of us, so she held my hair back with her right hand as she held his penis with her left and guided it toward my mouth. She massaged his balls while I went to work.

Joe

Damn, if I died tonight, I wouldn't even be mad. I had to figure out how to get Sam to put me in the rotation if she was on this shit now. Watching my dick disappear in her mouth was sexy as fuck. And I couldn't stop watching ole girl's plump ass and the way it jiggled with every move she made. They were going to be my chocolate and vanilla sundae tonight. I didn't know what to start with or where to put my hands, so I just let them do the work.

Once Sam came up for air, ole girl didn't miss a beat on my dick. The difference in sensations from Sam's mouth to hers was absolutely incredible. She let my dick hit the back of her throat while looking directly in my eyes. She was on all fours at an angle, so I was able to watch Sam lick her pussy from the back. "Ooooohhh sssshhhiiiitttt!" Sam had her ass in the air in that tight ass skirt as she pleasured ole girl while ole girl pleasured me. I started to feel the nut build up and I stopped ole girl from devouring my dick the way she was.

They both looked at each other and smirked as they got up and went over to a table that had a red tablecloth on it. They summoned me to come over to them. Sam placed blindfolds on me and then applied handcuffs to my wrists. The guided me to a chair, someone grabbed my dick and then I felt one of them insert me into their pussy as she rode me backwards. The other one licked and sucked on my neck, earlobes and nipples. It was sweet torture to not be able to see or touch whoever was riding my dick.

Sam

"You like the way Ionie's pussy feels? She's about to cum all over your dick, are you ready?" He shook his head yes as he moaned and tried to keep a straight face. Right before Ionie started to cum, I removed his blindfold and went in front of her and started sucking on her pussy as she came into my mouth. Once she was done, I asked him, "Did you like that?" He nodded again. "Now it's my turn! Get up and lie down so that I can ride your dick." He got so excited, he almost forgot that his hands were cuffed behind his back. We made sure to blow his mind for the rest of the night until we all fell asleep. We woke up, pleased each other once more before they both left.

I checked my voicemail and saw that Candy left me a message. "Sam, please call me back. I have something very important to tell you." Was she crying?

Chapter 28

Rob

"I had been praying even more since I still hadn't heard anything about Freddy. Today was the last day they would allow me to sit in my cell without showering and going to the cafeteria. I was dreading this day because that meant it was now open season for all these thugs that either wanted to beat my ass or fuck me. But I wasn't going out like a bitch. They were going to have to take it though, just like Freddy did.

CO

"Alright Williams, you know the drill. CO Fields is not here to save you today, so come on. Bring your funky ass on to the showers. You're becoming a health and sanitation issue."

Rob

"I got up slowly and allowed the CO to open and close my cell after cuffing me. He walked me down to the latrine and it was surprisingly empty. I started the water, grabbed my soap and made a lather while temporarily forgetting where I was. I imagined being at me and Aubrey's apartment while she washed my back for me. I put my head under the lukewarm water and felt something on my shoulder. My eyes immediately flew open as my head was then banged into the shower wall in front of me. My forehead was split open just like that and the mixture of my blood and the running water entered my eyes and caused my vision to become blurry.

I started swinging at the air, but never connected with anyone. I wiped my eyes as I held my forehead and noticed that there were two men scuffling. Was I tripping or something? All of a sudden, one of the guys started running out of the area we were in. I turned off the water and directed my full attention to the man that was left as I squared up ready for anything.

Inmate Jones

"You thought you were just gonna be able to hide behind Freddy, huh? It's a lot of niggas in here waiting for that dude to die. And waiting to catch you by yourself."

Rob

He shook his head as he eyed the spot where my dick used to be. I started to feel a bit insecure, but I kept my fists up ready for anything.

Inmate Jones

"Do you remember me? You look like you have no idea who I am."

Rob

"Nah man, I have no clue. But if you gonna do something, just do it. I don't have time for all this chatting and shit. Up here naked and shit, contrary to popular opinion I ain't no bitch." He just sat there and smirked as I tried my best to think of who this could possibly be.

Inmate Jones

"I was much skinnier when I was younger. We used to hang on the block real tough. I used to date Monroe's youngest sister. The one that wouldn't give up the pussy. Stingy bitch."

Rob

"Jeffrey Jones?" I started to relax at the realization that he just saved me from whoever was just here.

Jeff

"Bingo! I saw you on the news, damn that shit was crazy."

Rob

"What you doing in here?" I asked as I grabbed my towel. "I thought you ended up going to college or some shit once you moved away. I remember Miss Claudia hated my ass. And how is Cyreeta? That was my little homie."

Jeff

"They both good, and I wish I did. I was wiling like a muthafucka for a good minute after I left the hood. Moms married this 'Poindexter' looking dude when I was in my last year of high school. But he turned out to be shady as fuck. I came home one day and I heard a commotion. I thought my sister had friends over or something, they were always partying while moms was at work. But it was dude raping my sister.

I blacked out. They said I stabbed him over fifty times and because it was known that I didn't like him, that was the motive. Even though my sister was fourteen years old, a minor, and admitted that everything that I said was true, they still charged me as an adult and sentenced me to twenty-five to life. You believe that? I've been in here for eleven years, seven months and nineteen days. And I got a lifetime to go."

He shook his head at the reality of his situation and managed to perk back up. "But I've made my peace with it. I know what I did, and it is what it is. If it happened the same way, I'd do it all over again. But look, Freddy thought everybody was tryna take you away from him. I was just tryna let you know that you didn't have to put up with that shit. And when I heard about Monroe cutting off your... well you know. You ain't deserve that shit. Yeah, we used to do some fucked up shit, but you always had my back. Now I got yours."

Rob

"Ain't nothin' in here free, my nigga. What I gotta do for your protection?"

Jeff

"We'll get to that later. Go ahead and get dressed. I'll introduce you to the fam."

Rob

What other choice did I have? Like he said, everybody was waiting for Freddy to die. I put on some clean clothes and met him in the hallway. On to the next hustle, I guess.

Kristin

It had been a few days since the New Year's Eve party, and Joe and I had only seen one another in passing at work. I knew I wasn't going to be able to stay at this job much longer, so I had been job searching for other employment from my work computer. I was very relaxed today because Dr. Saul had taken some vacation time and wasn't due back to work until around the tenth. But guess who walked through the door around lunch time, this guy. My heart immediately began to race and I felt a sense of dread wash over me.

Dr. Saul

"Good morning Kristin, may I see you in my office please? I have a few forms that I need for you to file while I am out and just some overall business to fill you in on."

Kristin

He didn't even give me time to answer him, he just kept walking into his office. So, I took my time, walked to his office and stood in the door waiting for him to notice me. I was super nervous. I just did not want to be here.

Dr. Saul

"Come in please. And close the door and lock it behind you."

Kristin

His facial expression darkened immediately. Once I did as I was told, he told me to assume the position. I knew what that meant. I was to come and stand in front of him, but first I needed to remove all of my clothing except my socks. He had a weird thing about feet, and I just wished I could put them both on his face and keep them there. In the grand scheme of things, I'm sure that wouldn't hurt him as much as the things he did to hurt me.

He pulled a chain out of his bag and started to place it around my neck. I started to cry because I wasn't sure what was going on. He'd never used a chain or padlocks before. So just like the necktie, he tied one end around my neck and the other around my waist and hands. The padlocks kept the chains in place. After doing that, he made me suck his little dick and it was very hard to balance myself because I was still standing, couldn't use my hands and the chains were heavy. Every time I lost my balance, he would spit on my face and then slap it. He didn't care that my cheeks were turning red.

When he felt that torture was enough, he went inside of his backpack and brought out some type of spiked belt. I had to get on my knees in a chair while he beat me with that belt and if I screamed, he would choke me until I almost passed out. I was so tired and miserable that after some time went by, I couldn't even cry anymore.

He made me lay on my back with the chains still on which hurt so damn much and he roughly penetrated me until he released all over my chest. I wanted to die once he unlocked the padlocks and freed me from the chains. I went into his office bathroom and when I saw myself in the mirror, I knew that this would be the last time he ever had the chance to abuse me. He knocked on the bathroom door, startling me.

Dr. Saul

"Uh, would you please hurry, I need to lock my office and get going."

Kristin

He sounded so unapologetic, like everything he just did to me was normal or something. “I’m coming.” I gathered myself and exited the restroom. “Are we done for the day sir?” I always had to wait to be dismissed. He gave me the “until next time” and waved me off like the piece of garbage I felt like and I exited his office.

Once he emerged, he was like a completely different person- full of smiles and very polite to everyone as he left the building. I went into the storage room after everyone left for lunch, took a vial of morphine and injected it into my arm. I counted out about fifteen codeine pills and washed them down with the Crown I had in my purse. I laid on the bed that Joe and I cemented our “relationship” on. I started to drift off into a very relaxed sleep and I welcomed the feeling of euphoria. I made my peace with no longer being a part of this life as tears ran down the sides of my face. “I wish someone had loved me enough...”

Aubrey

I just couldn’t go to Florida with my mom and Mike. I would never forgive myself if something happened to them on account of Monroe’s fuckery. I can’t believe I fell in love with someone that I basically don’t know. This is just fucked up. I still couldn't believe the events that led up to all of this. This shit was so unreal. I wasn't talking to Monroe and he was trying his best to get back on my good side. I don't know if we will ever be able to recover from this mess. I love him, but I sure as hell don't like his ass right now.

Free and I decided to take a mommy trip with our babies to Barbados for a couple of weeks until things with Marie died down. We don't leave for a couple more days, but we both thought it would be a good idea to go to the mall together to purchase some last-minute items for the trip. Out of all of this fucked up shit, I was actually glad to have my friend back. We both matured and were able to let bygones be bygones. We were exhausted from shopping all day and was satisfied with our purchases and called it a night. Plus, the babies were knocked out and it was time to take them home anyway. We were loading my car, when I heard a familiar voice that made my heart drop.

Marie

"Hello ladies. Don't make any sudden moves if you don't want to die tonight. Put your hands above your heads and turn around. If you scream, I will shoot you both in the head and then I promise you I will raise your children in a life of utter despair. Do you understand me?

Aubrey

We both nodded our heads as tears started to stream down our faces. She was closest to Junior who was in his car seat sleeping with that gun in her hand. She started to give us instructions and we made sure to do everything exactly as she said. We left our purses in the trunk. Free tied my hands as instructed and sat in the front driver's seat and I sat in the passenger seat. Both babies were already strapped in their car seats and Marie sat in the back with them. She gave Free the directions to a home that was the only one at the end of a dead-end street. Everything around that house seemed deserted. We entered the home and she chained us both in different rooms and closed and locked the doors.

"Please don't hurt our babies, Marie."

Marie

"Well, you better hope no harm comes to my son. Whatever happens to him... well you get the picture."

Chapter 29

Sam

It had been two days since I called Candy back. I had been in a drunken stupor ever since then. Keith and Joe have been blowing my phone up and I just couldn't bring myself to speak to either one of them. Candy came by a couple of days ago and I made the mistake of opening the door to let her in. As soon as I did, she pushed me so hard that my tailbone still hurt from the fall that resulted from it. She yelled, cried, kicked and punched me. It felt like I was being hit by a couple of men, but I understood why. I could only blame myself. Once she finally left, I just laid there with my front door wide open until I could peel myself off of the floor.

I have a busted lip, both of my eyes are bruised, and I have black and blue marks all over my body. I haven't been using my best judgment for quite some time now. And to start my year off like this, is just very difficult. I feel alone and like no one will be able to understand what I'm going through. Who's going to love me now? I'm so scared, but I have to go to the doctor's appointment I scheduled for tomorrow. There's my phone ringing again, but this time it's my mom. How was I going to tell her about this?

<<ring, ring>>

Edith

"Samantha, I thought we agreed that you were going to be more present with this family. How is it that you haven't called your mother? I know you're not a little girl anymore, but baby I worry about you. Talk to me! I already can't speak with your sister as much as I would like. Come on baby, we spoke about this."

Sam

If only she knew how much I felt like a little girl right now. I just need her arms around me and her reassurance that everything is going to be okay. But things would never be okay ever again. I couldn't say anything, all I could do was weep into the receiver.

Edith

"Kitty, what is the matter? Please talk to me."

Sam

The words were just stuck in my throat, and I just sat there with the phone in my hand. Tears stained my face and the mucus was running down my lips. I needed my momma right now. "Mother, please come."

Edith

"I'm on my way Kitty. You just sit tight. Momma's coming."

Monroe

We were still at the back up spot throwing ideas around about how we were going to proceed. I would feel so much better in a couple of days once I knew that Aubrey and Free were on that plane and out of here. I wanted her to leave the same day her mom and Mike left, but she made it clear that she would leave once she got everything together for her trip. I was waiting for her to text me and let her know she was home. She wouldn't speak to me, so she texted every couple of hours to let me know how she was doing. She refused to let me send Goldie with them to the mall. Instead, I had him follow them anyway and just stay out of sight. I knew there was a chance they may see him, but better safe than sorry. I didn't think she would be able to get any more angry with me than she already was.

My phone's text alert came through and I noticed James reaching for his phone as well. We received a text at the same time from Marie. "I have your women and children. I care nothing about them or you. I want my son back, tonight." It was accompanied with a picture of the babies sleeping in their car seats. I knew it wasn't a fake picture, my son was wearing the same clothes that Aubrey put him in this morning before I left the house. "FUCK!" I turned over the table at my frustration.

I crumpled to the floor at the sight of that text and it seemed like my world was crashing down around me. I felt so helpless and the way I was feeling was mirrored on James' face. I heard the young boys coming back to the room we were in, so I got up and walked over to James. "Jay, we gotta be strong for our family. We're gonna find her and I'm gonna kill this bitch myself. I promise you that. Alright? Put your game face on, these little niggas can't see us fall apart."

James

"Where is Goldie? He was supposed to be trailing them." Shit! This meant that she got him too. "She is deliberately picking us off one by one. How the fuck are we supposed get in front of this? Dammit!" I have no idea how to combat this voodoo shit. Not even where to start. "Lemme see if I can find out what towers Free's phone is pinging off of. I'm going to talk to my police contact. He still owes me. Yo, where is Benny? You called him hours ago."

He's been MIA for a few days now, and he's supposed to be the most reliable one. Something was up with him, but I ain't got time to be tryna figure that shit out. This is the second time that my baby has gone through this in the span of a year. I realized that she's stronger than I could ever give her credit for. I'm proud of her as a woman and a mother, but I'm scared as a muthafucka right now.

Marie

"Nice to meet you Fresia. Robert couldn't get you out of his mind for the longest when I first took him over. You're a beautiful woman and you have a very bright future ahead of you, but the sooner you get rid of James, the better. Your true king will find you and you're going to be very successful. You should also sing more. That could be very lucrative for you. I would really like it if our children could have a relationship being as though they are true family. I hope you know that I don't want to hurt either of you, I just want my son back."

I knew she wasn't afraid of me, not like Aubrey. But that's only because Aubrey has seen first-hand what I am capable of. Fresia is a fighter, I just hope she doesn't do anything stupid. "By the way, James will never be able to give you children. I can't see how he was injured, but I do understand why he did what he did to my Robert by cutting his beautiful penis off. I can also understand why he doesn't want Robert to have a legacy. It's because he will never be able to."

Free

I just stared at this woman in disbelief. It was crazy I didn't feel afraid at any moment that she was in my presence. I actually felt a sense of calm, I truly believed she wouldn't harm me or my baby. I just hope this all works out. "How can any of this be true? How can you know any of this?"

She just smiled at me and I noticed that she was being genuine. "I promise you, neither Aubrey nor I knew anything about them taking your baby. But if I know my husband the way I think I do, I can promise you that he'll be returned to you safely."

Marie

"I appreciate that. Please promise me that you'll treat my children just as good as you treat your daughter and that they'll have a relationship as siblings." I felt that this night was about to get ugly. But I couldn't see my future, just others.

Aubrey

"Marie, Marie." It's way too quiet in this house. I wanna know if my baby is okay. How Free and Tamia are doing. Marie unlocked the door and stuck her head in like I was bothering her. "I was just wondering how Free and our babies are doing?"

Marie

“That’s just like your selfish ass to be so insensitive. You know I haven’t held my baby boy in my arms since the day he was born and all you can think about is yourself. Have you ever placed yourself in my shoes? No, because you’re a selfish bitch. Even when we worked at the clinic together, all you cared about was yourself. I bet you were in on this with your man. But don’t worry, I’m going to teach him a lesson.” I turned my back and started to close the door and lock it behind me until I heard *‘Her Majesty’* speaking to me. I turned toward her to see what foolishness she was about to express.

Aubrey

“Marie, I’m very sorry that you are going through this. I really am. I know we have never been close, but I would never wish this on any mother. I love Monroe, but this situation has really made me start to rethink some things. I don’t know what they were thinking, but if I had my way you would have your baby back right now! I can’t imagine what you’re going through. This is the first time that I’ve been away from my son even though it’s only been about an hour or so. And this is torture, I would give anything for him to be in my arms right now. I just want you to know, I understand why you’re doing this, and I would probably do the same.”

I meant everything I was saying. I saw her face soften toward me for just a second and then she was back to hurling the insults again. I just wish I had pushed a little harder to try and get to know her before. "Marie, I feel it in my heart that Monroe and James will do the right thing and return your son. Regardless of how you feel about me, I'm praying for a good outcome... for all of us."

Marie

"You're not thinking about me, you're just thinking about yourself and Monroe. But trust and believe, I have something for Mr. King."

Taisha

I've been on the run ever since I left Don's brother stranded. I went back to my room, gathered all of my stuff and checked out. I left his car at my hotel because I was ninety percent sure that he would be back looking to whoop my ass. I have no idea why Don was in his feelings this much that he wanted me dead. I mean, he already killed Travis. And Travis couldn't hurt a fly. And I didn't allow him to do anything to me that I didn't know was going to happen. I jumped into my car and started driving aimlessly. I would figure it out soon enough, all I knew was I was still feening, but that I was going to try my best to fight it.

My phone rang and scared the shit outta me! I forgot all about Officer Mason and asking him to stop by.

<<ring, ring>>

Officer Mason

"Ma'am, are you alright? I stopped by your room and they told me you checked out."

Taisha

"Officer, I'm sorry but I freaked out and I felt that I needed to relocate. I'm not sure where I am going right now, but I'm gonna figure it out. I just needed to get out of town. By the way, please call me Taisha."

Officer Mason

"Ma'am- Taisha, I tell you what, why don't you tell me where you are and I will meet you. We can talk this through and I'll help you figure out your next move." She was truly a beautiful woman. I know there is something that she's not telling me, but I've seen it all too often. I also know there is more to the story about her friend that was killed inside of her home. Hopefully, I will be able to get her to trust me. There was something about her that made me want to help her.

She doesn't remember, but we were in college at the same time. I know her ex-boyfriend is a big-time drug distributor and my department has had him on the radar for some time now. Monroe King is much smarter than his predecessor. He'll slip up eventually, I'm sure of it. Maybe if I can gain Taisha's trust, she may reveal information about his operation that can assist me in taking him down. That would fast track me to detective.

Taisha

"Okay, that sounds like a plan. I'll text you the address to where I am." He seems like a really nice guy, and I know I shouldn't even be worried about trying to be with someone right now. I just feel so safe when he's around. Lord please help me out of this mess called my life. I cannot continue to live in this manner and I'm way too fine to settle for anything less than I deserve. I just have to remain the course and get this monkey off of my back. But one little hit won't hurt me, right?

Chapter 30

Marie

Before I was able to catch up with Aubrey and Free, Monroe's little buff man noticed I was following them. I'm not sure why I wasn't thinking that they would have security around them, but he was quick to pull up on me when I started getting too close for comfort.

Goldie

"Hey bitch, what do you think you're doing? You thought nobody was gonna be looking out for you? Well you were wrong, obviously. You need to walk with me and don't make a scene."

Marie

We were in a crowded mall, and he was right behind me as he was trying not to look suspicious. I turned around and noticed he wasn't holding any type of weapon in his hands. And his face didn't look as confident as his voice sounded. I played his little game, because I already knew how this was going to turn out. "Where would you like me to go, little man?" I knew that got under his skin, so that's why I called him that. He grabbed my arm roughly and led me into a janitor's closet near the restrooms down a long corridor.

Goldie

"Get in there, bitch." I closed the door behind me and pulled out my gun and hit her across her head with it. "Call me a little man again, hoe. I can't wait til Money and James kill your ass, once and for all."

Marie

I wiped the blood from my brow as he pulled out his phone, I presume, to call Monroe. I waited until he was distracted enough before I grabbed his gun and disarmed him. He dropped his phone before he was able to complete the call. We struggled for a while, due to his strength. He had me in a headlock trying to cut off my oxygen supply. I scratched at his hands and arms, but he was able to maintain his grip. I felt myself slipping away, however I was determined to get my baby boy back and finally regained my second wind.

I grabbed a wooden broom and was able to crack it over his head, which made him loosen his grip from around my neck. He was a bit disoriented, so he wasn't able to regain control of the situation. He reached for his gun, but I got it first and then turned it on him. "Looks like I have the upper hand, huh *little man*? Get on your knees." He lunged at me and I shot him in his shoulder. "Yeah, I know you had something to do with relieving Robert of his beautiful penis. You better do as I say before I drag this out painfully and relieve you of yours too."

Goldie

"Please, please... Alright, just tell me what you want. Please, I need a doctor."

Marie

"I have no concern of your need for a doctor. You already know what I want, don't play around with me little man. I'm gonna ask you this once: where is my son?"

Goldie

"James and Money have him. I can take you to them, I promise. Your son is doing just fine. We didn't hurt him. Please, I was just following orders. I fed him and made sure he was okay. I know you can help me. Please help me, I wasn't going to really kill you. Please."

Marie

He started to beg and plead with me for his life as he held his useless arm. "Oh, now you want me to help you. You told me at the courthouse not to get my voodoo on you, but now you want me to help you?" I laughed a bit as I stood over him with his loaded weapon. "Ah, you didn't think I was going to remember you ridiculing me in front of everyone when I was just trying to ask you for help.

Answer my question before I shoot something else. Where... is... my... son?"

He looked around, like he was trying to stall. Then I remembered, I needed to catch up with Aubrey and Free. I needed some insurance. "Are you gonna tell me what I need to know or are we done here?" He turned up the begging but still didn't disclose the location. So, I shot him in his penis.

Goldie

"AARRRRRRRRGGGGGGGHHHHHHH!!!! AAAAHHHHHHHHHH, PLEASE!!! PLEASE OOOOWWWWWWWWWWW!"

Marie

He was getting too loud and I sensed some people getting closer to the room. "Goodbye, *little man.*" I shot him in his head. I picked up his phone, hid the gun in my purse and exited the closet as I locked the door behind me. There was a mall manager coming around the corner as I was walking back into the mall.

Mall Manager

"Is everything alright ma'am? I was told there were loud noises coming from this vicinity. Did you see anything?"

Marie

"No sir, I was just using the restroom. I didn't see or hear anything going on around me." I glanced down at my shoe and saw a droplet of little man's blood. "Is there anything else that you need to know? I need to catch up with my sisters."

Mall Manager

"No ma'am, I appreciate your cooperation and enjoy your shopping experience."

Marie

I continued on until I found Aubrey and Free. I overheard them saying they were almost ready to go so I headed to the parking lot to wait for them.

Candy

"I cannot believe this bitch gave this shit to me! I trusted her! Now I done lost my job at Sugar's because Curt said dirty pussy was bad for business."

Taisha

"Girl, who are you talking about? What bitch?"

Candy

"Do you remember that job I asked you to fill in for me that was out in the suburbs? The big house with the lady with the red hair."

Taisha

Candy sounded seemed so helpless. Raging one minute and sobbing the next. Sounds like I dodged a muthafuckin bullet! Candy done contracted Herpes and gonorrhea from the people she sent me to be fucking and sucking on. Damn! If that wasn't a sign that I needed to stop what I was doing, I don't know what is. "Damn girl. But look on the bright side, at least it's not that three-letter shit though. I couldn't even imagine that."

She was going off for a good while about that. I definitely understood why she was so upset though. They fucked up her livelihood and how she was getting her money. I had been living dangerously too by allowing these men to use my body in whatever ways they wanted. I would make me an appointment for a full check up tomorrow. It was a scary thought, but it was much needed.

Candy

"Yeah girl, I guess. But the one bitch I decided to go raw with. SHIT! Why the fuck I trusted this bitch, I have no idea. But I whooped that hoe ass though, in her own muthafuckin' house. What am I gonna do now? I already know word has gotten out, so I can't just be out here trickin'. But thanks for listening girl, let's link up soon."

Taisha

"Okay girl, take care of yourself." Damn, that was unfortunate. I really did feel sorry for her, but I have my own problems to worry about. In the meantime, I was getting ready to meet up with Officer Mason. He was so sexy, and it was just something so familiar about him which made me feel safe when he was around. Don's brother hadn't found me yet, but I was keeping a low profile anyway. I went past the hotel I stayed at before and his car was gone. That just confirmed that he is looking for me. He should be looking for the red headed bitch that gave him and Candy them damn diseases. That's what he should be focused on. Ole dirty dick ass nigga.

Rob

Jeff introduced me to his niggas and they didn't look too happy about me being part of their crew. I knew a few of them from the outside, and if I didn't fuck over their sisters, or their mamas, I had hustled them out of some product. Yeah, I know what they're thinking. And I realize with each passing day how much of a grimy nigga I actually am. Jeff was able to hook me up with one of the prison jobs that didn't require me to do too much and kept a little change in my pockets. I would organize, deliver and pick up library books from the inmates.

"Yo wassup, Jeff?" We dapped each other up. "What's good homie? Thank for the job, this shit is too easy. But I noticed a couple of the homies aren't too happy to see me. Do I have anything to worry about with them?"

Jeff

"Nah, I told you. Everything is cool. They know what's up. You know that cell blocks A, B, C and D will be combined when the Christian workshop comes through tomorrow, right? They do this once a quarter and you remember I still need that favor from you, right?"

Rob

"Yeah, I remember but you never told me what it was. Oh yeah, I did hear about the Christian Workshop. Officer Fields told me about it." I was actually looking forward to the workshop because I planned on getting baptized during the event. I was excited about it and my weekly bible study classes on Tuesdays and Thursdays had become life. And since it didn't look like Freddy was going to make it, it was a welcomed distraction.

Jeff

"Well, let me remind you that my boys and I are willing to offer you protection for the duration of your time here from all these niggas that's either tryna fuck you or kill you. I only need you to do one thing for me. Lemme ask you something first though. Do you remember my girl from around the way? You remember how much she looked out for us whenever we got into some shit?"

Rob

"Yeah, Renee was down. She always let us hide in her house when the popo was on us. And whenever I needed somewhere to stay, even after you left, she always offered me her couch. Renee was like my sis for real. I haven't seen or heard from her in some years though. How is she?"

Jeff

"Well, I'll get to that in a second. We had a son and he was two when I got knocked. In the beginning, she always came to see me with the baby and kept money on my books. At first, she said she would wait for me. But years went by and I saw her and the baby less and less. She would still send me a couple dollars from time to time, but eventually that stopped too. She started fucking around with this big-time dealer. Word is, he used to abuse her and treat her like his property. I was able to get back in touch with her and she told me that she wanted my son to know me and also give us another chance. By this time, Ayden was five. She brought him to see me and even though I had been out of the picture for a few years, this little boy loved his daddy.

One day, I was waiting for them to come see me, but they were a no show. I called her parents and my mom, but no one had seen her or heard from her in a couple of days. Luckily, her mom had Ayden, but Renee was supposed to pick him up days prior. I found out from an acquaintance on the outside that Big Don killed my girl because he said she *'belonged'* to him. I've been trying to get close to this nigga for years, especially since he's locked up here."

Rob

"I hear you and everything, but you still haven't told me what you want me to do."

Jeff

"Don is housed in cell block A, but since we're all going to be together tomorrow for the workshop, I need you to get close to him and kill him with this. I know y'all are close, but you were close to Renee as well. He took her from our son. I need you on this Rob. Don't fuck this up for me bro."

Rob

Jeff handed me a small shank that I was supposed to lodge into Don's side. Not only was I supposed to stab my friend, I was supposed to twist it so that he would bleed out faster. It came down to me taking Big Don's life in order to save mine. This shit was unreal.

Chapter 31

James

<<ring, ring>>

"Aye Money, this call is coming from Goldie's phone.

Monroe

"Answer that shit then!" What the fuck was he waiting on?

James

"Yeah, Goldie, you alright man?"

Marie

"Oh, he's tucked away in a very safe place. The question is, where's my son? Are you and Monroe prepared for a swap?" I heard my little man in the background crying for his mama. My heart dropped in that moment and I wanted so very much to cry, but I had to be strong just for a little while longer for the both of us.

"Is someone going to tend to my baby, or you just going to let him cry? Remember, I have both of your 'pickaninnies' here as well. I'm sure you don't want me to make them cry, now do you?" Unlike them, I wasn't above killing these women or these babies. Didn't make me any difference at all.

James

“No, Marie, we’re taking good care of him and all of that. Can we depend on you for the same? And how are our wives? Are they okay? Can I speak to Free?” I swear to God I’m killing this bitch tonight.

Marie

“Yes, everyone is just fine... for now.” It’s almost nine o’clock and I would like to get this over with as soon as possible. But I still needed to be smart. “I’m not ignorant to the fact that you all won’t hesitate to kill me, but all I want to do is get my son back. Very simple, however I do not trust you so we will wait for the sun to come up when the odds are more in my favor.

Monroe

“I want my family now, Marie. Is there any way that we can convince you to make the exchange sooner? I know you’d like to see your son sooner.”

Marie

“I’ve made up my mind. I’ll contact you in a few hours.” I hung up the phone. Of course, I wanted to see my baby sooner. But I needed to do this my way.

Joe

The clinic had been in a whirlwind since...what happened. The other dental technician, Julia, who took Aubrey's spot, found Kristin in the storage room. She said she had foam coming from her mouth and was unresponsive. When I returned from lunch, they were wheeling her out to the ambulance. Since I wasn't kin, meaning her husband, they wouldn't allow me to ride with her to the hospital. I had to follow behind them. I had to explain to them that she doesn't even have family in the DMV. From the looks of things, they didn't like that I was her boyfriend. These white boys prolly mad because my dick is bigger than theirs. Fuckin pencil dicks.

Anyway, I got there shortly after she did in the ambulance. I went to the information desk and had déjà vu. It seemed like it wasn't too long ago when Aubrey was here. I started to panic, my breath was shallow, I was sweaty and started thinking the worst. I paced nervously, as the receptionist was speaking to someone else until it was my turn. Once dude was finished, I walked up to her and realized I needed to calm the fuck down. I got out of my head and approached the receptionist at the desk. "I'm here to check on my girlfriend, Kristen Jones. Can you tell me how she is? When can I see her?"

Receptionist

"One second sir, let me check the file for that individual. Give me just a minute or two."

Joe

She rifled through some papers and then made a call. Her face kinda dropped a little, but then she recovered. Once she hung up the phone, she looked back up at me and said that Kristin was in surgery. When the doctor was free, he would come out and speak to me. I went and sat in the waiting room in the meantime. I called back to the clinic to update everyone on how she was doing. Julia told me Dr. Saul was taking it very hard. This nigga wasn't even in the office this week. He don't even know Kristen like that. I would have to ask her about that shit after she recovered.

Aubrey

There's definitely a difference in the way that Marie treats Free and I. But I can't complain, she does allow me to breastfeed my baby. She actually has conversations with Free but has us far away enough for me not to be able to hear what they were talking about. Marie was a mean bitch. I still didn't understand her dislike for me though. They were talking now, but the more they talked, the longer I was able to spend with Junior. I fed him, then he fell asleep after I burped him. I was rocking him gently when I heard the door unlock and open. She didn't even say shit, just took him out of my arms.

"Well damn, Marie. Please be careful with my baby." I whispered, as I rolled my eyes. I didn't mean to sound so rough but that was my son. She could do whatever she wanted to me, not him.

Marie

"Don't try me, bitch. You're lucky that I'm this nice to you. But don't press your damn luck." I locked the door behind me as I placed her baby back in his car seat, gently. I walked back down to the room Free was in and she was rocking her daughter. "Are you hungry? Would you like me to get you something? You need to keep your appetite up so that your breast milk nourishes your daughter."

Free was so different from Aubrey's spoiled ass. I could tell that Free didn't have it easy growing up, but she made the best of it on her own. I could also see that she was a dancer and even further back her mom had been taken from her violently. Everything was given to Aubrey. She was never humble and her attitude was like she was better than others. Especially me. I should just kill her off the principle.

Free

"No, I'm actually just going to take a nap until you're ready to do the swap. I'm really tired. But thank you so much Marie. I appreciate you being so nice to me, even though we're in this situation. I know it's not your fault." It most definitely was her fault. I wasn't stupid, I was just playing that way until I was able to get the fuck outta here. "You mind if Tamia stays in here with me? She just fell asleep and she usually gets fussy." I lied. She slept very good by herself at night.

Marie

"Not a problem. But if you need something, just let me know. I'll be out here." I didn't want her to be scared of me, but I could understand if she was. Free was beautiful, I could see why Robert was attracted to her. She was very womanly, her breasts were very generous, hips wide and a nice bottom. All of the things that attracted men to me, but somehow they always ended up wanting to leave. I still couldn't understand because Free and I were the same.

Benny

Once I arrived at the back-up spot, these niggas was looking at me like I broke the law or something. "Wassup?"

Monroe

"Yo, I called you almost two hours ago. What the fuck man? We in a fuckin' crisis and you taking your sweet ass time to get here. Aubrey, Free and our kids have been taken by Marie. She also killed Goldie. We tryna figure out the best plan to get them back safely and you out here doing who knows what. When I call you, I expect you to bring your ass immediately." I said as I got in his face. And this little nigga had the nerve to smirk up at me like I was one of his boys or something. "You got something to say to me?"

Benny

"Yo Money, back up alright? I don't appreciate you being in my face like that." Everyone in the room was looking at me like I was crazy or something. I ain't care though, I wanted one of these niggas to jump bad. And that included Money's snake ass. "No, I don't have anything to say to you at this moment. We'll address my concerns later. Right now, I'd like to do what I can to help y'all find your women and children. As they're the only people who deserve my attention at this moment." I said as I mugged Money dead in his muthafuckin' face.

James

"Aye Benny, I appreciate it man." I tried to minimize the tension in the room between the two of them. “As you know, Marie is dangerous and she’s already taken out a few men on our team already. We gotta get them back safely, but in addition to that, I wanna kill this bitch. She’s already taken too much time outta my life. Tired of her, but I don’t want to get her angry any more than she already is.”

Benny

“I’m with that Jay. We gonna have to come up with something she’s not expecting. Anybody reached out to Keith yet?”

Marie

I needed to dial Shawna to check on Celeste.

<<ring, ring>>

“Shawna, I know I was supposed to be back hours ago, but I’m still waiting for them to release Marchaud. There were additional tests that needed to be done and as soon as we’re done here, I promise you that I will be there to get my baby from you.” She hesitated at first and I wasn’t sure why. “Hello, Shawna, are you still there?”

Shawna

“Oh hey Marie, I’m already back at my place. I left a few hours ago after-“

Marie

"What do you mean you're back at your place? I trusted you with my daughter Shawna. Why would you leave my newborn by herself? What the fuck-"

Shawna

"Um Marie, calm down. I think you and your friend Reggie got your wires crossed or something. He and another one of your friends named Steve or something like that came and told me I could go home since you were going to be a bit late. They have Celeste. Was I not supposed to leave her with them?"

Marie

I immediately started sweating and pacing the floor. This was not how this night was supposed to go. "Um, no Shawna, I must've forgotten. Thank you though." I was going to kill her later. Very slowly. Oh, and Monroe and James think they're slick. I finally put two and two together, realizing Reggie and James are the same individual.

Chapter 32

Rob

Tomorrow was the day of the Christian Workshop. With my newfound belief in the Lord, I still struggled with my decision. Officer Fields visited me yesterday and brought me a new book to read. She seemed really happy to see me out and about, but she didn't know it was due to my old friend offering me protection. At this point, I was facing three counts of attempted murder charges. The maximum sentence for that is twelve years to life, per count. At this point I would be released in my sixties, if I was granted parole. If I killed my friend Big Don, I know I'd never see the light of day again. Either way I was fucked.

Jeff

That nigga Rob still hadn't given me an answer about whether he would kill that bitch ass Don or not. I figured I would give him some incentive. "Aye slim, haven't you been tryna get next to Rob since he's been here?" I was talking to this ole faggot ass nigga Darnell that is here serving a life sentence. I also knew that Rob had raped his little sister back when we were in high school. At least that's what she called it once her boyfriend found out she was giving up the ass. Since Rob was a little older than her, that was the story she started circulating. Darnell didn't realize it at the time, but his sister was a hoe. All of us had ran through her at one time or another. By ourselves or all together during a train, and she did everything. We all came out of it with crabs, but we recovered. Par for the course when doing dumb shit. We had fun doing it though.

"Well he's in the library right now and I know for a fact that there are no guards there due to shift change. Won't you go holla at him right quick."

Darnell

"I thought he was part of your crew? I don't want none of your niggas jumping on me because then I'll have to fuck them too. And I don't want no beef with you, dawg."

Jeff

"It's all good, just don't kill him and don't hurt him too bad. Can you do that for me?" He nodded and I made sure that Rob would see us walk by the library entrance so he would know I was serious about this business I needed him to take care of.

Aubrey

I heard Marie yell out and braced myself for whatever was going to happen next. I heard some footsteps and then doors slamming and then it was quiet again. The door lock to the room I was in started to turn slowly and for some reason, I was sure it wasn't Marie. I stood up and looked around for something to hit whoever with that entered. I figured I would just have to fight my way out of this shit. As soon as the door opened, I had my fists in the air, ready for whatever. There was a familiar feminine silhouette that entered the door before closing it behind her. I knew for sure it wasn't Marie, but it just couldn't be... Why would she be here?

Jordan

"Aubrey, Aubrey..." I whispered. "You in here, Aubrey?"

Aubrey

"Jordan, is that you?" I wasn't sure of her intentions, so I had to be careful with this bitch. I know she was trying to get me out of the picture and take my man and possibly my child. I didn't know what to feel at this point, but I wouldn't hesitate to whoop her ass in here tonight.

Jordan

"I've been following Marie, she took my baby away from me in the worst way. I saw her make you and Free get into the car and I followed you all here. I waited awhile before I came in because I know she got that *loco* going on with her. She put some type of spell on me and took my baby.

I don't even understand how she did it." I was crying now. I thought I was all cried out from this shit, but tonight, vengeance would be mine.

"I know you don't trust me, but there was no way I was going to sit back and allow her to hurt you or Junior. I've already called Monroe and James to let them know where we are, so you all will be out of here soon enough. I put Junior in your car and locked it with the heat on so he wouldn't be cold. Take these keys, go to the bottom of the stairs and when you hit the front door, run and don't look back. Get in your car and go."

Aubrey

"Jordan, I can't leave Free. I have to wait for her. Her baby is here too."

Jordan

"Aubrey, this is the plan James and Monroe came up with. Trust me, I'm gonna help her get out of here too." She looked at me funny, but she eventually started walking towards the door. She came back and hugged me which surprised me, but we did love each other once so I understood it. "Go!" I whispered.

Once I watched her walk down the stairs and walk out of my sight quietly, I walked down the hall to where Free was being held. Marie had left the house prior to my entering so I knew she wasn't here. I opened the door and saw Free cuddled up with her baby with her eyes on me.

Free

"What are you doing here, where is Marie? What did you do to Aubrey? I will kill you if you come any closer so stay your ass right where you are."

Jordan

I felt from the tone of her voice that she was very serious, and I could only imagine what she's heard about me. "We don't have much time. I called Monroe and James and they should be outside by now. Aubrey is already gone, I put Junior in her car and gave her the keys. Monroe and James told her to leave since Marie was more likely to hurt her, than you. You have to do exactly what I say. I know Marie will be back any second now." I told her what I was going to do and what she needed to do as well. Her eyes got big, but I asked her very sincerely to trust me as her and her daughter's lives depended on it.

I heard the door to the home reopen and close. There were footsteps and then there was a pause. I knew then, that she knew I was here. I stepped into the hallway and looked down the stairs and saw her looking back at me. "Hello Marie, we meet again. I know that you realize that you are now outnumbered and that you are less two hostages. Did you think I would just allow you to get away with what you did to me? That I would just go away, you bitch?"

Marie

"Jordan, I know by now you know exactly what I am capable of. You will not leave this house alive. You shouldn't have come here." I started to climb the stairs. I noticed she didn't fear me, her heart rate was steady and she wasn't perspiring either. "Such a brave, stupid girl. You will die for just being in my presence." Once I reached the top of the stairs, I raised my hands and started to chant a spell to place her under. She would assist me in achieving my goal of killing whoever got in my way tonight of retrieving my babies.

"Comnis jung teo mustil guyins. Comnis jung teo mustil guyins. Shukre teonis delivrus daoun. Shukre teonis delivrus daoun." I placed my hand back at my side and looked into her eyes as she smirked at me, as if my spell didn't work. That couldn't be... unless...

Jordan

"I guess you thought that bullshit would work on me. But after you took my baby, I was so angry and so hurt that I was forced to reach out to my elder. I'm not from Louisiana, but the form of voodoo you practice is juvenile, at best. I repeated the spell you chanted to him and was told that not only did you terminate my pregnancy, you rendered all of my reproductive organs useless so that I may never get pregnant again. I did nothing to you, I had no information to share with you, yet you still did what you did to me."

So, I returned the favor, but the spell I chanted caused her internal organs that sustained her life to shut down one by one and slowly. My elder also warned me, that I had been out of touch with my gift for too long and that when she died I would too. I didn't care, what was my point in living if I would never be able to have what I truly wanted: unconditional love.

"Sumnus, autib goonye dialo... Sumnus, autib goonye dialo... Sumnus, autib goonye dialo... Sumnus, autib goonye dialo..."

Marie

"Noooooooo!!!!" It wasn't the same form of voodoo that I practiced, but a more evolved magic that I had yet to tap into. I felt Free step out of the room and I focused all of my attention onto her as she got closer. I dropped to the floor, in excruciating pain, as Jordan did the same. I realized then that the spell she put on me affected her too. She wasn't strong enough to sustain her life force after that chant. As Free walked past me, I grabbed her ankle and placed a spell on her as well. Even though I couldn't chant out loud, I was still able to place my rapidly declining energy into the last spell I would ever place on anyone.

Free

I couldn't understand what was going on, as I was frozen in time until Marie released my leg from her grasp. Once she did, I understood her loud and clear. I proceeded to depart the house where I saw my husband and he hugged Tamia and I and ushered me into the awaiting car. Monroe and his goons ran into the home and I was taken away.

Jordan

"Why would you do that to her? She doesn't owe you anything!" I said to Marie as tears poured down my face. I understood her spell because we were now linked. I could tell she was nearing her end as my life force depleted at a more rapid pace. I saw Monroe arrive at the top of the stairs and he looked at me with a grateful yet pained look on his face. He picked me up and instructed Stevie to pull the car around as he carried me out of the house to the hospital. He instructed the other three remaining men to ensure she was dead and then to burn the house with her body in it. I heard a single gunshot and immediately, my head started spinning and my ears were ringing as well. This could only mean one thing. Marie was shot in her head. I looked up at Monroe and told him, "I love you" as blood started seeping from my ears and I died in his arms.

Rob

I was wrapping up in the library as I placed the last of the books from the cart onto the shelves. I loved this job as it provided me a very drama-free environment as you had to have a certain privilege to be able to utilize it. I would lock it up once I was done and hand the keys to the officer that would be by promptly at six o'clock. I expected him any minute and usually one of Jeff's crew was always floating around to remind others that I wasn't up for grabs. Now don't get it twisted though, I was nobody's bitch. I just knew when it was time to ask for help.

Darnell

I entered the library and there was one other prisoner there and the CO that was supposed to be on post nodded at me and walked the other way. I dismissed the dude that was reading and closed the doors while I made my way in the back where Rob was unaware of what was about to go down. "Hey Fish... did you mourn Freddy?" I saw him look toward the front to see where his help would be. He realized we were alone once I started walking toward him.

Rob

"Yo, the library is closed dude. You gotta go." My heart started beating fast, because I knew he wanted to cause me some harm. His hoe ass sister told him I raped her when she knew that she liked getting fucked by me and my crew. And she ended up burning us at that! "Aye dude, you gotta go. I'm not here for the fuck shit." He kept advancing towards me like I wasn't telling him to get the fuck on. When I saw Jeff and his crew walk past the entrance, I knew what was up.

Darnell

"Come on man, Freddy already opened you up. Let Big D get a sample." I pounced on him and had the upper hand for a minute as I tried turning him over so I could remove his pants. "Oh shit, it's true, you really ain't got no dick!" I got temporarily distracted and realized my mistake a little too late.

Rob

"Nah nigga, I ain't got a dick. But I do have something else you wasn't counting on though." And I proceeded to stick this metal rod in his throat and watched while his eyes rolled in the back of his head as the last moments of his life flickered out like a candle. Before the CO got there, I threw the shank on the floor across the room. I heard him coming, so I laid on the floor with my arms and legs outstretched like I was taught to do here when anything went down.

"Aye yo Officer," I yelled from the floor, "I believe the inmate needs medical attention."

CO

"Code 7, code 7… in the library, send the medics and lock C down NOW!"

Rob

The CO that I'm sure saw that nigga Darnell coming in here would have some explaining to do.

CO

"What the fuck happened Williams? Do you have any weapons on you?"

Rob

"Officer, I don't have any weapons on me. The inmate tried to assault me, so I took the shank he was trying to get at me with and did what I had to do. I don't even know where he came from." I lied to him, but it was better him than me. I saw Jeff out the corner of my eye too. Fuck him and his protection, I'll take all they asses out if I need to.

A few more officers arrived and took control of the scene as they carried out lockdown procedures in our cellblock. I was escorted to my cell and Jeff nodded at me as I went by and returned the gesture.

Chapter 33

Sam

"It's been a week since Candy came over here and whooped my ass. My doctor has since called me again, asking if I could come back in and talk a bit more about my results. My mother has been so respectful about everything I've shared with her. And I shared absolutely everything! She was quiet for a full five minutes, but after that she was back to mommy mode and she didn't ask me any uncomfortable questions. She just told me to come home. I told her I would, as long as she didn't discuss anything with daddy.

Joe and Keith constantly hit up my phone, but I was just not ready to speak with either of them. Surprisingly enough, I had no symptoms of what Candy accused me of giving to her. She didn't even allow me to get a word in. It wasn't as if I was the only one she was fucking, but I knew that there was the possibility. It was very rare that I strapped up. I knew it wasn't ideal, but it didn't feel the same. And I mean AT ALL!! I enjoyed sex so much, that I was willing to sneak out of my mother's grasp right now, but she didn't allow me to go anywhere alone. She even told me that she would be going to the doctor's office with me later today. I told her I was sure that he wanted to go over medication changes or something like that, but she just wasn't having it.

Joe

Kristin was declared brain dead upon arrival. She wasn't found in time to save her and the hospital reached out to her mother in Tennessee. Can you believe that the only thing this bitch was interested in was whether or not Kristin had an insurance policy? Got damn, I see why she would relocate to a whole 'nother fucking state to get away from her ass. I helped pack up her apartment so that her belongings could be donated to the shelters around the area. Her will described in detail what she wanted done with her estate. What was left of her life insurance payout after funeral expenses went to a charity designated for abused and abandoned women and children. So, her greedy ass mother travelled all the way to DC for nothing. And I laughed at her ass. Nasty, bitter, trifling ass woman. I mean, I know I wasn't exactly great to Kris all the time, but I would have never treated her like that.

The office was pretty somber. The practice owners didn't replace her right away. Dr. Saul didn't want anyone sitting in her chair. I still thought shit was fishy about the way his punk ass was acting these days. He always looked as if he was on the verge of tears or some shit. But anyway, I was pretty lonely and Sam wasn't returning my calls so I spent my time with Ionie's fine ass. She was coming over tonight and I couldn't wait until she whispered her moans in her strong accent into my ear. My dick was getting hard just thinking about that phat ole ass and that juicy ass pussy she was sitting on. Damn, I couldn't wait to sink my entire dick everywhere she would allow me too. I still didn't know exactly what Sam was into, but I was thankful for the introduction.

I headed home after a pretty somber day and saw that Ionie was already here at my apartment. She knew where the spare key was, so I told her whenever we were scheduled to meet up, just to let herself in. When I entered the house, it smelled of some good food cooking. I walked up behind her at the stove and started to lick and suck on her neck. She had on some boy shorts with a red crop top and no bra. She had my "Kiss the Cook" apron on and looked so sexy standing there cooking in my kitchen. She reminded me so much of my sister in law Shay, that I envisioned Ionie being my wife and the mother of my children.

Ionie

"I've prepared some fried plaintain, dumplings, rice and peas and jerk chicken like I know you like." I had just finished cooking and I was so happy to see him. I knew his girlfriend just passed away, and there was no need in both of us being lonely. "How are you today, Sweets? My yoni has been craving your touch since the last time

I saw you." I removed the apron, jumped up and wrapped my legs around his waist. He then sat me atop the kitchen island as he suckled my naked breasts after removing my crop top. We kissed one another until he was ready for me to wrap my full lips around his succulent pole. He removed his shirt and then the rest of his clothing and climbed up beside me. He peeled me out of my shorts and was pleased to find me wearing no underwear either.

I laid him back on top of the cold island and straddled him as I inserted his member into my yoni. It was if we were made for one another. He gripped my abundant ass as he impaled me with such pleasure. "Sweets, please don't make me cum in your kitchen.... sssssss, ooooohhhh you feel so damn good! Yeeessssss, yeeeeessssss baby, ooooooohhhhh." He just continued to drill me from the bottom whilst hitting that one spot over and over again. He knew just what he was doing. He watched the pleasure all over my face as my titties bounced up and down. "Baby, I'm about to cum... I'm gonna cum, baby! Oooohhhh!!"

Joe

"Give me all that shit baby." I just loved it when she climaxed. Once she started coming down, I inserted my dick back inside of the gushy until that nut built up. I removed myself and turned her over so that I could hit that spot again and released all up in that pussy while I watched that generous, sexy ass bounce all over my dick. She was the sexiest woman I had been with in such a long time. It just got better and better with her and not only could she cook and fuck me good, her conversation was even better. I knew I was sad about Kristin, so I needed to take it slow with her. But I was gonna make her mine. We jumped in the shower and she washed herself quickly, yet thoroughly so that she could warm up the food for us. I stayed in just a little longer to wash the stress of the day off of me. Once I dried off, I noticed something that resembled a bump on the shaft of my dick. "What the fuck is this shit? Ionie!!" Someone had some explaining to do.

Keith

I couldn't get in contact with Sam, but I had to go out of town for the week starting tomorrow. I developed this cough I couldn't shake, but I just kept pumping myself full of Vitamin C so that I could maintain during my trip. I would see my Primary Care Physician upon my return. I found it odd that Sam wouldn't return my calls, but I spoke with her dad and he let me know that she was staying with them since about a week ago.

I hadn't found Taisha's ass yet, but I stopped looking for her once I started getting sick. I'm still gonna fuck her ass up for stranding me. I laughed a little, because I can't even front like I wouldn't have done the same. She didn't know that my bitch ass brother changed his mind about killing her. Shit was actually very funny! I had been scoping her out and she had been spending quite some time with a young officer. Her ass was smart, but I would catch her by herself one of these days once her guard was down. My car just pulled up, so I left for the airport. Damn I felt like shit.

Free

Once we got back home, James wouldn't let me do anything for myself, nor would he let me out of his sight. "I'm fine Jay, stop fussing over me okay baby?" I laughed a little, but what I couldn't deny was that there was an overwhelming curiosity... dare I even say, a need to know about Marie's babies. I just felt like they were supposed to be with me. Even more than my own child. What is going on with me? What did Marie do to me?

James

Free hasn't been checking on Tamia the way she used to. There's a change that I sense in her. I've been feeding Tamia baby milk that I started buying from the store. But she's still pumping. She said Tamia is old enough to be weaned from her milk, but I still sneak and give her some from time to time when Free is sleeping. Free keeps asking about Marie's babies. She seemed obsessed with them or something. Monroe and I decided to drop them off to our friend at the Fire Station, but each time we decided to make the drop, Free was there. She wanted us to keep them, but why? She already had one kid by this fool, now she wanted his other children. This situation was fucked up!

Free

Aubrey kept trying to call me, but fuck that bitch, I don't want anything to do with her. She left me in that muthafuckin' house. What if Marie would have killed me or something. I'm truly done with her now. She was all about herself, just like Marie said. I felt like Marie wanted me to keep her babies because they had no one else. When she grabbed my leg, it's like we were one. I saw some of the things that occurred in her life. She was that bitch! I was bringing the babies' cribs and clothing from her apartment to our house tomorrow, unbeknownst to James. We were keeping these innocent children and I didn't want to hear anything else about it either. I could do this by myself, and I didn't forget that she told me he couldn't make any babies of his own anyway. So why not keep the twins and love them like they were ours?

Aubrey

After getting out of that house that night, I took my baby and went home. It was on the market, but I still had some of my things there. I was glad I'd kept it though. I wasn't exactly over the little bullshit that Monroe did with Jordan or the shit he had me wrapped up in with Marie over taking her baby. Then come to find out, they went and retrieved the other twin too. Like why the fuck would they continue to keep agitating this bitch with me, Free and our babies within her clutches? I mean, what gives?

This nigga was reckless. With my heart, with my safety, with our son's safety. I didn't know Monroe anymore. As soon as I got home, I turned my phone off, I put my car in my garage and the deadbolt was on my doors so he couldn't use his key. I refused to see him. I had already arranged to fly to the Virgin Islands for a little while to get away. My father's sister contacted me once she was old enough about eight years ago. She was younger than me, but she knew that I existed. She was twenty-two now and I figured that was as good a place as any for me to hide out until I figured out what we would do.

Monroe really had my head all messed up and I wasn't going to take it. I would leave tomorrow night, out of the back door because I knew he had someone watching my house. I saw the little nigga down the street, like I wasn't gonna notice him. Even though I used my mother's maiden name Collins in my everyday life, my passport had my father's last name, Pierre. I knew Monroe would check the manifests to try and follow me. My mother never wanted me to forget my roots. I changed my last name to hers when I was still in college.

After Junior and I boarded, I kept hoping that Monroe wouldn't track us. I ordered his passport but he was only 9 weeks at his point, so I hadn't received it yet. I mailed it to a PO Box that I set up under my name in the VI. Since we were technically still in the US, we didn't need the passports. But better safe than sorry. I tried to get Free to join me, but she wasn't taking my calls. I didn't leave her on purpose, I was following directions because they made sense at the time. Now I could see why she felt like I just bailed on her. It made me feel like shit, but I mailed a letter to her when I got to the airport. I wanted her to know that I would never do anything to jeopardize our relationship because she was one of my closest friends. I really hope that bitch Marie didn't get in her head before she died. She just needed to know my side of the story.

Sam

I was sitting on the table awaiting the doctor to come in and speak with me. I didn't understand why I needed to come back so soon, but here I was. "Hey Dr. Haughton, what's going on? Did I need more meds or a different medication or something? My mother is very worried and I just want her to be able to calm down, you know?" Dr. Haughton had been my doctor since I was a little girl. I was very comfortable with him. But something had to be wrong, his face says it all.

Dr. Haughton

"Samantha, I wanted to bring you in because a few of your test results hadn't come back until a few days after I saw you last."

Sam

He pressed the button on the wall and then one of his female techs came into the room and just stood there looking stupid. "Well, doc? Why is she here? Do you need to perform another procedure or something? Tell me and stop stalling, dammit!" I tried remaining calm, because my injuries from Candy hadn't all the way healed quite yet.

Dr. Haughton

"Sam, I regret to inform you that you have HIV. I've invited Janet into the room with us until the grief counselor can arrive for you."

Sam

After he said HIV, I just zoned out. I started to slowly walk out of the room and my mother looked alarmed and I could see her mouth moving and everything, but I couldn't hear her. Once I reached outside, I started running as fast as I could. My body didn't register that it was still winter, but I knew in my mind I had left my coat in the doc's office. I couldn't concentrate, everything was a blur.

Eventually, I started walking again after I stopped running to catch my breath. I got to the highway and thoughts were going through my mind a mile a minute. It was quiet, it was serene. There was a steady flow of traffic in both directions and then I saw an eighteen-wheeler approaching my direction. I waited until it got close enough... then I jumped in front of it. Please God, save my soul.

Epilogue

Aubrey

It's been six months since being in the beautiful Virgin Islands. Meeting my mom and my father's family was surreal. My father died shortly after I was born in a car crash and his mother that wouldn't let him marry my mother, was still alive.

She wants a full-blown relationship and because I look the most like my father out of all of his kids, she tries to brag on me or whatever. The petty side of me is like, "get out of here lady", but Denise Collins Roberson did NOT raise me to be that way. My mom had been here a few times to visit, but I didn't allow her to visit as much as she wanted to. And I dared my father's mother to be rude to her!

My father ended up producing eight children, of which I was the oldest. Most of us had his hazel eyes, and my sister Liz who reached out to me years ago looked like she could have been my twin. We became inseparable, and she absolutely LOVED Junior. I was totally heartbroken when I got here because I missed Monroe so much, but Liz helped me with Junior until I could get myself together. Finally, I felt comfortable enough to let Monroe know where I lived and to allow him to visit his son. Since being gone, I had found out so much about him that I had a 'feeling' in my gut about before but wasn't sure.

I always wondered where his money came from, because no auto mechanic could afford the things that he did. His family totally depended on him and he only allowed me to have the best. Currently, I was on my way to the airport to pick him up. I left Junior with Liz, because we had some things we needed to talk about without the distraction of Junior's little cute juicy self. When I pulled up to the small airport, I noticed Monroe looking so damn good that my pussy started to jump. "Down girl", I told her as I put the car in reverse so that he could place his bags inside and jump in.

Monroe

"Damn you look good, Beautiful." I wasn't sure if I could touch her, let alone hug and kiss her. She looked just as unsure as I did, and I looked in the back seat and noticed my son wasn't there. I missed him terribly. I can't believe I set the events in motion to once again push the love of my life away from me for a second time.

"I know that saying 'I'm sorry' doesn't make up for the betrayal you have felt solely due to my actions. I know I let my dick lead me to a fucked up situation with Jordan, but I'm prepared here and now, to do any and everything needed to let you know that I'm still in love with you only. You are and have always been the only woman for me, and if you told me right now to stay here with you and Junior, I would never return to Maryland ever again." I meant that shit with my entire being.

Aubrey

I pulled off of the road into a park and put my head on the steering wheel as the tears ran down my face. "You're the love of my life as well baby." I couldn't bring myself to look at him, but he exited the car, came around to the driver's side and held me. THIS is right where I belonged. We held the embrace for the longest time. Monroe kissed me and reaffirmed to me over and over that he would never hurt me again. "Let's get you to your son baby." And with that, we were back on the road. I couldn't help but notice that my pussy was throbbing, and I couldn't wait to feel him inside of me again. We still had a very long way to go, but I knew then and there that I could not live my life without him.

Keith

After leaving Samantha's memorial service, I reflected on the conversation that I had with her mom, Edith. She told me that her doctor told Sam, that not only did she have Herpes and some other sexually transmitted infection, that the additional tests came back positive for HIV. So far, I haven't tested positive for the HIV, but that doesn't mean I don't have it. With my doctor's urging, I will continue to get tested until I'm out of the "grace period".

I wish she would have come and talked to me. I don't think she ever knew how much I loved her, but I did know that she fought me every step of the way. I knew she never wanted to place a label on us, and maybe I shouldn't have tried to rush it, but I loved her. I still do, no matter what she was into.

I would just pour myself back into my work until I could muster up the courage to enjoy life again. I get that she felt helpless in the moment she decided to do what she did. I just wish she would have allowed me to be there for her. That closed casket will haunt me for the rest of my days. I cannot fathom what head space she was in that day. Once I thought everyone was gone from her grave site, I went back and gave my love the last flower she would ever receive before the workers filled that six-foot hole up with dirt to cover her coffin. "I will always love you baby… rest easy my love."

Benny

This bitch was gobbling my dick up just like I liked it. "Yeah, just like that." I took another pull of the blunt while watching her continue. She was this gorgeous ass Spanish chick I met a few months back, that reminded me so much of Jordan. But I knew that she could never be her. As this random woman swallowed my seed, my thoughts went back to the one night I spent with her. Jordan was sensual, sensitive, kinda distant, but her conversation was very intriguing. I knew that she was holding back some information, but when I found out what it was, I can't even front. That shit crushed me. I don't even know why. How was it that after spending a few hours with this woman, she had already captured me within her clutches? Could it be because she reminded me of the woman my mother once was, before the drugs took hold of her? Maybe.

After the boss's women and children were returned to them safely, I officially parted ways with Money. It wasn't before we had the chance to talk though.

Five months ago

Monroe

"Ayo Benny, can you meet me at my office at the shop? I wanna holla at you about some things."

Benny

Reluctantly, I agreed. Because I also knew I needed to get some things off of my chest. I didn't make him wait, I needed to get this over with. I showed up and noticed James and a few of the other guys hanging around. We were cordial, but I know they remember from my exchange with Money on that night everything went down with the crazy lady, that our relationship had changed. Once I got to the door, I knocked a couple of times and he told me to come in. He asked me to have a seat, I declined.

Monroe

"Suit yourself." I was at my mini office bar and proceeded to fix myself a drink. "Would you like one?" He declined that also. I walked back over to my desk and sat on top of it as I took a swig from my glass. I began to speak since he did not. "I wanted to thank you again for helping with the efforts to save my family. Although Aubrey decided to leave the area for a while, I have still decided to proceed with my retirement plans. If you are still interested, I can set you up with my contact and the connect-"

Benny

"Look Money, I've always respected you." I said as I interrupted him. "But I will not allow you to continue to diminish the respect that I thought we had for one another. All I want to know is, why would you introduce me to a chick you were fucking? I admired the relationship that you and Aubrey had. And to find out that you was on that same fuck boy shit that I see from the corner boys, I just didn't understand. I don't need nobody's sloppy seconds. That's not my style. I thought we had the respect of men between us. Imagine the surprise and stupidity I felt when I saw you fucking

ole girl the day the crazy bitch burned your shit down."

Monroe

How didn't I pick up on this? "Look Benny, I apologize. The truth of the matter is, Aubrey and I both were in a relationship with Jordan. She took shit too far, which I should have seen coming but you're right. I allowed that same fuck boy mentality to allow my dick to think for me instead of honoring our brotherhood. For that, I apologize to you. Please do not allow this misstep to fuck up the business front that we have established together. Can you accept my apology? I have to leave this shit behind in a few, and if you want the empire, it's yours."

Benny

"This is unbelievable. You expect me to take your word that all of y'all was in a relationship together? So why would you have her locked in the warehouse holding room? This ain't making no sense right here, fam. I actually overheard all that shit, I've decided just to part ways personally and 'professionally'. I'll find my way. Is that all you wanted to discuss?" He told me yeah and continued to drink out of his glass. I left his office and linked up with Keith.

My goal wasn't to be in the drug game forever, but I knew that with the knowledge I had already acquired, coupled with what I'm sure Keith would teach me, I would be able to reach my short and long-term goals in a timely manner. I exited the premises after dapping up James and the crew and wishing them well. This would be the very last time I would make time for Monroe King.

Present Day

Keith filled me in on Sam's death and some of the details surrounding it. Once I left his house, I called Candy and she told me the rest of the story. Shawty had that virus though? I was getting tested asap. Candy said she didn't test positive for that, but what she did test positive for ended her career as a stripper at Sugar's. I knew the owner, Curt, wasn't having that shit. Damn, it's unfortunate. I'm just glad that I continued to curve her ass. I knew she fucked that nigga New Year's night even though she was there with Keith. Rest in peace, lil nasty bitch.

Free

I felt myself slipping away a little more each day. I knew it had something to do with whatever Marie did when she touched me that night. I felt no connection to my baby, Tamia. All I wanted to do was feed Marchaud and Celeste and ensure that they thrived. Even when I tried staying away from them, there was this invisible force that wouldn't allow me to keep my distance. But I was determined to figure this shit out.

My husband moved completely out of the master bedroom and moved Tamia's crib in there with him. He ensured he closed and locked his door at night, and he didn't let her out of his sight. If he left the house, she did too. I wanted to commit myself to an institution, but anytime I tried to make a move, something always held me back. The babies were now seven months and James wanted me to place them up for adoption. I knew my marriage was in jeopardy, but these babies needed me much more than he did. Right?

Joe

Even after our talk about the bump I found on my dick, Ionie was sexing me nonstop. She didn't seem phased once my physician confirmed that I had contracted Herpes. I was never missing getting my dick wet. She ensured that I was always taken care of. My grief had just started to decrease over Kristen, and then that shit with Sam. Why couldn't she have called me? Did she think all I wanted from her was sex? We may not have been good in a relationship, but we had always been friends.

"Ionie, did you hear what I said about Sam? She's dead. She committed suicide because she found out she had HIV." Ionie just kept poppin' that hot pussy on my dick with that ass was bouncing in front of me looking so damn good. "Babe, stop. Come on, let's talk." But she just kept going.

Ionie

I heard his ass, but why did we need to stop and talk about this shit right now? It wouldn't make a difference if we talked about it now or in ten minutes after I had the chance to squirt all over him. She was still gonna be dead, her ass wasn't coming back. Shit, this dick was good, and I didn't even have to go back to the club because he was always in the mood just like I was.

In my past life, I had a whole husband and three children in the city. That life wasn't for me no more. When I was introduced to 'Sexual Healing', the sex club I frequented, I was literally in bliss. I just watched at first, but by my third visit, I was high and had a little liquor in me, so I was ready to participate. Gay men's sex intrigued me for some reason. But there was this one guy that was midnight black with this beautiful skin. He looked like he was sculpted by God himself. Muscles and body, perfect in every way. He sexed men and women, everyone wanted him. He even had his own suite in the club. There were always spectators around when he was sexing. My yoni was always dripping wet when I watched him.

I was about three months in when I was "chosen". His club name was Zeus and the way he scooped me up and pleasured me that night, I knew I had been going there for a reason. He must have enjoyed me as well, because anytime I was there, he made sure to include me whether he was sexing a man or another woman. I was on the verge of climax as I fantasized about Zeus while still sexing Joe. I rode him like my life was in question.

We didn't need to talk about whether or not Sam passed HIV on to us... I knew I had it. I passed it on to her and now him. "Ooooohhhh, sssssssss yeeeessss baby, I'm cumming. Ahhhhhhh shit baby!" He started to cum inside of me as well which made my experience even more pleasurable. It would be unrealistic for me not to contract it with all of the free sex I was having. I left my husband so that he'd have another chance at love with someone else without the worry of this death sentence. While I missed my children, I wasn't going to burden them with watching their mother die slowly.

"That was good baby, now what did you want to talk to me about?" I asked Joe as I laid beside him.

ABOUT THE AUTHOR

Troii Devereaux was born and raised in the Washington, DC metropolitan area. Her passion for fiction writing flourished in middle school, when her eighth-grade teacher encouraged her to read one of her creative writing assignments to her homeroom class and the other eighth grade classes as well. *Troii* is an entrepreneur, self-published author and CEO of AKT Publishing, Inc. Her pseudonym, *Troii Devereaux*, is used for the books containing adult material, whereas she will use her given name to fulfill her dream of writing children's books.

After her retirement following a 20-year military career, *Troii* decided to make her passion for writing a full-time endeavor. She has served in Maryland, South Korea, Japan, Germany, Qatar, Guam, Texas, New Mexico, Afghanistan and California over her tenure in the Air Force. When she is not working on a new book or screenplay, she spends time with her husband, family and friends. *Troii* is also a full-time student pursuing a degree in Management, with a concentration in Marketing. Her hobbies are reading, writing, traveling and continuing to find inspiration for future novels and screenplays to share with her fan base.

With a bold and unabashed voice, *Troii Devereaux* delves into fictional situations encompassing topics such as sexuality, violence and fantasy. She brings romance, drama and erotica to her readers in the breakout series, "*Never Be Anotha...*". The first two installments of the trilogy were released in 2019. While there is a very sexy and entertaining context behind her stories, *Troii* wants her readers to recognize the serious aspects to encourage individual confidence in their sexuality, unapologetically.

Previous releases:

Never Be Anotha: Resentment, Book 1 (May 2019)

Never Be Anotha: Repentant, Book 2 (Nov 2019)

Made in the USA
Coppell, TX
07 February 2026